MYSTICAL MUSIC

MYSTICAL MUSIC

Chords of Prophecy
Book One

KAITLYN BOLYARD

Blind Goose Publications

To the magick within us all

Contents

Madame Rosivda's Divination Shop

Marek Dabrowski lived only a few blocks from The Den, where he worked and usually enjoyed the walk. Today, though, Marek regretted forgetting his umbrella. As soon as he stepped outside, the rain soaked him to the bones. It came in great icy sheets, cascading from dark, heavy clouds. He could complain, but there was no one to complain to, and besides, it fit his mood perfectly. Nothing seemed to be going right. It had been weeks since anyone had put money in his tip jar, even change, and Mr. Robins had noticed because that shrewd little man saw everything.

The conversation went something like this.

Mr. Robins approached when he heard a moment of silence between songs. Marek looked up at the man's triple chins and frowned. What could it be now? Not loud enough? Too loud? He moved his hands from the piano keys and settled them in his lap.

"You know what I've noticed?" Mr. Robins asked.

Marek didn't bother answering. The question was rhetorical.

"I've noticed you haven't been making me much money."

Marek bit his tongue, forcing himself to listen instead of speak.

"And you know what else I've noticed? The hotel down the street, our main competitor, is always brimming. People come in just to hear the music. They listen, and they buy things from the gift shop. They listen and buy a coffee or a drink. They're just coming in at all hours to hear that guy play."

Now Marek nodded, acknowledging he was listening.

"Why don't they come to hear you, I wonder?"

Maybe this required a response, but Marek wasn't sure what to say. He wanted to rebuff with something snarky about the other pianist's flippant style, his lack of artistry, the way he played pop songs throughout his set, nothing classical or challenging. But he knew this explanation would fall on deaf ears.

"Don't you have anything to say?" asked Mr. Robins.

"What would you like me to do? Do you want me to change anything?"

"I have an idea. Why don't you take the night off while I figure this out? In fact, why don't you take a few nights off? Come for your afternoon hours but no nights until Friday. How does that sound?"

It sounded horrible. It sounded like Marek wouldn't be able to make rent if this became a trend. "Alright. Will you have someone else play instead?"

"We'll just pipe in some music for the night crowd. Maybe I'll eventually replace you with a DJ."

Marek looked away, hiding his emotions like always. "What time should I stay until today?"

"It's - what - almost three?" Mr. Robins checked his costly watch. "You can kick off at four. Same thing tomorrow."

Marek nodded and returned to the piano keys. His arms felt heavy, his fingers numb. The music sounded the same, though, as it always had: orderly, measured, mathematical. He could play while his mind wandered to other things. He could play on autopilot without thinking about anything.

Even though it was a short walk, the storm had drenched him already. If the rain were warmer, that'd be one thing, but this freezing rain made his bones ache. He shivered and felt like a naked skeleton dancing down the street. Within moments, the rain felt cold and hard. Little white pellets fell heavy from the sky, bouncing up from the sidewalk at his feet. He glanced around, looking for someplace he could dip into or even an awning that would protect him from the assault.

As he glanced up, he caught a neon sign in a window. This was the first time he had noticed it on his walks to and from The Den. In a dark window, the glaring neon read "tarot readings." In scrawled lettering, the sign above read "Madame Rosivda's Divinity Shop." He wondered for the briefest moment what a divinity shop could be, and then a great gust of wind whipped into his face, and he hurried for the door.

Inside, it was much, much warmer. The temperature change made Marek nauseous for a moment, but as he caught his breath, he glanced around the small entryway and breathed in the earthy scent of patchouli. He knew a guy once, in college, who always smelled of it, that and a dank weed smell that clung to his clothing. Marek shook his head, trying to clear it of the memory, but distinct scents could always bring him back to specific moments. He was standing outside, waiting for class to start, being offered a hit off a ragged little joint, refusing the offer politely, and never becoming friends due to that refusal.

A voice broke his reverie. "Good afternoon, " it said. "How can I help you?"

He glanced around, seeing no one. What he did notice, however, were candles lined up haphazardly on a low table, each of them burned down beyond recognition, a mass of wax that looked dangerous. He stepped further into the room, hesitating. A doorway was ahead, with only a beaded curtain separating this room from the next. The beads glistened in the dim light, and he couldn't reasonably determine if they were purple or pink.

Just then, a round, robust woman pushed her way through them. "Well, come on then," she said. "You came in here for a reason, didn't you?" She beckoned for him to follow her. Her eyes were an indeterminate shade, not quite green or blue, maybe closer to hazel. He couldn't tell if she was young or old, either. The shape of her implied a middle-aged woman, but her face looked too young, too unlined.

Unable to voice his questions, he followed her through the beaded curtain into a smaller room in the back. Despite its size, the room felt cozy and comfortable. At the center sat a round table covered in red cloth with yellow embroidery running down its edges, fringe reaching the floor. A trio of candles sat in a wide triangle at the center of the table, but they had yet to burn down as far as those in the entry room. These stood tall and proud by comparison.

"Well, come on in, then," she said.

She motioned toward a low chair, and he sat down hesitantly. His wet coat still clung to him like a second skin. She glanced back at him as if looking for the first time.

"Oh dear, you're soaked, aren't you?" she asked.

He nodded, still shocked, unable to speak.

"Let me take your coat and get you some tea."

He struggled to pull his arms from the sleeves but eventually escaped them. Madame Rosivda draped his coat over one shoulder, disappeared into the front with it, and then returned. His breath slowed as he started to relax into the cushioned chair.

"Looks like you've had quite a day, Marek," she said.

He stared into her strange hazel eyes, but now they looked grayer, he thought. "How do you know my name?"

"Did you not see my sign out front? Do you not know where you are?"

He shook his head.

"I specialize in divination," she said. She settled into the seat across from Marek as if this were a sufficient explanation.

"I don't understand."

"How would you like a tarot reading, Marek?" she asked. "The first one is free."

Now, his words finally found him. "I'm just trying to sit out the storm," he said. "I appreciate your hospitality but don't need a tarot reading. I don't believe in that stuff."

"Just a taste?" she asked. "The reading is free; you might as well try it."

She was interrupted by a high-pitched screeching from the other room. It sounded like a tea kettle. But where was the heat source, Marek wondered? Did she have an entire kitchen hidden somewhere here?

"Oh, I forgot your tea." She hurried away again. By the time she returned, Marek was feeling much warmer and drier. She carried a hot cup of tea with a saucer and set them gingerly on the table.

"White tea with peach," she said. "Most customers enjoy it with just a half spoonful of honey."

Marek took the cup from her and sipped carefully. The steam and heat warmed and filled him with a sense of calm. "Thank you."

She had her back to him, poking through a cupboard in the corner, and came back with something wrapped in a black silk scarf. She uncovered it and revealed a deck of cards. The tarot, he assumed.

"I don't need a reading," he said.

"What else will we do with the next twenty minutes until the storm dies?" she asked.

"I suppose we could talk," he said.

"Do you have anything, in particular, you want to talk about?"

"I admit I don't. Not really."

"Do you permit me to give you a reading, then? It's just a simple one, nothing complicated. We'll make it a single-card reading."

"I've never heard of only drawing a single card."

"Just to get a general read on you," she said. "Nothing complicated."

"I suppose that would be alright, but don't expect to wow me."

"I did know your name, didn't I?"

"How *did* you know my name?"

She pointed to the identification card clipped to his pants. "I also know that you work at The Den."

He laughed. "Sneaky," he said.

"I use the resources at my disposal."

She removed the scarf from the tarot cards and placed them on the table between them, in the small space between the triangle of candles.

"You can shuffle the cards," she said.

2

The Emperor

He pulled them into his hands. They were larger than a standard deck of cards, and there were more of them, so he struggled to shuffle them. Eventually, he grew more comfortable and managed a few good bridges. He then set them down on the table.

"Cut the deck," she said.

He split it fairly evenly in the middle, setting the top half next to the bottom.

She reached over the table, flipping the top card from the bottom half and placing it face up on the second stack. Marek could see a king-like figure sitting on a golden throne, his hand placed calmly on the head of a lion who sat at his feet. In the other hand, he held a jeweled scepter. He looked strong and determined. The card read "The Emperor."

"What does it mean?" he asked.

Madame Rosivda looked carefully at the card, then back at Marek. She drew a shallow bowl from a hidden compartment in the table, setting it in front of him.

"Pour a little of your tea into here," she said.

He complied. He had drunk it almost down to the dregs, but

there was just enough to fill the bottom of the bowl with a thin layer of liquid.

"Now, I want you to look into the water as I tell you a story."

He glanced at her, uncertain, but followed her instructions. As he gazed at the liquid in the bowl, it began to shimmer and quake. Ripples spread across its surface. He glanced up at Madame Rosivda; his eyes were worried.

"Don't look at me," she said. "Look at the liquid and listen."

He returned his attention to the bowl, which had grown calm again. Maybe he had imagined the ripples and waves. Madame Rosivda began to speak, her words low and soothing. He soon fell into the rhythm of them and forgot his surroundings.

"There once was an emperor whose only concern was keeping his coffers full," she said. "Each new birth in his kingdom meant another soul who would pay him taxes. He never put those funds back into upkeep, into caring for his subjects. Instead, he kept it all to himself, hoarding gold like a dragon.

"When he learned his subjects were falling ill from a mysterious disease, he grew worried, but only because so many died, which meant less would pay their tithes. A medicine man came to offer a cure, but it would cost him. The emperor thought the price was too high, so he refused.

"His subjects continued to die, and there were so many deaths they started throwing the bodies in great heaps and burning them. The smell reached him, but the emperor hardened his heart. He refused to give in, buy the medicine needed, and save them.

"Eventually, the only people left alive were those who lived in the castle because they never had contact with those who had contracted the disease. The emperor's hoard of gold had dwindled, and little remained in his stores. He couldn't tax his court because all the money they earned came from the commoners, who were dead. None of them had any funds any longer. The kingdom could no longer survive without those he had neglected below him. There was no one to harvest the gardens, kill wild game, or prepare meals. Broke and starving, the emperor regretted denying them medicine, but it was too late."

As Madame Rosivda's entrancing words faded, Marek looked up from the liquid in the bowl, which seemed to have nearly evaporated. "Am I the emperor?" he asked.

She stared back at him. "Do you think you are?"

Marek leaned back in his chair and sighed. "None of this makes any sense," he said. "Is this supposed to make sense? Are you going to explain it to me?"

She shook her head. "It will make sense, but it might take some time. The cards are subtle, not straightforward."

"I don't understand."

"You might need some time to sit with it. The answers will come to you." She gathered the cards into a single pile and carefully wrapped them with the silk scarf, squirreling them into the cupboard. "But it sounds like your storm has passed," she said. "You might as well be on your way."

Marek sat shocked for a moment, unable to stand, to think clearly. Her tale had mesmerized him, but it all seemed like a lot of nonsense. What was the moral of the story? He felt no real connection with it.

Madame Rosivda helped him with his coat and sent him on his way. The clouds had cleared, and the sun shone down. He had all evening to think about the story of the ill-fated emperor. At least he would have something to distract him from the hours he wouldn't be working.

When Marek stepped into his apartment, he wanted to play, even if it was on the cheap keyboard he had bought at a garage sale last summer. The apartment was much too small for even an upright. He wouldn't have managed to get it up the stairs.

He powered up the plastic mimic pretending to be an actual piano and flipped to the section of a song he had been working on. His fingers couldn't find the keys on these few bars, or he wasn't agile enough to hit them at the correct times. He struggled with it for a few minutes, sighed, and gave up. He returned to something more familiar, a song he had played a million times before, and let his mind drift.

As he moved methodically through the song, his thoughts drifted to Mr. Robins and his decision to cut his hours. He could give lessons again. He didn't always have the patience, but his students were always eager to learn. Or at least their parents were keen for them to learn.

At four years old, he hadn't exactly been a prodigy, just a stubborn little boy whose parents insisted he play. He caught on quickly, though, and soon gave recitals and played at all the family gatherings. It wasn't long before they determined this was his calling. He didn't have much to do with that decision. His immigrant parents wanted nothing else for him. His older brother would become a doctor; he would become a pianist.

After leaving the hotel the following day, Marek walked by Madame Rosivda's shop and decided to enter. She was bustling about when he entered, relighting some of the candles that had burned to almost nothing.

"Hi there," she said. "You came back."

He nodded.

"Does that mean you found your emperor?" she asked.

"Not exactly."

She turned to face him, smiling. She wore purple lipstick today and a purple scarf wrapped around her head. "Well, I'm glad you're back. Come, come."

She led him back into the little room with the round table, where the tarot cards sat waiting. She asked if he wanted tea, and he politely declined.

"How much for a reading?" he asked.

"I feel like you weren't satisfied with your last one, so I'll strike a bargain with you."

"Oh, no, you want my firstborn son," he said.

She laughed. "Nothing of the sort. I know you don't have one, so I might be waiting for payment for years. Let's try something much easier."

"What did you have in mind?"

"You owe me a song."

"A song?" He hadn't told her about being a pianist. All she knew, or should know, was his name and where he worked based on their last conversation.

"Yes, a song. You can interpret that as you wish, but must share a song on your next visit. That is your wheelhouse; this is mine. Barter is the best kind of trade."

"But I play piano and can't exactly bring that here."

"You have a keyboard."

Marek wiggled in his seat, suddenly feeling uncomfortable. Now, it felt like she knew far too much. Or maybe she knew just enough to make him uneasy.

She slid the tarot deck toward him. He shuffled and cut the deck, placing both halves back into the middle of the table. The candles sputtered, like lights flickering, momentarily.

"See, you think I am doing the reading," she said. "But you are the conduit. Without you, I couldn't get this started, and the cards would reveal nothing if your hands didn't touch them."

Marek just stared. He still had no expectations. To him, this was just a way to kill some time and nothing more. He had found himself with too much time and needed to use some of it.

3

Judgment

Madame Rosivda turned the card, revealing an angel with blue skin playing the trumpet. His golden wings, two sets of them, rested like a feathered cloak on his shoulders and back. The clouds were slowly clearing, revealing a pale pink sky.

"This is Judgment," said Madame Rosivda.

"Like from Revelations?" Marek asked.

"Revelation angels are much more terrifying. Many more wings and eyes, truly monsters to any human eye. The tarot refers to a judgment of a different kind. Now, I must be more creative because you didn't want any tea. This time, I want you to look into the flame of this center candle here." She motioned toward the one which sat just in front of him, slightly to the right. He let his gaze rest on the flame. "Focus on the candle carefully as I tell you a story."

Marek let his gaze grow soft, the candle fading in the background of his vision. It flickered again like a breeze blew, but the air remained still. Then, it seemed to burn even brighter as Madame Rosivda began to speak.

"Long ago, an angel of God blew his trumpet to welcome the dawn. Each morning, even before the cock crowed or light glowed on the horizon, he would play a few resounding notes. The sun would hear his call and begin to rise, bringing daylight to the plain below. By the time the light reached the people, they believed it had arrived on its own, but little did they know that the light would remain hidden from them without this angel.

"The people in the nearest village hunted often, and the wild game near them soon grew sparse. They had tracked the deer population to near extinction, so the hunting parties had to travel farther and farther away to hunt. They often left early in the morning to go on an expedition and return to the village by midday to feast upon their kill. One hunter, in particular, felt a great excitement each time they traveled further than before. He set off alone one morning, hoping to kill a proud buck with his bow and arrow before the sun began to rise on the horizon.

"Between the trees ahead of him, he heard rustling movement and crept forward slowly. He spied the angel there, bringing the horn to his lips and blowing to wake the sun from its slumber. The hunter wiped his sleepy eyes, hardly believing what he had seen, but sure enough, as the angel finished playing, the sun began to rise. The hunter returned to his village without a kill but shared what he had seen with the rest of his usual hunting party.

"The next day, they left even earlier than usual. Each man had barely slept, eager to capture the angel in a trap. They believed if they could only trap him, they might be able to ask for a blessing from him. They were desperate for the deer population to grow, and this might be the way to bring that abundance back to their village.

"They approached where the hunter had seen the angel the day before, carrying a great net. When they arrived in the clearing, they found the angel sleeping on a large rock, his trumpet at his feet. They consulted one another and decided that capturing the angel himself might be more complicated than initially thought. Yes, he was sleeping, but if they startled him, he could fly away from them. The trumpet, however, lay some distance away from him, and if they were careful, they might be able to take that and then request a favor for its return.

"The bravest among them crept forward, careful to make no noise.

The angel rolled over in his sleep, moaning softly. The hunter may have been brave, but that didn't mean he wasn't afraid. He was just able to push through his fear. He wrapped his fingers around the golden trumpet, snatched it away, and then hurried back into the woods.

"The hunters watched and waited for the angel to wake. Eventually, the angel stretched his arms above his head and sat on the dew-laden grass. He reached for his trumpet, but it was not there. He looked around, confused. Then he stood and began to pace around the clearing, searching for his instrument. He flexed his great wings, slowly rose into the air, and circled above.

"The men whispered among themselves, debating who should approach, and then eventually pushed the not-so-bravest among them forward. The angel swooped down and approached him on foot.

"'Are you looking for this?'" the hunter asked, holding the horn high above his head.

"The angel nodded, not speaking.

"'I will return it to you,' said the hunter. 'In exchange for a favor.'

"The angel spoke, but his voice was deafening. The hunter dropped the trumpet to cover his ears, and the angel swooped in to reclaim it. He flew high up into the heavens and disappeared from view.

"The hunters were crestfallen. Their chance to have their wish granted had passed. They returned to their village in defeat. The next morning, the next, and the next, the angel did not return to call the sun. Their village lay in darkness, and now they had few animals to hunt, and their crops failed."

Marek fell out of his trance with a start. It was like that strange falling feeling you have when dreaming and waking suddenly. He stared at Madame Rosivda, who gave him a coy smile.

"Do all of your stories end in death and destruction?" he asked.

She laughed.

"Well, do they?"

"Just your luck, I guess. I assure you, my tales are not all doom and gloom, but there are a few. It is how you perceive them. Yes, this was an unfortunate tale for the hunters and the people of the village, but the angel saved himself. Who knows what they may have done to him."

"I still don't understand any of this," Marek said. "Who do these people represent? How does it relate to my own life? When will any of this make sense?"

"Like I said. Sometimes, it takes a little while to process. In the future, I suggest not coming two days in a row, back-to-back. While I love to have visitors, and it is great to see you in particular, Marek, taking a break between readings might suit you better."

Marek sighed. "Are you trying to say I'm too dense to get it?"

Madame Rosivda laughed again.

"Don't make fun of me," said Marek.

"I'm not," she said. "You just need time."

"I have way too much time on my hands now."

"Go home," she said. "Work on that song you owe me, and come back next week.

"Does it have to be a new song?" he asked.

"Only if you think it does. I wouldn't know the difference."

"Wouldn't you?"

"I appreciate your belief in my psychic powers, but I assure you, there are many things I don't know." She stood and escorted him back into the entryway.

He wanted to stay, chat about anything, and avoid the real world waiting for him just outside the door, but he couldn't find any words to delay his leaving. Instead, he stepped out into the chilling air. He'd need to turn the heater on at home soon as the days grew ever colder and shorter. "Thank you," he said. The words felt weak and insufficient.

"No problem, dear. Now, you must be on your way. I'll see you next week."

Over the next few days, Marek's life felt highly dull. Each day was the same: he spent his mornings at the hotel, mindlessly running his hands over the piano with Mr. Robins scowling over his shoulder and the afternoons struggling through the few bars he still couldn't quite master on his keyboard. Marek wished he had a hobby outside his work, but he had always been so single-minded that he never gave anything else much time. He wished he could sit in front of the television or find joy in cooking himself dinner. Instead, it was grand piano to electric piano, to rubbing his hands with oil to rest and recharge for the next day. He typically ate frozen dinners heated in the microwave, giving no thought to the food he ate other than something to sate his hunger quickly.

One night, after driving himself to the point of frustration attempting to learn new material, he decided to walk to clear his head. The moon shone large and heavy in the sky, taking on a reddish-orange hue. It was a cloudless night, but the wind blew sharp and cold. Marek pulled his jacket tighter around him and quickened his pace. From a distance, he could hear a horn bee-bopping down the street. There were often buskers, but usually not this late at night, and it had been a long time since Marek had heard anything other than an acoustic guitar. As he grew nearer, he saw a tall man with a long, curly ponytail. His hair fell to the middle of his back, and his trumpet shone in the streetlight. The man swayed, dancing along to his music, and his hair swung to one side, revealing an angel wing pattern on the back of his jean jacket.

Marek tried not to stare. Although he hadn't made any connection to the Emperor card, this was so obviously Judgment that he had to pause and catch his breath momentarily. He walked closer and stopped to listen. The horn player's eyes sparkled, welcoming him as he continued to play. Marek pulled his billfold from his pocket, removed a wrinkled bill, and dropped it into the hat, which sat at the horn player's feet. The man smiled as he lowered his horn.

"Thank you," he said.

"Your music is wonderful," said Marek. "Do you usually play so late?"

"Not usually. I got wrapped up in the music and lost track of time."

"Happens sometimes. What is your name?"

"I'm Abaddon," he said.

"That's a unique name. I'm Marek."

"You're not exactly Joe Smith, yourself."

The two men exchanged a look of recognition. They spent so much of their lives spelling and pronouncing their names for others. It created an immediate connection between them. A barely spoken one, but it was enough.

"Do you live around here?" asked Marek.

"That's a strange question to ask a stranger."

"I didn't mean it as anything. I just thought maybe you'd like a drink."

"I should be getting home."

Marek sensed Abaddon's uneasiness. He was trying to be friendly but must have said the wrong thing. Maybe the horn player thought he was trying to come on to him. That wasn't his intent at all.

"Just a friendly drink. One before calling it a night?"

"No, man. It's quite late. But maybe I'll see you around?"

Marek searched Abaddon's eyes and found fear there. The man looked away, staring at the sidewalk between them. Somehow, Marek didn't even know how to make friends anymore. He let his hopes die and fade away. He turned away and started down the street, trying to pretend this awkward interaction hadn't happened. Maybe he had been too eager? He hoped that he would run into the trumpet player again, though. It would be nice to have a musician friend again. It had been so long since he'd had anyone to share music with - to play with, even if it was just accompaniment.

Just as Marek was about to round the corner, a voice called out to him.

"Hey, man. Sorry, I'm just tired." Abaddon smiled sheepishly.

Marek shouted back. "It's alright. I'll see you soon." Somehow, he was sure of it, too.

That night, Marek dreamed for the first time in a long time, and when he dreamed, it was of a large man sitting on a throne. The man stroked his long beard and looked out upon the land he ruled over. Darkness spread across the land, enveloping everything. The emperor rose from his throne and returned to his chambers, closing the doors behind him. He could no longer look at the destruction he had wrought.

When Marek woke, he did not feel refreshed but more exhausted than when he had first laid down.

Marek returned to work each morning to play at The Den but felt like a zombie, devoid of thought and emotion. It had become a chore for him, no longer enjoyable if it ever had been. It didn't help that Mr. Robins would spend minutes at a time standing a short distance away, scowling at him. It felt like his boss constantly judged him and found him wanting. The customers and other passers ignored him as if he were just a part of the furniture and not a living, breathing human being. How had it come to this?

Marek had played piano all his life but was never a virtuoso. He mastered the movements, the keys responding to his fingers, but he could never feel the music as some musicians claimed to. Instead, it was a transaction, an exchange between the sheet music, his fingers, and other people's ears. Those around him seemed to get satisfaction from it, but he never did. He sometimes felt a sense of accomplishment when he finally mastered a complex piece, but it was from the successful completion, not the music, that he drew that satisfaction.

Marek closed the fallboard, hiding the keys away. He would take a break now, stretch and massage his hands, and briefly walk around the lobby. Although his stomach had begun to growl, he needed to stretch and move around a little before returning to play. This time, instead of standing and lurking from the lobby floor, Mr. Robins stood on the steps of the grand entrance. Few guests used these steps because they were long, winding, and burdensome but looked glamorous. Until Mr. Robins, the goblin, stood on them.

Mr. Robins beckoned to him with one gnarled finger.

Marek sighed heavily and moved toward him.

"So," said Mr. Robins. "I managed to book Timmy from across the street for Sunday."

Marek struggled to keep calm.

"We're gonna give him a trial run."

"What are you saying?" asked Marek. He could feel his face getting hot.

"No need to come on Sunday. You get the day off. Have some fun."

Marek glared at his boss. With Mr. Robins standing a few steps up, he matched Marek in height for once. It was disconcerting and disorienting. Marek wanted to yell but didn't want to make a scene.

Mr. Robins touched the lion's head, which capped off the railing. He looked pretty pleased with himself, with a sly grin spreading his lips.

"I don't feel well," said Marek. "I think I need to go home."

"Suit yourself. As you can see, I don't need you anyway." Mr. Robins motioned to the rest of the lobby, which was empty save for the receptionist sitting at her desk in front.

Marek walked out, eager for the cool air on his skin. Things were only getting worse. He needed to start planning a backup plan in case Mr. Robins decided to fire him. He quickly walked the few blocks home and returned to the song he had been struggling with. Marek wanted to see Madame Rosivda but remembered she had demanded a song. This adagio could be the piece if he could only get his fingers to move how he wanted them to.

After a few more tries, he hit it correctly for the first time, then again and again. He played over the section until he felt comfortable that he would be able to replicate it without too much struggle. Then he strapped the keyboard to his back and walked down to the divinity shop. When he entered, Madame Rosivda was actually in session with another customer. Somehow, Marek had forgotten that she must have other clients, especially since no money had exchanged hands. Unless she were independently wealthy, she would need to make her money somehow.

Marek practiced his fingering without turning the keyboard on to avoid disturbing them. He ran his hands over the plastic keys. It was never quite the same as playing a real piano, but it served its purpose. Most of the candles had burned themselves out, but the smoke smell remained, distracting him. Marek felt impatient; how long would he have to wait?

Just when his nerves were beginning to rattle him, a tall, svelte woman stepped through the beaded curtain. His eyes were immediately drawn to her, especially because she wore a tight evening dress in the middle of the day. As she walked through the entryway and out the front door, he couldn't help but stare. She was gorgeous, with deep honey-colored skin and long, curly hair that fell to the small of her back. What would it feel like to touch her there? He wondered. Eventually, Madame Rosivda emerged, scolding him.

"You like Olive?" she asked. Then she shook her head. "Of course you do. Everyone likes Olive."

Marek was at a loss for words. He felt like he was dreaming, and reality hadn't washed back over him yet.

"You brought me a song?" she asked. "How wonderful!"

Marek stared after Olive, unable to look away from the door she had just passed through.

"Wake up, lover boy. She's gone, but I can introduce you next time if you would like."

Marek shook his head, trying to clear the burning from his brain. He had never seen a woman so beautiful, or at least one who made him flush with desire the way she did. He didn't believe in love at first sight, but lust was another matter altogether.

"Yes, I brought you a song," he said. "Do you have a chair or a stool I could use?"

Madame Rosivda bustled in and out of the back room, bringing a short, three-legged stool for him to sit on. It wasn't comfortable by any means, but Marek would make do. He hoped to replicate the success he had mustered earlier in his apartment. He pulled the sheet music from his bag and set it carefully in front of the keys. He sat, and his fingers found the keys. He managed to play with no mistakes the first time through, but the sound felt hollow, without substance.

Madame Rosivda nodded, thanking him for the song, but also offered him some criticism. "That was nice, Marek, but have you ever considered writing your own music?"

He smirked. "What, not good enough for you?"

"I didn't say that." She turned away from him, tending to her dwindling candles. He wondered how long it would be until she gave up on the dilapidated wax mess and replaced them with fresh ones.

Marek stood and began breaking down the keyboard and returning it to its case. Madame Rosivda finished relighting her candles.

She ushered him into her backroom and offered him some tea, which he accepted. When she returned with the steaming hot mug, she asked him the question again. "Have you ever written a song?" she asked.

"Actually, no," he said. "I've never been that creative."

"No interest in it?" she asked.

"I feel more comfortable playing music other people have written."

"What a shame," she said. "I think you'd be rather good at it."

"What makes you think that?"

"Just a hunch."

She unwrapped the tarot cards from their back scarf and handed them to him to shuffle. The ritual had already become routine for them. Suddenly, Marek felt the urge to tell her everything that had happened, about how he had found the "angel" she had told him about, the angel playing his horn in the street. But before he could begin, she began speaking again.

"So you met your angel? The angel of Judgment?" she asked.

Marek stared. "How did you know?"

"There are many things I know. You should have gathered that by now. What did you think of Judgment?"

"Not exactly what I expected," said Marek. "And he had a strange name. What was it? Armageddon? No, not that. Abaddon, I think."

"Abaddon?"

"Yes, that sounds about right."

Madame Rosivda frowned at Marek across the table. "Do you know what that name means?" she asked.

"No, I can't say that I do, but I'm going to guess you're going to tell me."

"I don't want to worry you, but it is not a name that brings good fortune."

"So you're saying I should avoid him?"

Marek looked away. The whole thing had made him uneasy, and the poor man seemed afraid of him. He should let it go. It was a strange coincidence that he would run into a trumpet player after drawing the Judgment card. But a trumpet player with angel wings on his jacket? It seemed too coincidental. It must mean something, surely.

"Abaddon means 'Place of Destruction.' The Bible depicts Abaddon as the Destroyer, the angel of the Abyss in Revelations. In many cases, he appears as a demon rather than an angel," said Madame Rosivda.

"Can't say I'm up on my Christian mythology," said Marek. "And who would name their child such a thing?"

"Some people name their children without considering the meaning. That's how we wind up with Shitheads. Parents like the sound of the word or phrase but don't name their children carefully."

"Wait, did you say shithead?" Marek laughed. "I don't think that falls in the same category as this."

Madame Rosivda grew more serious. "In reality, it is more likely they did know the meaning of the name to choose something so specific from The Bible. Many people aren't well versed in Revelations but may have a specific connection. I suggest asking your friend about it if you're feeling particularly adventurous. Why did his parents name him this, and what does he think it means."

"I had no idea it had such significance," said Marek. "It just seemed like an interesting name to me." He paused, shuffling the cards, cutting them, and laying them on the table.

"Now that we've been talking about him, Abaddon may be the focus of this reading. I should have told you to clear your head," said Madame Rosivda. "Would you like some time to sit and sip your tea before we continue?"

"I think it will be fine," said Marek. "I am curious about him. But I'm also curious about the Emperor. I don't think I've encountered him outside my dreams yet."

Madame Rosivda had reached over the table, ready to flip the top card, but now she paused, staring into Marek's eyes. He felt naked, stripped, and uncomfortable. He could never hold eye contact very long with anyone. He looked away, off into the corner of the room, where he spied a few cobwebs clinging to the ceiling.

"Tell me about your dream," she said.

"Well, it was similar to the story you told me. The emperor was sitting on his throne, looking over his kingdom. But as he sat there, darkness came over the land, slowly creeping up and making everything dark."

"Describe this darkness more. What did it look like? How would you describe it?"

"Kind of like a rolling fog or smoke. It was black; I couldn't see through it."

"Were you the emperor or watching him?" she asked.

"I'm not sure," said Marek. "My dreams are so strange sometimes. I only really remember them when they are strange. Sometimes, it feels like I'm watching the action play out rather than participating. Like watching a movie of myself. But I wasn't the emperor myself; I don't think so."

"I see."

"Do you think the emperor is a real person?" Marek asked.

"What do you think?"

"I think he might be." Marek took a drink of his tea. He had already drunk most of it while they talked. "Any chance I could get a refill?" he asked.

"Certainly."

While she wandered off for more tea, he began to daydream. He often played songs in his head. His thoughts returned to the piece he had just played for Madame Rosivda. Except, in his mind's eye, he played the grand piano in The Den. He could feel the heat of Mr. Robins' eyes on his shoulders. The man was constantly watching. Even after all this time, Marek couldn't quite get used to it. It was a bit like being an animal in a cage. Most of the time, people didn't outright stop and stare. Usually, they walked on by like he was wallpaper or furniture, but not Mr. Robins. Maybe that made it so disconcerting - that he wasn't used to that reaction. And it had been years since he had performed in concert - so there had been no audience for quite some time.

In his daydream, Marek finished the song and then stood to leave.

As he often did, Mr. Robins beckoned to him not to offer praise but criticism. But when he turned to face the staircase, it wasn't Mr. Robins who greeted him, but the emperor from his dream, tall and robust. While Mr. Robins inspired only annoyance and frustration, this man inspired fear.

Madame Rosivda returned with another steaming hot cup of tea. Marek jerked awake, and she saw his sudden movement. "Are you alright, dear?" she asked.

"I think I know who the emperor is," said Marek.

"Oh, do you, now?"

"I think it is my boss."

"What makes you think that?" she asked.

Marek thought for a moment. Was there anything outside of this brief daydream that connected Mr. Robins to the emperor? Again, they looked nothing alike, but there was something similar in character.

"He's money-grubbing for sure," said Marek. "Only cares about the bottom line."

"What's the hesitation? Does he not *look* like the emperor?"

Marek brought his fist down on the table, sending it wobbling. "That's exactly it, I think. He doesn't look like the emperor, almost the opposite, but the attitude is there. The selfishness, the only thing that matters to him is money."

"Divination is not always a straightforward thing," said Madame Rosivda. "It seldom is. Not all cards will fit nicely into your definition of them."

Marek reflected on this. "I can't expect every card to be a character in my life, can I?"

"Not hardly. Do you know how many cards are in a tarot deck?"

"No idea, but I know it is more than fifty-two."

"There are 78 cards," she said. "Twenty-two major arcana and 56 minor arcana."

"What does that mean?"

"So far, you have only drawn major arcana. These cards tend to relate to major events in your life. The minor arcana are similar to a deck of cards with four suits: wands, chalices, swords, and coins. Each suit has face cards, the page, knight, king, and queen, and numbered cards from one through ten."

Marek was interested but more eager to see what the next card would hold for him. "Let's get on with it, then," he said.

She handed the deck back to him. "After all this talking, I suggest you clear your head and shuffle again." Marek struggled to clear his thoughts. He reshuffled the cards, laid them on the table, cut the deck, and laid both stacks at the center.

4

Death

Madame Rosivda turned the card, revealing a young woman holding a plump, golden baby. This card appeared upside down to Marek, so he struggled to make out the picture. The baby had wings, like an angel, and reached out to yellow butterflies as they fluttered by. The woman's cloak held the night sky and stars around herself and the child. Poppies hung from the ceiling above them, but the child paid them no mind. He was much more interested in the butterflies. While the child looked delighted at the world around him, the mother looked down upon him with sorrow. What was she so sad about?

"This is the Death card," said Madame Rosivda.

"Does that mean someone is going to die?" asked Marek. "And what does it mean that it is upside down?"

"Relax, " she said. "This card infrequently means actual death; if it does, it is typically not the seeker's death."

"Am I the seeker?" Marek asked.

"Yes."

She pulled out the shallow bowl and motioned for him to pour his remaining tea. The liquid settled, but as he watched, it quaked and shivered. He wanted to ask why it did that, make sure it wasn't just his imagination, but she had begun telling a story about the card, and he fell into a trance, not unlike his earlier daydream.

"There once was a young woman," she said. "Who was visited by an angel in her dreams. The angel spoke in her dreams because if he came to her in his proper form, she would likely be terrified of him, and he wouldn't be able to speak with her calmly. He told her she would soon conceive a child with heavenly origins. He warned that the child would be with her for only a short time, but she must love him wholeheartedly and make his time on Earth as wonderful and loving as possible.

"When she woke, she remembered the dream but tried to push it aside. She had no lovers, so how would she conceive a child, much less a Heavenly child? But as the weeks passed, her stomach grew, and she felt the infant kick within her womb. Immediately, she loved this child and sang to it each day. She feared the birth and the short life the child would have, as the angel had predicted, but she felt such a strong attachment to the baby, even before his birth.

"When the baby was finally born, his skin was a strange golden hue. He seemed to almost sparkle in the sunlight. He was also born with two small stubs on his back. She worried that this was a congenital disability that would lead to his death, but when the doctor suggested removing them, she wouldn't let him approach with his scalpel. The boy was born the way he was meant to enter this world, she believed, and wouldn't allow the surgeon to make any alterations.

"Within the first week, the stubs grew into wings, complete with feathers, and she feared someone would take her child from her if anyone else knew. She kept him constantly swaddled, only uncovering the wings when she bathed him secretly. As he grew, the child always wanted to be outside, but she didn't want anyone to know about his wings, so she only took him into the courtyard rather than out in public.

"The baby was especially interested in the yellow butterflies which would alight on the flowers, floating from one to the next. She feared that he would eventually learn how to fly himself and leave her. So she held on to him tightly as he watched the butterflies with awe and amazement.

"But eventually, this baby grew into a young boy, and she could not always carry him around. She made him unique clothing with slits for his wings so that he could stretch them and be comfortable. It had become too complex to hide them entirely, so everyone in the household knew about his uniqueness, but they kept him hidden from the rest of the town. He was only allowed to go out in the courtyard, where he chased butterflies and frolicked among the flowers.

"The young woman would sit outside with him, watching him play, until one day, he began to jump into the air, testing his wings as he floated down. She warned him that he could try his wings out but that he shouldn't leave the confines of the courtyard.

"He whined, as many young men do, accusing her of not loving him. He claimed she wouldn't imprison him this way if she truly loved him. She would let him go exploring. She would be proud of his flying. He accused her of being jealous that she didn't have her own wings. She punished him by sending him back inside, saying she would not let him out until he learned to control himself.

"But the following day, he snuck out into the courtyard, flew up into the rafters, and sat there, looking down on the small garden. When she awoke, she found him and tried to convince him to come back down. He would not, but he cried salty tears, realizing he would need to leave her there. He couldn't deny his nature, and he needed to fly.

"She begged him not to go. He was too young to survive on his own, she argued. He was still just a young boy and needed her protection. He told her she was wrong, that he was an angel and needed to return to Heaven to be with his kind. He lit off from the rafters, and she watched as he rose higher and higher into the sky. He flew above the clouds, and she never saw him again."

Marek held onto the image of the young, winged boy for a moment, wishing that he, too, could fly away into the clouds. Even if just for a moment, he would love the ability to escape from his life. "What does it mean?" he finally asked.

"What do you think it means?" Madame Rosivda rose from the table, gathered the cards together, and wrapped them in the black scarf before returning them to their place in the cabinet.

"Why do I always feel more confused after we do a reading?" asked Marek.

Madame Rosivda shrugged.

"I thought I was supposed to feel more clarity."

"You will, eventually. As I said before, it takes time. The cards are a starting point, not a resolution. So many of my clients haven't quite grasped that."

"What does it mean that the card was upside down?" he asked.

"Death is typically a card about loss. That it came up reversed relates to you handling that loss. If the card were upright, you would accept that loss in a way that would allow you to move on. When the card appears reversed, the loss will take more time to get over. It may delay the querent from moving on and living their life."

"It feels like these cards relate more to other people than me," said Marek. "I'm not sure how this connects back to me."

"The world doesn't revolve around you, Marek. Sometimes it might seem to because you can't escape the flesh vessel you are in, but overall, you are a small player in a much larger story."

Marek left with more questions than answers, as he had the last few times. As he made his way home, the keyboard felt heavier than it should, in its case slung over his shoulder. Madame Rosivda wanted him to compose a song for her, so it might be some time before he could return. At least she wasn't charging him money because he didn't have much, but he felt she would be disappointed if he tried to pass off another song as his own.

Several feet ahead, Marek spied Abaddon busking on the corner. Several people walked by, barely paying the trumpet player any mind, as if he were a beggar rather than a performer looking to make some money. Marek approached, smiling, and listened to a song before trying to initiate a conversation.

"You're persistent, aren't you?" asked Abaddon.

"What do you mean?"

"Never mind. What's that you've got in your bag?"

"A piano."

"A whole baby grand?"

"Not quite. Keyboard."

Abaddon smiled up at him. "Well, bring her out, why don't you?"

"Oh, no, I couldn't. This corner is your spot."

Abaddon winked. "Well, yes, but I thought maybe we could jam."

"I'm classically trained."

"What does that mean? You can't play with other people?"

"I'm no good at improv." Marek wished that weren't the case, but it was entirely accurate. He had never been able to play off the cuff the way many musicians could. He could play songs he had memorized but not improvise.

"Well, how about this," said Abaddon. "You play something, and I'll contribute to whatever you're playing."

Marek hesitated. A couple holding hands crossed in front of them. The man turned to mock them. "You guys playing or what?"

Abaddon just nodded. "Give us a second to set up, boss." He turned back to Marek. "Well, what do you say?"

Marek set his case on the ground, unzipped it, and pulled the keyboard out. Once again, he had no stool, so he set the keyboard up to standing height. It would be a near miracle to play comfortably. He felt so nervous, and his fingers were almost shaking. Just with Abaddon watching, with his wide green eyes, he felt so incredibly naked. That was it. Bare, like in those nightmares when you're late for school and when you get there, you aren't wearing any pants. But Abaddon was surprisingly patient and ran through a few scales while he waited. The trumpet's clarion call was perfect, and Marek wondered what kind of improvisation he would provide to what would most likely be Mozart or Bach.

Finally, Marek's hands found the keys. He ran through his scales, although it wasn't like he needed to tune his instrument like other musicians, just limber up his fingers. He launched into a song he often played at the beginning of his sets at the hotel because it was so familiar to him. Abaddon listened for a few seconds, nodding like a metronome keeping time. Tik up, Tock down, Tik up, Tock down. He waited for a few bars before jumping in, like a little girl on the playground watching the rope twirlers before jumping in for double Dutch. He pressed his thick lips to the mouthpiece, and the sound that came out sounded like the voice of an angel.

Marek had to shut his mind down to imagine he could not hear Abaddon's trumpet so he could continue playing with accuracy. But part of him wanted to stop playing and listen to the other musician. Eventually, the song fell away from him, his fingers ceased moving, and he did just that. Abaddon ran away with the music, playing a soulful solo that echoed off the surrounding buildings. Passersby stopped and turned and stared. A group of teenagers, usually distracted by the sound of their voices, stopped to listen. One of them began dancing, and his movements were rhythmic and jerky as he moved one part of his body separate from the others before moving on to the next – his arms and legs moving independently.

When Abaddon had finished, the crowd gathered broke into loud applause, and Marek felt like a tiny fly just watching, somehow separate from the scene surrounding him. Several audience members approached with crumpled bills to put in Abaddon's hat. Marek stared dumbly at his keyboard. If only he could be creative like that. Somehow, his music always felt restricted and restrained. He never felt the piece like others did, sometimes making him question whether he was even in the right profession. Maybe he should have become an accountant or something.

When the crowd had dispersed, Abaddon turned to him. "What happened, man? I wasn't trying to steal the show, but you just stopped playing."

Marek was taking down the keyboard, folding its legs, and sliding it back into its pouch. "I told you I'm no good at this kind of playing."

Abaddon likewise wiped and stowed away his instrument. "What kind of playing do you do?"

"I play in a hotel lobby. I used to do the nine yards of recitals, tux with tails."

"What happened?" asked Abaddon.

"I'm not a cute little prodigy anymore."

Abaddon winked. "I think you're kinda cute."

Marek could feel the heat rising in his cheeks. It was always lovely to be complimented, even if he didn't reciprocate the feeling.

As they each finished putting away their respective instruments, Abaddon made a suggestion. "How about we get that drink?" he asked.

"You didn't seem too eager for one the other night," said Marek.

"Well, no. I didn't know you then, did I? You were just a strange man walking by at night. Now that I see you in the light of day, I think differently of you."

"Where to?" asked Marek.

"The Royal Club."

"What's that?"

"Jazz lounge. We can grab a few and listen to music while we're at it. But we'll have to grab a taxi unless you want to tote that thing for ten blocks."

"I think a taxi will be fine."

While the taxi slid silently through the night, Marek watched buildings fly past the window. He had come to this town looking for new opportunities but hadn't found any. If only Marek could get beyond his insecurities, maybe he would have been able to join a musical group or play with people like Abaddon and ride on their coattails to the top. He wasn't strong enough to advocate for himself and never had been. When he first started playing piano at the ripe age of four, he hated it with a passion that burned deep in his chest. He was a child, of course, and that had something to do with it. He'd much rather run around than sit still for an hour a day learning to play. But would he have pursued something else if his parents hadn't pushed him into this life? It was a question that haunted him.

Abaddon nudged him then, leaning his shoulder into him. The warmth and scent of the other man reached him and woke him from his reverie. "Hey, Marek, what are you thinking about, man? You've been awfully quiet."

Marek turned away from the window, giving his attention to his companion. "Nothing."

"You seem engrossed in this nothing." Abaddon laughed, glancing out his window. "We're nearly there."

Marek nodded.

Moments later, the taxi pulled to the curb, letting them out into the night. A bit of pink still hung at the horizon's edge, but the clouds had gathered in, darkening the sky. For a Thursday, quite a few people gathered on the streets, walking, lingering, and gathering in amorphous groups that came together and then separated again. As the taxi pulled away, Marek looked up at the sign for the club, which looked like an old-fashioned theatre marquee. It read: The Jazz Club and listed some upcoming acts, including Tango Louise and The Beats. He had never heard of them, but that wasn't surprising. They were likely local bands that hadn't made the big time yet and likely never would.

Abaddon motioned him forward, pushing his way through the revolving door. Inside, a lush red carpet ran the length of the lounge, winding up to the stage. Marek watched, feeling like a voyeur, as Abaddon veered to the right, sidling up to the bar. A few other patrons already gathered there, bent over their drinks. The lights were dim, the mood calm, a bit exhausted even. The night had hardly begun.

Abaddon looked back at Marek over his shoulder as the bartender approached. "What do you want? First round's on me."

"Just beer-flavored beer. I'm not picky."

"You want a cocktail menu?" the bartender offered. He was a rail-thin man with a mustache too big for his face. He had waxed the tips into a sinister but somewhat crooked curlicue.

Marek bellied up to the bar. "No, really, beer is fine."

Abaddon stared at him. "Really, man? Live a little. You don't have to get barrel-aged stout, but at least have a whiskey or something."

"I don't drink hard liquor."

"Then have it with water."

Abaddon ordered a concoction with no less than fifteen ingredients while Marek sipped his whiskey. It wasn't bad, just not what he was used to. He had never been much of a drinker, even in college. He preferred to keep his senses sharp, but the world he experienced with those senses wasn't always ideal. Maybe he'd be better off a little numb to it all.

When the bartender finished Abaddon's drink, finishing it with a foam of egg white, a lavender bud, and a shake of edible glitter, they stepped away to find a table. A small tea light sat in a glass container at each table. Marek couldn't help but compare them to Madame Rosivda's candles. In comparison, these were pinpricks of light, barely recognizable as a flame. He followed Abaddon to a table so close to the stage that he could reach out and touch it if he wanted to. No musicians were playing yet; they'd have to wait at least half an hour for the entertainment to begin.

The stage was reminiscent of a community theatre stage, a bit dusty, painted a flat black with the signature red curtain drawn across the backstage area. A single spotlight focused on a microphone, waiting for someone to perform in its glow. Marek knew this was a jazz club but wasn't sure what the working definition of jazz would be here – it was a genre that was always difficult to define accurately.

He glanced back to Abaddon, who sipped his drink from a curlicued pink straw and smiled back at him. "Now I'm glad I passed on the cocktail," he said.

Abaddon smirked, straightening. "You wouldn't appreciate the work that went into this beauty, then."

"I wouldn't be caught dead drinking that."

Abaddon pinched the straw with two fingers, twirling it through the foam, sending the edible glitter cascading down into the depths, changing the entire concoction into a rich purple.

"Does that thing have a name?" asked Marek.

"A Friend of Dorothy's."

"Who's Dorothy?"

"If you don't know, you're clearly not one of her friends."

Marek grunted in reply, taking such a long swig of his whiskey that it made him wince.

A waitress wearing a tight black dress approached. The shiny pleather clung to every curve of her body like someone had painted it onto her. Marek felt his eyes widen. It was only natural to appreciate such a thing of beauty, he told himself, and yet he hated the animalistic part of himself that had such immediate reactions.

"Looking for something to satisfy your appetite, Abaddon?" she asked.

Marek wondered for a moment, just precisely what she was offering.

She leaned over the table, and Marek glimpsed her cleavage. Abaddon reached up to run one finger over her cheek, and she laughed, a sound like tinkling bells.

"Just the regular, darling," said Abaddon.

She turned to Marek, straightening. Her short black hair framed her face perfectly. She extended one hand to him, and he struggled to take it. Given her interaction with Abaddon, they shook hands overly formally. Her hand was tiny and cold, her fingers like fragile icicles.

"I don't believe we've met," she said.

As Marek sat dumb and starstruck, Abaddon gave the introductions.

"Nyx, this is Marek. Marek, this is Nyx, and no, she's not on the market."

Marek stuttered, trying to protest that he had no such intentions.

Nyx laughed again. "No worries. I'm used to it. What can I get you, gentlemen?"

"I'll have my usual," said Abaddon. "My friend will need a menu."

Marek protested. "I'm not that hungry," he said.

Abaddon spoke for him again. "I'm sure you can manage a little snack." Then, in a conspiratorial whisper, he added, "Would you believe he's not a friend of Dorothy's."

Nyx looked Marek over again as if assessing his value. "Yes, I would believe that," she said, "but I can't believe he's here with you."

Marek watched her walk away, entranced. He couldn't resist a

"I'm so sorry."

"It's fine. It's not, but what can you say about it? I'm sorry for bringing it up. When I've been drinking, it all comes back up again. I can't keep it pushed down, you know?"

Marek nodded.

"Why are *you* so down?" she asked. "Bet you can't top my sob story."

"No, I can't." He sipped at his whiskey. It was about time for another refill or to call it a night, but he would wait for Abaddon to return before heading out. "I'm naturally an Eeyore."

"An Eeyore?"

"From Winnie the Pooh. I'm just always gloomy, no matter what is happening. But nothing great has happened lately either."

"Part of it is just perspective."

Abaddon returned, smelling like dank weed and smiling profusely. "What have you downers been grumping about?" he asked.

"Nothing," said Marek.

"Just the same old things," said Nyx.

Abaddon wrapped his arms around their shoulders, pulling them closer to him. "I'm so high. You're killing my vibe already." He paused then, looking from Nyx to Marek and back again. "How about some shots?"

They bellied up to the bar for a round of shots and then refilled their drinks. The live performances had ended, and the lights dimmed as bass bumped through the speakers. Abaddon showed off his moves, undulating between them, swaying with Nyx to the beat. Marek took his turn, feeling her slip comfortably into his arms. Before long, the pleasant buzz of drunkenness overtook them, and they forgot their darker conversation.

5

The Three of Chalices

Madame Rosivda turned the card, revealing a trio of mermaids embracing each other at the hips. They smiled at one another as if they shared a secret. Their fins floated around them like layered dresses, and their tails intertwined beneath where they swam. In great curlicues, their hair swayed with the water. It was the Three of Chalices.

"Once upon a time," said Madame Rosivda, "There were three mermaids, sisters, who were separated from the rest of their pod by a violent storm. As the waters calmed, they realized they could not find any of the other merpeople and that they were, indeed, alone. They did not know if the others had perished in the storm or if they could not find them. They learned to hunt and survive independently, building a more profound connection than ever because it was just the three of them. After several years had passed, with no link to anyone else, they began to feel lonely.

"Early one morning, a fisherman came to the beach and cast his line into the water. One of the mermaids got snagged on his hook, which clung tight to one of the scales in her tail. He began to reel in, and she struggled to escape him. When he saw what he had caught, the fisherman couldn't believe his eyes. She begged him to release her, which he did willingly. He surely wouldn't eat her, at least. But in return, he asked her to visit him the next day. Reluctantly, she agreed.

"The next day, the fisherman returned, but he did not come alone. Two of his friends came with him. When the mermaid came to visit him, she also brought her sisters. The mermaids swam onto a large rock that protruded from the surf and sang for the fishermen, who were all in awe of their mysterious beauty. Entranced, the fishermen abandoned their rods and swam out toward them.

"As they drew closer, the mermaids allowed them to cling to their tails, pulling them further out into the surf, farther than they could swim on their own. But when they reached the rock, the mermaids swam away from them, escaping to the depths where they couldn't follow. The men climbed onto the stone for fresh air and found themselves trapped there. They couldn't swim back. Eventually, the first mermaid returned with this promise: if the men would join them and agree to father their children, they could live with them in peace and harmony in the depths of the sea. If not, they would abandon them there to die of starvation or exposure, whichever would take their lives first.

"Given this choice, which wasn't a choice, they agreed to join the mermaids. 'But how will we breathe?' they asked, 'For we lack gills, as you can see.' The mermaid gave them each a necklace of golden shells, and as soon as they placed them around their necks, gills grew from their skin, allowing them to breathe under the water. They swam with them to the depths of the sea, where they learned to live the way the mermaids did, eating fish and fathering an entire pod of merchildren."

Marek seemed to be hanging on at The Lion's Den by a thread. While he still played music in the lobby each morning and afternoons on the weekend, it felt like Mr. Robins was always watching. Didn't that man have anything better to do? Instead of concentrating on the music, Marek let his mind wander. He wondered what being a merman or even a man with gills would be like. The longer he thought about it, the sillier it felt. It was a daydream, just a way to occupy his thoughts. He still hadn't written a song for Madame Rosivda. As a musician, that shouldn't be such an impossible task. It should be a cinch, but maybe he just wasn't that kind of a musician. Perhaps he wasn't meant to be creative like that.

Abaddon had begged him to come to Open Jam at The Royal Club that Thursday. Maybe he'd make it. Perhaps he wouldn't. Maybe he'd just go to listen. Marek had made no promises. But something needed to change. He knew Mr. Robins could fire him any day now, and he should be looking for a new gig already. Of course, the Open Jam operated more like an open mic and was an unpaid gig. But, if he could get in good with other musicians, more opportunities might open up. Marek pictured himself busking with Abaddon on the corner and remembered how much of a failure that had been. He felt so out of place, like he didn't belong there. Besides, even a keyboard wasn't the most portable instrument. Why couldn't he have learned something sexier, like the saxophone?

In the middle of a set, Mr. Robins snuck up behind him, tapping him on the shoulder. Marek nearly jumped out of his skin. Mr. Robins leaned over him, his foul breath in his ear. Marek resisted the urge to flinch away.

"I know you're in the middle of things," he said, "but we should go for a little walk. What do you say?"

Marek nodded, no words at the ready. He slowly stood as his manager took a few steps backward. "Where to, boss?" he asked.

Mr. Robins grabbed Marek's arm at the elbow as if escorting him. Could this get any more awkward? Sure enough, it could; as they walked past the registration desk, the clerk there, a young man with a massive beard named Daniel, gave them a little wave. Marek wished he could disappear. It was a good thing only a few people were milling about the lobby at this hour, but it still felt ridiculous. Mr. Robins finally let Marek's arm drop and walked briskly ahead. He left Marek to follow him through the revolving door.

They stood in the fresh, cool air of the street, and suddenly Marek wanted a cigarette, bad. He had finally managed to quit a few years ago, but when stress hit him suddenly like this, the craving always returned. It felt like an unscratchable itch. Instead, he licked his lips and swallowed hard.

"It will be getting cold soon," said Mr. Robins. "Hope there won't be too many bums hanging around this year."

Marek remembered a man coming into the lobby to warm himself. Staff constantly asked him to leave, but Marek felt some sympathy. After all, he had nowhere else to go, and the entrance was technically a public space. You just couldn't go up the stairs and bother the guests. Then, one day, he stopped coming. Marek wondered if he had just given up or if something had happened to him. Winters here could get dangerously cold, and he had been quite old. He might have died on the streets, but what did Mr. Robins care?

"Marek?"

"Yes, sir."

"You know you don't need to 'sir' me, right? I mean, I do appreciate it, but -"

"Yes, sir."

Mr. Robins let out an exasperated sigh. "Alright, then. I didn't bring you out here just to smell the daisies. We're going on a little field trip."

"Where to?"

"The Ziggurat."

Marek held back the groan that built up inside him. This little trip couldn't be good news. The Ziggurat was their competitor, across the street and down about a block. Mr. Robins walked briskly, but Marek could easily keep up with his much longer legs. He needed to slow his pace to avoid stepping on the man's heels. They walked silently, but Marek could feel his heart beating loudly in his chest. His breath came rapidly as well. What sort of madness was this?

Mr. Robins stopped abruptly in front of The Ziggurat. The Middle-Eastern-style pillars shone golden in the mid-morning sunlight. It felt like they were standing at the entrance to an ancient temple rather than a high-class hotel. Wind whipping through a large fountain sent spray their way. Marek winced, covering his eyes from the mist.

As a bellhop opened the doors for them, Mr. Robins turned to Marek. "Time to see what the competition is up to."

Even this early, the lobby was teeming with people, and the heat radiating from the crowd made Marek feel nauseous. He swallowed hard again, feeling the warmth rise on his face. The pianist here swayed back and forth as he ran his fingers over the keys. Marek could imagine him wearing oversized sunglasses, accurately portraying Ray Charles. The crowd likewise moved with the music. Not a single person stood still. All eyes were on Timmy; all hands were full of drinks, some alcoholic. Even this early in the morning.

Mr. Robins nodded approvingly. "Now, this is a party," he said.

Marek's eyes fell to the floor. It wouldn't be long now. He knew he'd soon be history.

They stood there, taking the scene in for what felt like forever. Mr. Robins looked around, smiling broadly. Yes, it was the competition, but he had his bid for Timmy. He planned to offer more money and give him the weekend shift at The Den. The music was loud and made Marek's ears hurt. Suddenly, he felt like he couldn't breathe and rushed back into the street. Mr. Robins followed him.

"See," Mr. Robins said, "Why can't you gather a crowd like that?"

Marek couldn't hold back any longer. He felt the anger rise in him like an unstoppable storm. "I know, alright?" His ordinarily calm demeanor erupted into an angry outburst. "I know you want to get rid of me. It's only a matter of time. You want that guy in there, not me."

"I never said that."

"You might as well have!"

Mr. Robins raised his voice, trying to match the tone of Marek's. "You still have your weekdays. You're still on the payroll. You've been a loyal employee. I'm not ready to let you go just yet."

"Aren't you, though? Isn't that what you're plotting? How to replace me with him? Why lie about it? Why draw it out like this?"

"What are you trying to say, Marek?"

Tears welled up in Marek's eyes. He hated the way the tears came when he was angry or frustrated like this. It felt like a weakness. It felt like defeat. "Let's just call it what it is," he said.

Mr. Robins looked up into Marek's face, searching his eyes, seeing the tears gathering there. "It's just business."

"Just business, my ass. Let me do you a favor." He started stomping away but shouted back over his shoulder. "I quit."

It felt like a dream. No, more like a nightmare. It didn't feel real. Marek could feel himself picking up speed as he hurried down the street, but he couldn't believe the words that had just left his lips. He wasn't one to make spur-of-the-moment decisions like this, but he also knew he couldn't take it back. Marek was so much in his head that he didn't even notice Abaddon busking down the street or hear the siren call of his trumpet. He barrelled right into the trumpet player in his haze, knocking him to the ground.

"Hey, man, what the hell!" Abaddon struggled back to his feet. His trumpet had clattered to the ground, and a purpling bruise was already rising around his lips. Marek must have knocked the instrument back into his face.

Flustered, Marek offered a hand to his friend, lifting him from the ground. His words had left him again. All he could muster was half-hearted. "I'm so sorry. I never meant to -"

"What do you think you're doing?!"

"I don't know. I'm sorry."

Both men leaned against the brick apartment building, catching their breath. Each for slightly different reasons. Eventually, they turned to each other and laughed out of sheer exhaustion. They couldn't stay enemies for very long, even fake ones.

"What would you say to a drink?" Abaddon asked.

"A drink sounds excellent right about now," said Marek.

* * *

Instead of classing it up at The Royal Club, Abaddon suggested they hit up Vito's, a dive bar with much more affordable drinks. The goal was to drink away the day's worries. As soon as they walked in, Marek could smell the faint odor of vomit and urine. A few grizzled drunks haunted the dimly lit space. It was, after all, midday on a Tuesday. Abaddon ordered a round of shots for the bar, quickly earning them a handful of friends. Marek ordered a beer-flavored beer and sipped cheap whiskey alongside it.

There was Wheel of Fortune on the small television above the bar, and they took turns guessing letters. They played dice for shots. They drank and laughed, and Marek's head grew pleasantly fuzzy. Eventually, they ordered burgers, which tasted like the grill char. It was like eating ash, but it filled the hunger and helped soak up some of the booze. They drank more.

Eventually, the sky darkened, and Marek began to wish for his bed. He felt like he could sleep for at least a week. Abaddon had other ideas, though.

"I should take you to the Strutting Cock," he said.

"Is that a gay bar?" Marek asked.

Abaddon slammed his beer down on the bar. "What gave it away?"

"I think I'll pass," said Marek.

"We could go back to my place."

"You got beer there?"

"Mostly wine, but we could pick something up on the way. Besides, it's just a short walk from here."

"Is it?"

"No lie."

"It's been fun, but I should call it a night."

"What? Already?" Abaddon's face lit up with a mischievous grin. "The night has just begun, my friend. You can't call it quits already. Besides, where do you need to be in the morning?"

Marek tried to think of some excuse, but he couldn't.

"It's not like you've got work to worry about."

"True."

They stumbled from the bar and stopped at a liquor store. Marek picked up a bottle of whiskey. It was quickly becoming his new favorite drink. Abaddon opted for vodka, promising he had mixers at home.

Marek didn't plan on touching the stuff anyway. Abaddon also whispered that he had other things available if Marek was interested. Like weed, like pills, something that would help him forget everything.

"I don't need to get totally wasted," said Marek.

"But you want to. Might as well."

Abaddon lived in a small fourth-floor apartment, little more than a single room with a tiny bathroom adjacent. The single room was a bedroom, living room, kitchen, and dining room, all wrapped into one. Marek found himself wishing they had taken a cab back to his place. They sat on the loveseat, which served as Abaddon's couch. It was cozy but not entirely uncomfortable. Marek didn't mind the closeness, but he needed some fresh air as they got deeper into their drinks. He also needed a cigarette.

"Any place we could go to smoke?" he asked.

"Finally ready for some smoky treats?" Abaddon smiled. He was always down for a toke.

"I was hoping for a cigarette."

"I think I've got those around here somewhere, too."

Abaddon searched the surface of his coffee table, cluttered with sketchbooks, art supplies, and old newspapers. Then he dug into the loveseat cushions, eventually producing a half-full pack of menthol lights.

Marek looked at them with disgust. But it was still a nicotine fix.

They threw their coats over their shoulders and headed for the roof. It was a ten-story building, so the wind whipped around them, but the fresh air felt good, especially after the drinking. Marek handed Abaddon a cigarette, and they lit up.

"Are you sure we can be up here?" Marek asked.

"Sure. Everybody comes up to smoke since the landlord raised the rent on anybody caught smoking in the apartments."

They stared at the city below, the smaller buildings dotting the landscape around them. Stars created little pinpricks in the sky above. Abaddon sat on the ledge, letting his legs dangle over the side. Marek had always been a little bit afraid of heights, though. Well, not heights, more falling. He stayed safely on the other side. After finishing his cigarette, Abaddon pulled a joint from his pocket, lit it, and inhaled. He didn't even cough as the smoke escaped his lips.

"You sure like that stuff," said Marek.

"You judging me?"

"No, just an observation." Marek leaned into Abaddon's shoulder, reaching for the joint. Their fingers touched as it changed hands. Marek brought it to his lips, inhaling deeply. The heat caught in his throat, and he started coughing a deep, death rattle.

Abaddon laughed, but it was good-natured. "You ever gotten high before?"

"Once. Years ago."

Abaddon grabbed the joint back, relighting it. "Try to hold the smoke in before letting it out. Let it burn in your lungs for a bit. It takes a while to get used to, but it's not that different from a cigarette."

"Except for the getting high part."

"Yeah, except that."

Eventually, Marek joined him on the ledge, forgetting his fear of falling. They watched the cars moving below.

"You hungry?" Abaddon asked.

"I could eat."

"There's a taco joint we could check out if you want. We can grab food, maybe get some *cervezas*. I got some friends I could call and have a little party."

"Celebrating what?"

"Your freedom, of course." Abaddon drew him close, wrapping his arms around him tightly.

Usually, Marek would pull away, but the warmth felt nice, felt needed. It wasn't the time to be alone, now, with his dark thoughts. He needed this human contact. He needed to feel wanted. When Abaddon released him, he felt strangely lonely, separate again, but soon they were out on the street again, walking toward a new future. They shared another cigarette on the way, passing it back and forth between their lips. The joint was starting to affect them now. They giggled like schoolchildren, and Abaddon skipped ahead down the sidewalk while Marek struggled to keep up.

When they arrived at the taco place, Marek felt like he was starving. They ordered a handful of tacos each and devoured them, washing them down with more beer. As Marek sat digesting, Abaddon started texting and calling some friends. Marek watched, amused, as Abaddon urged them to come out on a Tuesday night.

"Any luck?" Marek asked.

"I don't know what's wrong with these people."

"Some people have real jobs."

Abaddon tapped his hands on the table, growing impatient. They drank a few more beers. Eventually, Abaddon turned to Marek, his face aglow.

"I've got an idea," he said. He grabbed Marek's arm and pulled him outside. Marek struggled to keep pace as Abaddon nearly ran down the street.

"Where are we going?"

"Paradise."

Marek could barely catch his breath before they arrived at what looked like a club. As promised, it was called "Paradise," but he had no idea what he was getting into.

"What is this?" he asked.

"A dance club!"

"I don't dance."

Abaddon's eyes grew wide. "You don't jam or improvise or dance? What kind of musician are you?"

"A classically trained one."

Abaddon snorted. "Well, honey, you need to feel the music; get it in your veins."

"I'm not injecting anything in my veins."

"I'm not asking you to shoot heroin, my man. Just loosen up a little."

Before he could protest further, Abaddon pulled Marek inside. Behind the bar were two shirtless men serving up cocktails. It looked like they had rubbed their chests down with baby oil. Marek could smell the musk of their cologne, the sandalwood, and white amber, warm and welcoming. Abaddon ordered drinks for them, a sunset-colored concoction that tasted like mangos and strawberries. Marek took a sip, and even with the alcohol, it tasted like juice.

As they turned to the dance floor, a smoke machine released great clouds of pink and purple. Black lights and cascading lasers crossed the room, and a gathering of bodies moved en masse to the music. The bass became Marek's heartbeat. He swallowed the rest of his drink, leaving it on one of the tables, and they joined the fray. He lost Abaddon for a few moments as he moved further ahead. The warmth of other bodies welcomed him in. Between the lights and sound, it was challenging to differentiate one person from the next. All he could feel was the beat and the movement, and soon, he was dancing, no longer worried about the placement of his limbs or the closeness of another person. It felt miraculous.

After a few songs, Abaddon returned to him, talking in his ear.

"How are you feeling?" he asked. "I have something for you."

Abaddon dragged him from the floor, handing him a small pill. Marek leaned in so he could talk in his friend's ear.

"What is it?"

"You're so untrusting. Just a little molly. Trust me; you'll like it."

Marek placed the small pill on his tongue and swallowed.

"Wanna dance?" asked Abaddon. They returned to the dance floor.

Before long, Marek felt like his and everyone else's bodies were one organism. He felt so incredibly close to all these strangers, to Abaddon. There were no longer boundaries between one person and the next, just closeness, heat, and pulsation. While he danced with Abaddon, he watched a few cages above filled with nearly naked men and women. Three tall, long-legged women with long, flowing hair were in one of the cages. He looked up at them and saw sisters, saw mermaids plotting together to capture his soul. He would freely give it.

6

The Three of Wands

Madame Rosivda turned the card, revealing a forest with golden leaves and grass covered by deep yellow clouds. In a clearing, three star-topped wands pierced the ground. In the middle of the triad was a tiny fairy flitting back and forth, his wings struggling to keep him afloat. He wore a pink cap, jacket, and pantaloons, with pointed slippers to match. It was the Three of Wands.

"Once upon a time," she said, "there was a little fairy who had a big job to do. This fairy prepared to welcome a great wizard home from his journey. In times past, this wizard had ensured the safety of the fairy village by placing a protective barrier around it. This barrier hid the town from view. You could not see the village until you had passed through this barrier. But as time passed, it grew weaker and weaker and eventually dissipated, no longer offering the town protection. Now that the wizard was returning after nearly a century, the fairies needed to convince him to re-cast the spell.

"The fairy was young (by fairy standards) and inexperienced with talking to wizards. He was selected because he served the fairy king, who was too busy with the tasks of being king. As the wizard ventured closer and closer to their village, the fairy flew about frantically, trying to get everything ready. When he heard the wizard's approach, he finished placing the final touches, three long star-topped wands arranged in a triangle in the clearing. When the wizard stepped between them, he would be trapped there, and the fairies would be able to make their request. His remaining task was to ensure the wizard stepped into the trap.

"When the wizard approached, the fairy flew up to him, landing on his left ear. The wizard tried to swat him away, but the fairy avoided his slapping hand and landed on the wizard's other ear. The wizard exclaimed, irritated, and moved to slap the other side of his head, smacking himself as the fairy flitted away. The wizard swore and stumbled forward. He spotted the fairy when he then landed on his nose.

"The fairy avoided his hand again, and the wizard tripped into the trap set for him. A yellow glow surrounded him, and he couldn't move from the spot where he stood. He pressed his hands against the sphere of light which contained him but could not escape from it.

"'What do you want of me?' he asked.

"The fairy flew close to the wizard's ear again so he could make his request. You see, fairies, being so small, also have small, high-pitched voices that the average human ear cannot hear. A wizard can listen to it if he tries, but only from a short distance. But the wizard swatted the fairy away when he flew into his ear again, sending him flying through the air. The force knocked the breath out of him, and he fell to the ground, dead.

"Seeing what had happened, the other fairies feared to approach, so instead, they left the wizard trapped there. They didn't want him to cause any more damage to their village."

* * *

Marek spent the next few days playing chords on the electronic piano, playing with different sound effects and electronic options. He wished he could replicate the heartbeat bass of the club but could only manage a few notes which made him yearn for that moment of ecstasy he had felt a few nights before. Marek had gotten closer to Abaddon than intended, but it wasn't like they had sex or anything. While it had been a while since Marek had sex with anyone, he was sure he was primarily attracted to women. Unfortunately, that hedging word "mostly" came from the fact that he had been uncertain for the first time. But that could have been influenced by many things - by the alcohol, weed, and drugs in his system, by the environment and the music, and by Abaddon himself.

Marek shook his head. He hadn't spoken to Abaddon since that night and hoped it wouldn't be too awkward at the open jam. Abaddon had invited him but maybe didn't expect him to come. He would just see what happened. Marek wasn't even sure if he would play anything. He planned to bring the keyboard but didn't have a plan. He would just see how it went and go with the flow. Thinking this, Marek questioned himself. When did he ever "go with the flow"? The answer was not until recently, at least. He knew that, eventually, he would need to find a steady source of income, but maybe quitting his job wasn't the worst thing that had happened to him. Perhaps it was what he needed.

Marek arrived with his keyboard slung over his back. A ragtag mix of musicians gathered around the stage, but he didn't spot Abaddon. Marek hung back, not introducing himself to everyone, feeling awkward and out of place. He'd just sit and watch, he decided. He didn't need to be directly involved; he could just observe. Maybe he'd play next time. As others pulled their instruments out and played scales, he sat at a small table some distance away. He hoped not to be noticed.

No such luck, though, as he noticed Nyx approaching him. She looked strange in baggy pants and an oversized sweater. He barely recognized her.

"He's here," she said. "Man of the hour!" She wrapped him in a bear hug and held on longer than what was comfortable.

"What do you mean?" he asked.

She leaned in to whisper in his ear. "A little birdie told me you're a free man."

Marek scoffed. "Hardly."

She frowned, mimicking his expression with an exaggerated furrowed brow.

"Not working tonight?" he asked.

"That obvious? I'm here for the jam."

"You're here on your night off?"

"Where else would I be? Let's get some drinks, frowny face. First round's on me."

Marek reluctantly followed her up to the bar. The headache from Tuesday night's drinking had been excruciating. Maybe he'd just have one, possibly two, tonight. He might not have a job to wake up for, but he didn't need to break himself.

They bellied up to the bar, and Nyx caught the bartender's attention. She ordered a dry martini with an extra olive, and Marek ordered his whiskey. They returned to Marek's table.

"So, other than living the good life, what have you been up to?" she asked.

"Eh. Not much."

"Abaddon told me some things."

"Like what?" Oh, god, thought Marek. Was his friend the type to kiss and tell? Marek only half-remembered what had happened earlier in the week. He was sure Abaddon had kissed him, and he hadn't pulled away, but it was just a kiss. Marek had been drunk and high and sad, and it didn't count. Now he was thinking he shouldn't have come. Would Abaddon expect something?

"Your face is telling me more things," she said. "What happened between you two?"

"It was nothing."

She smiled. "But there was an 'it' to be 'nothing'?"

Marek groaned.

"It's alright. You don't have to spill the beans." She slipped out of her teasing and back into a mellow contemplation, her smile growing slack. "This your first time at the jam?"

"Yeah."

"It's kinda chaotic until everyone decides what they will play and with whom. We all wind up on-stage in a ridiculous orgie by night's end."

"A what?"

"Of instruments."

"You play?"

"Jazz flute. Not well, mind you, but I can hold my own."

"What makes a flute jazz?"

"You'll see."

The first group, a three-piece with drums, guitar, and bass, began playing. Marek settled into his seat, trying to relax. Nyx flitted away into the crowd as soon as she finished her drink. It was just as well. Marek didn't feel like talking. He watched each ensemble set up and play, some with unique combinations, like an accordion with an electric guitar. One musician brought an ocarina, which reminded Marek of playing Legend of Zelda: Ocarina of Time as a teenager. He was well into his cups already, more than the planned two drinks. He started to wonder where Abaddon was. Maybe he wouldn't show. Possibly things would be awkward between them now.

The host for the evening was the bartender he had seen the first night at the club. He looked the same, maybe even more dressed up than he had been. Below his too-large mustache, he wore a flower-patterned bow tie. He would make a good model, thought Marek, if he only shaved. The man was skinny enough to wear any clothing like a hanger without stretching it out. Marek had heard that models were so thin for the reason that clothes could wear them rather than the other way around. Their bodies didn't distract from the clothes they wore down the runway. The bartender's name was Ronnie, which also suited him. Nothing too flashy.

Marek caught himself mid-thought. Why was he spending so much time thinking about the appearance of a man? Was he attracted to men, after all? Even if that were the case, it wasn't like he wasn't attracted to women. Maybe it wasn't an either / or situation. Perhaps he liked both. Marek's head began to spin. He had drunk too much already. Perhaps he should just call it a night and go home.

Just then, he noticed who was on stage. Nyx with her flute and Olive with her, well, with her everything. Neither wore a dress and seeing them wearing their street clothes was strange. Nyx had removed her oversized sweatshirt and wore a raggedy t-shirt. Olive wore flannel, which seemed so out-of-character that Marek had to do a double-take. Was it her? But as soon as they began performing, he heard her voice and knew he wasn't mistaken. Marek had never heard someone play flute in jazz before. Nyx's lips pursed over the mouthpiece, but instead of a high trilling, the sound that came from her instrument was a low hum. She was blowing more into the instrument than across the opening. The result was a whispered, almost raspy tone that accompanied Olive's deep, sultry singing. A sleek barrette pulled Olive's long, wavy hair back from her face, and he could see her strong jawline, cheekbones, and dark, inviting eyes.

Marek felt entranced, pulled into a calm meditation from his earlier anxious worry. He barely noticed the entrance of someone's tow-headed child running back and forth across the room or Abaddon joining him at the table. The little hairs rose on his arms, and an electric shock slowly rolled over him. He couldn't say how Olive's singing affected him this way because no music had ever reached in to send his heart pumping so quickly. Eventually, he would need to get up the courage to speak with her, but simultaneously, he doubted it would ever happen.

When the two women left the stage, Abaddon touched his arm lightly.

"Hey, man," he said. "Sorry, I'm late."

Marek nodded.

"You okay?"

"I'm fine."

"I see you checking out Olive." Abaddon leaned back, a broad smile crossing his face.

"You're not jealous?"

"Me? Jealous? No, I like to share." He winked at Marek. "Besides, what do I have to be jealous of?"

So they weren't going to talk about it. That was fine with Marek. He didn't know how or what exactly to talk about in any case.

Nyx came over to the table, wrapping Abaddon in a hug. "I didn't think you would show," she said.

"I was just napping."

"Didn't think to set the alarm?"

"Alarms are for cogs in the machine. I sleep when I want, wake when I want, drink when I want, fuck when I want."

"Yeah, yeah," she said. "Care for a drink?"

They disappeared off to the bar, leaving Marek with his thoughts. Someone had given the rambunctious child the sign-up list. He was babbling off the next musical group, stumbling over the words. When the two returned, a trio of singers had graced the stage. They were young, teenagers most likely, each with her hair pulled back into a high ponytail, each with a microphone. Abaddon had another glittery drink, and Nyx had another martini. Marek glanced at the dregs of his glass. The ice had melted, leaving it mostly water. For some reason, the girls hadn't started singing yet. They looked anxiously from one to the other.

Abaddon motioned to Marek. "Did you bring your keyboard?"

"Yeah, but I don't think I'll play anything."

"I think they're looking for accompaniment."

Nyx chimed in. "You should help them out."

Before Marek could protest, Abaddon was already shouldering the keyboard and pushing him toward the stage. Marek groaned as he followed. This exact situation was what he *didn't* want. Abaddon even set up the keyboard for him, snagging some sheet music from the girls and finding a stool. Reluctantly, Marek sat and glanced at the music. It was easy enough. He wouldn't need to practice this or even think much while playing it. That didn't change that he was now the center of attention, placed right in the middle of the triangle the girls formed on stage. He looked up momentarily, noticing sparkling star barrettes each girl wore in her hair, and suddenly felt even more uneasy. He was the wizard trapped in a fairy circle, unable to escape.

7

The Ten of Chalices

Madame Rosivda turned the card, revealing a seaside scene with a dark castle rising in the distance. In the pink sky, an angel with two sets of wings floated down, her eyes downcast as she watched a groom and his bride embracing. The star on her headband shone brightly, but the couple did not notice, as they had eyes only for one another. It was the Ten of Chalices.

"Once upon a time," she said. "There was a young couple who were about to marry. They had little means but did have the support of their families despite their young age. They planned a small ceremony by the sea, inviting only immediate family and some of their closest friends. However, just before they exchanged vows, an angel descended from the sky.

"The angel came with a warning for them. She told them that in a year, they would lose one another. The angel did not specify if this loss would come from a separation, a challenge to the marriage, or death. Despite the angel's warning, they continued the wedding and tried not to worry. As their anniversary drew nearer, the wife went to a medicine woman with her concerns, asking if she could do anything to prevent their impending doom.

"The medicine woman lived on the far edge of the forest, far from the little village where the young couple lived. The journey took most of the day, so the wife brought a small lunch of bread and cheese to eat on the way. She sat on a low boulder when she stopped to rest, spreading her meal around her. Enticed by the sweet cheese, a fairy approached, landing next to the woman. Although she could not understand the fairy, the woman shared some bread and cheese, which the fairy gratefully accepted before flitting back into the forest.

"When the wife arrived, the medicine woman greeted her with a hot cup of tea and invited her to stay the night. It was getting quite late, so the wife agreed but insisted she leave the following day. The husband, arriving home to an empty house, set off into the night searching for his wife. In the darkness, he tripped over the great roots of an old, knarled tree and fell into a great ravine, dying.

"When the wife woke, the medicine woman told her she was too late and had already lost her husband. The wife cried, cursing the skies, and begged the medicine woman for a swift poison. The older woman refused and imparted to the wife another bit of knowledge. A child was growing already in her womb, and she must live to protect her child's life."

Marek finished drinking his tea and asked Madame Rosivda a single question. "Do any of these stories have happy endings?"

After playing accompaniment at the open jam, other musical groups and singers who needed backup invited Marek to play with them. He knew he would never be the featured performer at this rate, but the extra money was excellent. They mainly provided him with sheet music to follow along with or specific chords to play, so it didn't require much thought. Mostly, he played side gigs at small get-togethers rather than special events. He had played at a few kids' talent shows, some solo & ensemble competitions, and small venues that paled compared to The Royal Club.

Abaddon had encouraged him to busk on the corner, but he mostly refused. He still didn't do well with improvisation, or composition, for that matter. He still owed Madame Rosivda a song, but she seemed to appreciate his company so rarely charged him for the readings she performed for him at least once a week. He had played her a few songs as a practice, but nothing he had written himself. He wasn't sure if he'd ever get there, but he also questioned if it mattered. He might not be thriving, but he was surviving. And that was good enough for now.

He and some of those he accompanied would perform at the Open Jam on Thursday nights. It was unpaid but a chance to play on stage with an audience. Marek didn't have jitters anymore, but some did, especially younger ones. The three girls he had first played with, Amelia, Ivy, and Bella, were regularly there, and Marek would offer himself as an accompaniment to anyone who wanted or needed it. Playing on stage was starting to feel more was starting to feel more natural again, like something he didn't need to be afraid of, but he still felt nervous with new people.

One night, between sets, Nyx came strutting towards him. Her eyes glistened with excitement.

Marek could barely keep his eyes open. He had played a late set the night before and should be sleeping. "What do you want?" he asked.

She scoffed. "Nice to see you, too."

"Sorry. Just tired."

"I have a proposition for you."

"What do you want?" he repeated.

She ruffled his hair, mussing it. "Maybe not, then. You don't seem interested."

Marek straightened. "Just tell me."

"How would you like to play accompaniment with Olive?"

Marek gulped. He still hadn't said more than two words to Olive and wasn't sure he'd be able to concentrate enough to play anything in such proximity to her. He could feel himself blushing, his face getting uncomfortably hot. "I don't know..." He let the sentence trail off into nothingness.

Nyx slid into the booth next to him. "Oh, I see."

"See what?" His voice was sharp and annoyed.

"You like her, don't you?" she asked.

Marek didn't reply, just stared off into the distance. Come to think of it, he hadn't even seen Olive tonight. Where was she?

"Don't worry," said Nyx, following his gaze. "I was talking about next time. She's not going to make it tonight."

"Oh." Marek's heart started to slow as he took a deep breath.

"I love how expressive you are," said Nyx. "I can understand how you and Abaddon are friends."

Marek grunted in response. She slipped away into the crowd.

Later in the evening, Nyx brought over some sheet music so he could practice before playing on stage. Now, he just had to practice.

Back in his apartment, Marek fought with the keyboard like it was a beast he couldn't tame. His fingers couldn't find the right keys, and with every mistake he made, he pictured Olive looking down at him disapprovingly. Her green eyes still entranced him, and her singing sent shivers up his spine. It wouldn't be so bad if he could just learn to relax, but even being near her put him on edge. Even thinking about her made him fidgety.

He texted Abaddon instead and grabbed a cab.

When he arrived, Abaddon had created a nest of pillows and blankets covering his living room floor.

"What's this?" asked Marek.

"Amazing. Find a spot."

Marek settled onto a pile of pillows. He bounced a bit, feeling like a small child. One thing he could always count on his friend for was some silliness. "Got any weed?" he asked.

"I've got better."

Marek watched as Abaddon crossed the floor and opened his freezer. He returned with a small baggy of what looked like small squares of paper. He handed one to Marek and placed one on his tongue.

"What is this? Acid?" Marek asked.

"You don't have anything going on for a few hours?"

"Nothing."

"Alright. I am just checking because this stuff can last a while. And yeah, it's acid. You never done it?"

Marek shook his head.

"Just put this in your mouth. Suck on it for a bit."

Marek put the paper in his mouth, amazed it didn't taste like anything but stale cardboard. He pushed it around with his tongue, sliding it from one side of his mouth to the other.

"Am I supposed to swallow it?" he asked.

"Just keep it in your mouth for a while. You don't have to swallow." Abaddon winked.

"You're gross," said Marek.

Abaddon shrugged and returned the rest of his stash to the freezer.

They watched a throwaway movie about an hour later, and Abaddon started waving his arms around.

"Ah, it's finally starting to kick in," he said. He followed his arms with his eyes. "Do you see the trails?"

Marek didn't see anything or at least nothing like what Abaddon described.

"You don't see them yet?"

"Nothing."

"Maybe it just hasn't hit you yet."

"Am I supposed to see things? Like things that aren't there?"

"You might. We took a small dose, but I usually see trails or things that look somewhat fuzzy. Sometimes, the carpet breathes."

"Breathes?"

"Yeah, it looks kinda like a big blue muppet breathing, pulsing."

"A muppet? That sounds terrifying."

"Nothing scary here, my man." Abaddon scooted closer to Marek and put his arm around his shoulders. It felt warm and pleasant. "Just relax."

They watched the rest of the movie, and then Abaddon turned on some ambient music. Laying with his eyes closed felt much more comfortable. At first, Marek started to feel a bit nauseous, but as he listened, really listened, that feeling faded. He closed his eyes, and instead of the usual darkness behind his lids, he saw swirls of color.

Abaddon shook him gently. "Don't fall asleep."

"I'm just resting my eyes. Besides, why can't I fall asleep?"

"I wouldn't recommend it. It makes the trip last longer, and you might have some wild dreams. You just have to ride it out."

"How long does this stuff usually last?" Marek asked.

"Could be up to twelve hours."

"Twelve hours?! That's like a full day!"

"I did ask if you had anything going on."

"I thought you meant like three, maybe four hours. Not twelve!"

"Calm your tits. It'll be fine. We'll just chill and listen to some music. Nothing to worry about." He playfully punched Marek's shoulder. "I got you."

Marek tried to settle back into the cushions. The evening wasn't exactly what he had planned, but he'd try to roll with it. What was the worst that could happen?

* * *

Later, Abaddon cranked the music up with some electronica and danced around the small apartment. Marek felt like he couldn't move from his spot. He closed his eyes and thought he couldn't open them again. He felt himself shrinking, imploding. Before long, his sense of self shrunk to the size of a small molecule, a crumb, floating around inside the sea of his body. He was much too small, a speck inside his skin's great, expanding space. He pushed up against his limbs, willing them to move but without control. Then, with sudden panic, he realized he needed to pee and feared he would piss himself.

Abaddon shook him awake. "You alright?" he asked.

"I think I might be sick." Suddenly, Marek could move again and rushed to the toilet, retching violently. When he had finished expelling everything in his stomach, which wasn't much, he shut the bathroom door behind him and sat to relieve himself. Marek didn't trust his ability to stand over the toilet. His knees felt so weak that he could just melt into the floor in a great puddle of blood and muscle, his skin refusing to hold all his organs. If this was what an acid trip was, he didn't like it.

When he had finished, he stood and suddenly realized he was naked. He couldn't figure out where his shirt had gone when he had removed his pants. He feared that he had lapsed again, done something untoward with Abaddon. He didn't mean to, he told himself. He was drugged. Was that Abaddon's plan all along - to take advantage of him? He tried the door, and it seemed to be locked. He couldn't get the handle to turn. Oh god, what was happening? Tears sprang to his eyes. He didn't like this. He didn't like it at all. He wanted to be home, curled up in his bed, the blankets pulled up around him. He wanted to feel warm and safe.

He struggled to think. Abaddon was his friend, and he tried to reason with himself. Why would he do anything that Marek didn't want to do? Maybe Marek just didn't remember. Oh, god, now he was thinking of himself in the third person like he was watching from above. Omniscient, omnipresent, yet unable to do anything about it. He was just looking down on himself, cold, scared, frantic. He pulled a towel down and wrapped it around himself. That solved the naked problem, at least. He felt slightly better. He looked at himself in the mirror and didn't recognize the face looking back at him. Was that what he looked like? He tried the door again, and the doorknob wouldn't budge. He paced back and forth, and the bath rug started breathing. It pulsed in and out, just like Abaddon had described. It was alive.

A knock came at the door. "Are you alright?" Abaddon asked.

"No. Not really."

The door flew open, and Abaddon's arms were around him. "What are you doing?" he asked. "Why are you naked?"

Marek sobbed. "I don't know."

Abaddon pulled the shower curtain aside, revealing Marek's clothes crumpled in the bottom of the tub. "You don't remember taking your clothes off?"

"No. I thought maybe you stripped me while I was sleeping."

Abaddon pulled up Marek's jeans and recoiled at the vomit that covered them. "Here, let me get you something to wear. I'll be right back."

He returned with an oversized hoodie and some basketball shorts. "Just don't get sick on them."

"I'm so sorry. I feel like an idiot."

"Hey, no worries. I shouldn't have pushed you to do acid with me. You'll be fine. Just get dressed."

Marek pulled the shorts around his waist and the hoodie over his head. He was starting to feel human again, but his head ached. He shouted to Abaddon in the other room. "How much longer is this going to last?"

"A few more hours, at least.

"Ugh. I just want it to be over."

Abaddon pulled some pillows from the floor and set Marek on the loveseat. He changed the music to a calming ambiance and put some anime on the TV. He turned off the sound and captions on the anime and suggested they play a game.

"You don't want to fall asleep again," he said. "We're going to voice the characters instead."

"That sounds dumb," said Marek.

"Just give it a try."

Soon, they chatted back and forth, making up stories and scenarios for the characters. Marek started to feel better with the distraction and was finally normal again. He watched as the sun began to rise and warm the room with a brilliant yellow.

"I think you can safely sleep now," said Abaddon. "You can stay here - I've got an air mattress. Or I can call you a cab."

"I want to sleep in my bed."

"Fine by me. I'll call that cab."

When the cab arrived, Marek slipped in, still wearing Abaddon's clothes. He stared out the windows, and everything felt so surreal. He could tell the acid still held him, but the effects weren't as strong. He just wanted to get home into the familiar space of his apartment. He paid his fare and took the elevator to his floor. As he pushed open the front door, he decided to try playing the sheet music Nyx had given him rather than going straight to sleep. At least one thing the last few hours had provided was a chance to get out of his head.

He looked at the music with fresh eyes, not thinking or worrying about Olive but aware only of the notes. His fingers found the keys, and he played almost flawlessly. He played through the song several times until he was confident, even with how much she would distract him. Strange fruit, indeed, he thought, rereading the title, and caught himself wondering what she would taste like on his lips.

A few days later, the night arrived when he would accompany Olive. It was low-pressure, for sure, just the open jam. It wasn't a paid gig or anything, just one song. And he had practiced the song so many times he wasn't even nervous, not about the music at least. Abaddon arrived on time, for once, and allowed Marek to drink water, not even pushing beer on him. He seemed cowed from the acid experience and reluctant to give Marek any substances. They didn't discuss it, but their conversation felt more subdued than usual.

Eventually, Marek broke the silence. "You tired?" he asked.

"A bit, yeah," said Abaddon.

"You showed up on time, for once."

"What are you trying to say?" Abaddon used his straw to stir his drink. His mischievous grin had returned. "Playing with Olive and me tonight?"

"You're playing with her as well?

"Yeah. The trumpet echoes the final wail. You'll see," said Abaddon. "Are you finally gonna make your move?"

"What do you mean?" Marek feigned innocence.

"I know you've got a thing for Olive. You have since day one."

"I do not." Marek could feel his cheeks going hot.

"Aw, look at you. Blushing and everything."

"Don't make it into a big deal."

"Just pointing out the obvious, man."

Marek gulped down his water, wiping his mouth with his sleeve. He grimaced.

"I'm sure you'll be fine," said Abaddon.

"I will. I could play the music with my eyes closed."

The time finally came, and Marek moved toward the stage to start setting up. As he opened the keyboard, adjusting the legs to the correct height, Nyx approached him. She motioned for him to put the keyboard away.

"You won't be needing that," she said.

"Now you don't want me to play?" he asked.

"No, sweetheart, I've got something better." Nyx beckoned to him, and he followed her backstage, behind the red curtains, where a baby grand piano sat waiting.

Marek couldn't help but gasp. He hadn't played a proper piano since his time at The Den. This one was small but a million times better than a keyboard. "When did the club get this?" he asked.

"It's been hiding in the wings for a while," she said. "But they just got it tuned. It had been sitting unused for a while. Probably would have sounded awful."

Marek ran his hand over the top of the piano, brushing dust from its surface. "It could still do with a clean. Got a rag?"

Nyx shook her head.

"How are we gonna move it?" he asked.

She pointed to casters attached to the legs.

"Well, isn't that convenient?"

They unlocked the wheels and gingerly moved the instrument out to center stage. A small round of applause erupted from the audience. Marek struggled not to blush. He placed his sheet music on the music shelf and opened the piano lid. He brought the bench out and sat. He felt much more comfortable on the padded cushions than his usual wooden stool. Playing this instrument was going to be glorious.

He looked around and saw Olive adjusting her microphone and Abaddon practicing his embouchure by buzzing his lips. They would begin in just a few minutes. Marek counted out the beat softly and began to play. He tried to focus on his playing, but that soon faded to the back of his mind as Olive's deep, sultry voice filled the space. Strange fruit, indeed, he thought. He had only been given his part of the piece and didn't know the words, although Nyx had told him it was initially a Billie Holiday piece. It was dark and haunting. Listening to Olive's plaintive singing nearly broke him.

"Southern trees bear strange fruit..." she began. Marek barely heard the words and felt the emotion straining her voice.

On the last note, Olive's voice rose high into an agonizing wail, which Abaddon then punctuated with his trumpet. The cry tapered off into silence, echoing through the auditorium. The audience sat in awe momentarily, then erupted in applause. Marek could feel tears welling up in his eyes. He wiped them away, trying to pretend they had never been there. He pushed the piano further back on the stage before approaching Olive.

"You're beautiful," he said, stumbling over the words. "I mean, that was beautiful."

Olive graced him with a smile. Her whole face lit up.

"I mean, both. Both were, um, are beautiful."

"Thank you," said Olive. Even her speaking voice dripped from her lips like honey.

"Can I buy you a drink?" he asked.

"Sure."

Marek followed her to the bar. He'd give anything to link his arm in hers but didn't want to be too forward. Ronnie took their order, and they silently watched as he mixed up a cosmopolitan for Olive. Abaddon followed behind, breaking the spell.

"You guys were amazing," said Ronnie.

"Olive was amazing," said Marek. "I just provided background noise."

"Thank you," said Olive. "It's been a while since I sang that. I'm glad I didn't mess it up."

"Hey, what about me?" asked Abaddon.

"You were okay," said Marek.

"Just okay?"

"I mean, you held your own." Marek smiled at Olive. "Let the lady have her spotlight for a moment."

"How about a shot?" asked Abaddon.

"What'll it be?" Ronnie lined five shots up on the bar. They couldn't all agree on the same drink, so Ronnie pulled out five bottles. Abaddon had tequila, Olive had Rum Chata, Ronnie had Buffalo Trace, Marek had Jameson, and Nyx had a lemon drop. They clinked their glasses together and downed their drinks. Then Marek and Olive found a table in a dark corner of the club.

Marek couldn't stop himself from staring. Olive was the most gorgeous woman he had ever seen. Her skin was a golden hue that shone in the dim light. He couldn't reasonably determine her ethnicity. She wasn't white, or not entirely. He looked so pale and devoid of color in comparison to her. Her hair was dark and wavy but not kinky. Her eyes shone a deep, emerald green. Without thinking, he asked a question out of ignorance.

"What are you mixed with?"

She laughed, a deep, throaty sound that returned to him with life and vitality. "Sperm and egg," she whispered. "Just like you."

He realized his error. "I'm sorry; I didn't mean it to come out like that."

"It's alright. I'm several things, but I don't know exactly. My parents abandoned me when I was small. I don't remember them, and I don't know my family history."

"I'm so sorry." He couldn't seem to find the right words.

"It's alright," she said again. "As I said, I don't remember. It's hard to miss someone you never knew."

They sat in awkward silence for what felt like a full minute. "What about you, Marek," she asked. "Where does a name like that come from?"

"It's the Polish version of Mark," he said.

"Really? So, I'm guessing your last name ends in 'ski'?'"

"Dabrowski."

"Marek Dabrowski," she said. He liked the sound of his name in her mouth, the way her lips and tongue formed the sounds. He'd love to hear her say it in a different context.

"And you?" He barely recovered from his reverie.

"Olive Laveau."

"Like the voodoo priestess from New Orleans?"

"Exactly," she said. "I'll put a spell on you."

"I think you already have."

Their conversation only lasted long enough for them to finish their drinks, but in that time, Marek's infatuation with her only grew broader and more profound. Instead of a small stream, it was a raging river, carving out a canyon in his heart.

Thankfully, he didn't need to be the one to suggest another meeting. Olive did that for him. A cousin was getting married in two weeks, and she had signed on to be their soloist. What she needed was someone to accompany her musically. It wasn't a date, not by any means, but it was a start, and right now, Marek needed to see her more. He couldn't let her continue to be a fantasy. She was genuine and here, just a few feet from him. He didn't want to clip her wings, but he didn't want her to fly away. He needed her, his perfect angel, and he needed her close.

They got together to rehearse a few times. She already had her part down pat, but he needed to remember the correct fingerings for the chords. Strangely, the song for Olive's solo was in a minor key, often reserved for more somber occasions rather than celebratory moments. The bride wanted her mother to cry, or so she said.

When the day finally came, Marek rented a fancy tux and met Olive at the church beforehand for one last run-through. She looked amazing in a long red dress that clung to her in all the right places. He struggled not to stare, to imagine what it would feel like to caress her curves in a dimly lit room. Instead, he turned his attention to the music, letting his mind wander only to the notes he needed to play.

Soon, guests began to arrive, and he paced the long corridors of the church, feeling somewhat out of place. After all, he knew no one but Olive, but she was already chatting away, caught up in the day's excitement. She neglected to introduce him to anyone, but he took it in stride. He didn't exactly want to play meet and greet anyway. He enjoyed watching her light up as she embraced old friends and family.

It was a big wedding, with several hundred guests crammed into the little chapel.

As the beginning of the ceremony drew closer, no one could find the groom. He supposedly had been at the gym that morning, as witnessed by one of the groomsmen who had served as his spotter during his weightlifting. Then he went on a run, promising to drive himself to the church. He was already about twenty minutes late when the bride began to panic.

Olive excused herself to calm her cousin, leaving Marek sitting awkwardly at the piano, waiting for some sign that they could finally begin. He would play the procession, Wagner's traditional wedding march, and Olive's solo. The wait proved agonizing. Twenty minutes grew into a half hour and then forty-five minutes. Guests whispered and speculated. Would the wedding be called off? Had the groom stood up the bride? They began to mill about, some watching eagerly on the front steps for the groom's car to pull up, but no one came. The groom's family couldn't get ahold of him. He wasn't home, no one could find him on his usual running route, and he wasn't answering the phone. At an hour and fifteen minutes, a few guests threatened to leave.

Then, an agonizing wail erupted from the bridal suite. The bride's mother rushed over, throwing the door open, revealing her disheveled daughter, her veil thrown to the floor. Olive's cousin had sunk to her knees. Mascara ran down her face as she cried and screamed. Other female family members rushed to her side, carefully closing the door behind them. What was happening?

Marek froze. He was as eager as everyone else to learn what had happened, but one thing was clear: there would be no wedding. He stood awkwardly, leaning against the wall of the nave, watching as chaos broke among the guests. His ears rang from the sudden cacophony of voices, punctuated by the bride's agonized cries. When his focus broke, he struggled to breathe. Instead of staying to maybe, eventually, speak with Olive, he stepped outside. The day was perfect, the sun shining brilliantly above, the air cool but not cold. He went down the steps and called for a car to bring him home.

Olive called him later, asking where he had disappeared, but he didn't answer. He listened to her voicemail at least a dozen times over the next few days but couldn't find the words to say what he needed, to comfort her. The groom had died in a car accident on his way to the wedding. Marek buried himself in that tragedy and hated himself for not knowing what to say or how to react. Eventually, he visited the one person he knew wouldn't judge him: Madame Rosivda.

8

The Page of Swords

Madame Rosivda turned the card, revealing a deep blue landscape filled with low, rolling hills. In the distance, a great plume of smoke rose into the sky, obscuring the entire horizon. In the foreground, a young man wearing an outfit reminiscent of Robin Hood cast aside a flimsy sword haphazardly. A small butterfly caught his attention, and he turned his face towards it, the feather on his cap bending with a slight breeze. He reached out, trying in vain to touch the beautiful insect. It was the Page of Swords.

"There once was a young man tasked with guarding his master's property," said Madame Rosivda. "He was the son of a shepherd who had worked for this family for decades. As a shepherd's son, he had aspirations of one day becoming a knight, and so his father humored him, buying him a sword, but he had no one to train him. Instead, the young man would swing the thing around haphazardly and remain woefully unprepared for an actual fight. To keep the boy out of his hair, the shepherd sent him out into the farthest fields, telling him to protect the property. In reality, there was nothing to protect the property from, but the boy did not know that and relished the opportunity to feel useful for once.

"As usual, the boy began playfighting and pretending that he was a knight, tasked not with protecting a relatively small plot of land but with defending the kingdom. After some time, not much time at all, he grew tired and cast the sword aside. He looked about and spied a small white butterfly floating above him. Before the sword, his previous obsession had been nature and all its creatures. The butterfly reminded him of this, and he could not resist. He wanted to capture the insect as a specimen and pin its little wings down for further examination.

"The boy failed to notice a small smoke plume rising just over the hills. The small hut he shared with his father had caught fire and was already blazing away, but he focused on the butterfly. It wasn't until smoke filled the entire horizon that the boy noticed, and then he ran. The fire trapped his father, and he was too late. He would have caught the fire much earlier if he had only been paying attention. Instead, he hardened his heart at his father's death and became a roving mercenary, taking coins in exchange for eliminating unsavory figures. He never did become a noble knight."

"I'm the careless boy, I bet," said Marek.

Madame Rosivda shrugged her shoulders. "It might be one possible future for you."

"Have you seen Olive lately?"

"I can't say that I have. Olive has been almost suspiciously absent as of late. But you are a fine client. Not a substitute, but a fine client."

"I'm sure it helps that I can afford to pay you now."

"You know me too well." She gathered the cards back together and escorted him to the door.

It was another gloomy January day. Marek hadn't left the apartment for weeks. He played the same chords repeatedly, not even managing an entire song. He wanted to call Olive but still had no idea what to say to her. Eventually, he got a call from Abaddon, checking in.

"You still alive, man?" Abaddon asked.

Marek scoffed. "Yeah."

"Haven't seen you around in a while. Where have you been?"

"Nowhere."

The conversation was short. Marek hung up, feeling that he should get out, but it was cold, windy, and miserable outside. It was as good an excuse as any. He must go grocery shopping soon, but a frozen pizza would suffice. He stretched out on the couch while the oven preheated. Just after he heard the beep, a knock came at the door. Marek pushed himself into a seated position. Who knew where he lived? It must be someone trying to sell something. They'd just go away if he ignored it, but he needed to get up to put the pizza in. Even that felt like a nearly impossible task. When he stood, his legs grew wobbly, his knees weak. The knock came again. They were persistent. He'd have to tell them to fuck off. He changed directions and went toward the front door.

The knocks grew louder, more urgent, and less polite. When Marek finally opened the door, Abaddon nearly fell headfirst into the apartment; he had grown aggressive. He stumbled into Marek, pulling him into a big hug.

Marek pushed him away. "What the hell are you doing?"

Abaddon gave him puppy-dog eyes. "Just checking up on you."

"Well, come in. You're letting the cold in just standing there."

Marek went out to the kitchen to put the pizza in.

"What're you making?" asked Abaddon.

"Just a pizza."

"When's the last time you went outside, man?"

"It's cold." Marek grabbed another beer from the fridge. He had filled the trashcan, started a collection of empty cans on the counter, and stacked empty boxes along the floor. He hadn't cooked anything, so there weren't any dishes, but the place looked like a college dorm—trash collected along the kitchen tile. Dust and cobwebs decorated each corner.

Abaddon sat on the only clear spot, the far end of the couch. Marek sat down next to him. "When's the last time you showered?" Abaddon asked.

"What are you trying to say?"

"Come on, man. Let's get out of here. Living like this isn't healthy."

Marek glared at him.

"I'm serious. You need to get out."

"And go where exactly?"

"Anywhere. Seriously. You'll feel better, I promise. How'd you wind up this way anyway?"

Marek took a long slug of his beer.

"Don't want to talk about it?"

Marek nodded.

"Well, first thing first." Abaddon grabbed the beer out of Marek's hand. "Put that shit down and get your stinky ass in the shower."

Marek grumbled and slowly made his way to the bathroom. Abaddon turned the water on, letting it warm up as Marek stripped. Marek couldn't remember the last time he had showered, maybe last week sometime, but he felt like hot garbage. The weight of the past few days melted away as soon as the hot water hit his skin. Before Abaddon left the room, he glanced back one last time. "Make sure you shave, too, man. You're starting to look homeless with the raggedy nonsense."

After nearly half an hour, Marek emerged, smelling of soap and aftershave, wrapped in an oversized towel. He hadn't removed his beard but had trimmed it into shape. He had also shaved all the dark little hairs from his neck.

Abaddon looked him up and down. He stood to examine him more closely. "Nice, nice," he said.

"I'll go get dressed," said Marek.

As he turned, Abaddon smacked him so hard on the ass that he nearly fell to the ground. "Don't take too long, Princess. We've got places to be!"

Marek threw on some clean jeans, a T-shirt, and a button-down. He groaned as he pulled some socks onto his tired feet. "Where are we going?" he asked.

"You'll see," said Abaddon.

The venue was dimly lit, and there was a two-drink minimum, which Marek would adhere to gladly. He didn't expect a Christian rock band to take the stage. He whispered loudly to Abaddon when the television screens flanking the stage began scrolling the lyrics.

"What is this? You took me to church?"

Abaddon shrugged, a mischievous grin crossing his lips.

"Not quite. Just give it a try."

"You better be trying to bang the drummer."

"Who me? You think so little of me!"

"Really? We're playing this game?"

But as they listened, Marek quickly realized he had misjudged the situation. Even with the teleprompters, the music was far from topics of Jesus and salvation—quite the opposite. If anything, these people were Satanists or more indulgent. With lyrics like "Let me lick your wounds" and "Fuck me like a demon," it definitely couldn't be classified as Christian. The scrolling songs didn't seem to make sense, given the context.

"Why do they run the lyrics on the screens like that?" Marek asked eventually.

"More immersive experience," said Abaddon. "Or something." He clapped Marek on the back. "Can you learn just to relax, man? Do I need to buy you another drink?"

"I mean, I won't say no."

"You won't?"

"You know what I mean. To the drink."

"Wishful thinking then, I guess."

Abaddon returned with another beverage for Marek, but it was weak. As Marek gulped it down like water, Abaddon observed him.

"You need to learn to relax, man," he said.

Marek put his feet up on the table. "I am relaxed."

"You're putting on a show. I can tell."

"What, you read minds now?"

"Maybe."

"Ugh," Marek groaned. "Why do you care? You barely know me."

"Don't I?" Abaddon leaned toward Marek, then reached out to hold his face.

"What are you doing?" Marek tried to edge away, but Abaddon had a good grip on him. Before Marek could stop him, he kissed his lips firmly, then let him go. "What was that for?"

"I know you better than you think."

Marek could feel himself blushing, the warmth rushing to his face.

"You're curious, aren't you?" Abaddon asked. "You've thought about it, at least."

"Thought about what?" Could he pretend they hadn't just kissed? Again? He hadn't thought of anything but Olive for the past few weeks. She had filled his every waking moment, but it felt like a lost cause. He couldn't even get up to call her after everything had happened.

"There you go again. Back into your head. I can see the gears turning."

"So maybe I am. You don't make me curious. You make me confused."

Abaddon stared into his eyes. "At least I make you feel something." Seeing it empty, he glanced at Marek's glass, grabbed his hand, and pulled him closer to the stage, where the loud band drowned out all Marek's thoughts, confused or otherwise.

Maybe it was that he was surrounded by so many other souls or the last drink sending him over the edge, but Marek finally let his worries slip away. Instead, he felt the beat of the music, the bass line, the ecstatic electrical guitar, and the lyrics starting to make a chaotic sense. He felt a strange connection, not only to the music but to Abaddon, and not just to him but to all the people gathered here. It felt like some kind of church, all trying to let go, find the flow, and escape. He no longer felt alone. Tiny bits of confetti fell around them, like so many small, white butterflies.

9

The Page of Wands

Madame Rosivda turned the card, revealing a swirl of pink and golden stars. Amid the vortex, a young fairy skipped, wearing slippers and a sleeping cap. He carried a wand, which he held aloft, and a burning candle haphazardly balanced in his other hand. He stared into the flame, but his balance looked precarious, as if he may trip and fall at any moment. It was the Page of Wands.

"There once was a young fairy who doted upon his mother. Earlier, he had flown far away to explore, to test out his wings, and see what the world had to offer him, but when he heard she had fallen ill, he returned. She was bedridden, partially with grief for him when he had left, and now he returned to her bedside, wiping her brow with a cold cloth as the fever raged through her body. He brought a candle to her bedside when she called to him, and they spoke in whispers in the dim, flickering light.

"But the fairy quickly realized it was too late. Nothing the young fairy could do would save his mother from her illness. He felt the weight of responsibility heavy on his heart. The only thing that could have helped would be that he had never left her side. She was too far gone. Even when she did open her eyes, she didn't seem to recognize him. Instead, she lived in a fever-induced haze, her eyes rolling into the back of her head. She did not recognize the world around her, much less him. She saw him as a kind nurse tending to her but did not recognize him as her son."

"That's it?" asked Marek. "Another sad story?"

Madame Rosivda stared at him, a scowl crossing her face. "If you don't want to hear my message, don't come," she said.

"It's not that," he said. "But it's always so vague."

"Maybe your mind is cloudy."

"Maybe. I was hoping to get some insight on Olive. I haven't seen her around, not even at The Royal Club. No one seems to know where she is. I'm starting to get worried."

"Is this what you focused on when we began the reading?" Madame Rosivda asked.

"Hell, if I know. My mind has been - I don't know where my mind has been."

"Maybe it's time for some self-reflection."

"That's why I came to you. Your readings usually help get me back on track, but all this talk of sick women and fairies sounds nonsense today."

"Nonsense?" Madame Rosivda frowned as she gathered the cards, covering them with their black scarf before returning them to the cupboard. "None of this is nonsense, dear heart. I can't believe you would say that after all this time."

"I am sorry. Truly. I just..." Marek's voice trailed off, fading away.

"You need to get your head straight," she said. "Have you tried meditation?"

"What, sitting still and trying to think of nothing?"

"Not quite. I can walk you through a quick breathing exercise."

"If you think it will help."

"It might." She directed him back into the front room, still full of at least a couple dozen burning candles, and then brought two round cushions, which she placed on the floor. She motioned Marek toward one of them. "Sit cross-legged on this."

Marek looked doubtful but followed her direction. They each settled onto the floor, and Marek found himself again wondering how old Madame Rosivda was. Her joints didn't crack or pop as she sat. She didn't seem to show any hesitation or discomfort. She kneeled so that she sat upon her own feet, seiza-style, which was a feat Marek wasn't sure he'd be able to accomplish with ease.

"Am I sitting the right way?" he asked.

"Don't worry," she replied. "I've been doing this for years—that, and yoga. I don't expect you to be as flexible as I am. You're fine, dear."

Marek found himself worrying that he wasn't sitting right and that this was a tremendous waste of time. He should be practicing and rehearsing for the open jam that night. He hadn't played an entire song since the wedding and could feel his fingers growing lazy.

"First, you need to work on clearing your mind," Madame Rosivda said. "For many people, that is the hardest part. For you, we'll try square breathing."

"What's that?"

"Shh. Patience, grasshopper. I'm about to tell you."

Marek chuckled at the reference to the Karate Kid but genuinely tried to let his thoughts settle, let the anxious worrying fade away. Of course, the more he thought about the desire to get rid of the worry, the more he worried.

"We start with breathing in with the nose for a count of four. Then, we hold our breath for another count of four. We let the breath go through the mouth for four and then wait for four more counts before breathing in again."

"So, everything in fours?"

"Exactly." She counted the beats for him as he breathed in through his nose.

Marek felt like he couldn't hold his breath, even for the four seconds she suggested. He breathed out heavily.

"Let's try again," she said, starting the count backward from four. "Breathe in, three, two, one. Hold for three, two, one. Breathe out through your mouth: three, two, one. Then hold again, for three, two, one."

Marek gasped, unable to keep time.

"You seem to be struggling," she said. "Let's try something simpler."

"Like what?"

"Just pay attention to your breathing. Don't count it; don't try to control it. Just breathe naturally."

Marek breathed in, then out. In and out. Quickly, then gradually slower, until he started settling into it.

"For the next minute, just count your breaths. Don't try to control it; just count." Madame Rosivda closed her eyes. "Don't focus on me; focus on your breath."

Marek sighed loudly. This exercise felt like a waste of time. He could be using this time to get some work done. Instead, he was sitting on the floor on a cushion like a child in kindergarten, trying to follow Madame Rosivda's directions and failing. He counted into the teens and then lost track, started again, made it to twenty, and lost the count again. "I don't have time for this," he said, pushing the cushion aside and standing. He stretched and looked down at Madame Rosivda, still sitting peacefully with her eyes closed. "Did you hear me?" he asked.

"Yes," she replied, slowly opening her eyes. "You're not even trying."

"I'll see you next week." He pushed out the front door, feeling the cold air hit his face. It wouldn't be that cold without the wind, but there was always a bitter wind this time of year. It whipped past him, through his clothes, as if he had jumped into a pool of ice. He shivered, wrapping his arms across his chest, and started walking. He knew even Abaddon wouldn't be out busking in this weather, and he wondered how many people would bother coming out to the open jam. There were always fewer people when the weather was terrible. It might not be snowing, but the cold was enough of a deterrent for some.

When he opened the door to his apartment, he found himself wishing he had a roommate or even a pet to greet him. It was always so quiet and lonely living by himself. His family home had been a place of constant movement and activity when he was younger. In years past, he had had a live-in girlfriend who was always waiting for him with a warm embrace and dinner in the oven. That felt like another lifetime.

He checked the freezer and remembered he needed to go grocery shopping. He didn't feel very motivated to leave the house just now. Instead, he moved to the bedroom, the rumpled blankets of his bed not made from the morning. At least if he crawled in, he would be warm. He stretched out, pulled the blankets over him, and snuggled in. Moments later, his heavy eyes pulled him into a deep sleep.

He dreamed of angels and fairies and other winged things. They flew in great curlicues over his head, and he remained grounded, unable to join them in their flight. They mocked him, dipping down to run their fingers through his hair, tug on his ears, and laugh in his face. Each time he reached out to try to snag them, pull them down to the ground, they flit away, cartwheeling through the air.

He woke with a start when the phone rang. He rejected the call because he didn't recognize the number, but they called back immediately. It must be something important, or at least someone persistent. Night had descended already. Was there something he was supposed to be doing, someone he was supposed to meet? His foggy brain, still clouded with winged things, couldn't seem to grasp hold of it.

"Yeah, what do you want?"

"Have you heard from Abaddon? He was supposed to be here tonight. Now that I think of it, so were you."

It took Marek a moment to place the voice. As his pause grew longer, she spoke again.

"Marek? Are you alright?" It was Nyx. It had been a minute since he'd seen her, either.

"How'd you get my number?"

"I asked one of the girls. You're not exactly unlisted around here."

Marek struggled to sit upright in the bed. His face felt half-numb from sleeping on his side. He ran one hand through his hair, remembering the fairies and angels grasping at it in his dream. He could use a haircut, he thought to himself.

"So, what's going on?" he asked.

"You tell me. You've missed the past few weeks, but Abaddon is usually here. Sometimes, he's late, but he's always here. It's going on 9 p.m., and I haven't seen him. I thought maybe you had."

"I haven't seen him today, at least."

"Have you seen him in the past few days?"

"Yeah, we went to this weird concert. Why are you so worried?"

"I don't know if you know this, but Abaddon used to, I mean still is, an addict. It doesn't take much for him to slip back into it. I hope he's just doped up at home and not off somewhere. He isn't answering his phone."

Marek struggled out of the bed and made his way to the window. He looked out over the city, already teeming with nightlife. "I mean, it doesn't entirely surprise me, but I thought what he was into was pretty tame, mostly. Weed and party drugs, nothing too concerning."

An edge of anger crept into Nyx's voice. "It's heroin, Marek. Haven't you ever noticed the tracks in his arms?"

Marek shook his head and remembered she couldn't see the motion through the phone. "N-no," he said haltingly. "Maybe we should go check up on him."

"I figured I'd try you first since you two have been so buddy-buddy lately. Meet you at Abaddon's apartment. If he's passed out, I might need your help busting the door in."

Marek wasn't sure how much help he'd be, but he agreed. Now, his brain also ached with worry. He ordered an Uber to pick him up and hurried downstairs to wait. For some reason, even when things happened quickly, they felt so slow to him, like trying to swim through mud. As each minute ticked by, he felt his heart racing faster and faster, and he cursed the driver for taking so long to arrive. Eventually, he focused on his breaths again, counting each inhale and exhale as Madame Rosivda had taught him. It gave him something to distract himself but didn't help the rising panic.

The driver finally arrived, and Marek piled into the backseat. He didn't bother buckling in but leaned against the door, staring disconsolately out. The driver tried some light banter, but Marek wasn't having it.

"I'll give you a good tip if you can hurry it up a bit," he offered.

The man glanced back at him in the rearview mirror and nodded. "What's the hurry?" he asked.

"I've got a friend who might be in trouble."

"Am I taking you into a dangerous situation?"

"No, not necessarily, but it'd be good to get there sooner rather than later."

"I got you."

The rest of the ride moved more quickly as the driver careened around each turn, not running reds but pushing against each yellow they approached. He weaved in and out of the traffic, finding the quickest route through the flow of cars. Marek felt like they were trying to beat the clock, but time moved inexorably forward, each minute holding him back from Abaddon. If he lost his friend, if it came to that - Marek tried to pause his racing thoughts, but they came unbidden. As the car pulled up in front of the apartment, Marek jumped out without a word and ran to the elevator, which was out of operation. He sprinted up the stairs, breathing heavily until he reached the door to Abaddon's apartment.

Nyx was there already, ineffectually turning the doorknob with a force that looked like she'd break her hand if she pushed harder. Mascara ran down her face in fat, black streaks. She moved aside to let him try. The first thing Marek tried was running and throwing the total weight of his body against the door. His attempt accomplished nothing but sent a sharp pain running through his shoulder. Then he ran at the door, leg extended, dropping, kicking against the wood. Again, the wood had no give and only caused him pain. Marek wished he had more relevant skills and had trained for this, but who trains to break down doors except for police officers and Boy Scouts? Did they even teach skills like that in the scouts? Marek doubted it.

He spotted a fire axe encased in glass. He threw his fist into the case, his knuckles making contact and his skin splitting apart. He grabbed the axe and desperately hacked at the door, feeling ridiculous and in-effectual as he made small gashes in the wood but still couldn't break it down. Nyx watched him for a minute and then asked him to step aside. She wore three-inch platform combat boots, which might serve as a better weapon in this case. Kicking with force, she wedged her foot just to the left of the doorknob, and the door finally sprang loose. They both rushed in, brushing shoulders as they pushed past each other, and Nyx took the lead, descending upon Abaddon's nearly lifeless body propped on a pile of pillows.

Marek spotted the evidence: a plastic strap wrapped around Abaddon's forearm, a needle lying haphazardly alongside him. Abaddon's face fell slack, his eyes half-open and incredibly dilated, his lips an unnaturally pale blue. Nyx shook their friend, trying to bring him back to consciousness. His body flopped like a dead fish. Marek reached for his phone and began to dial for an ambulance.

Nyx stared at him and started yelling. "We don't have time for that. We have to get him downstairs. Get him to the hospital."

Marek grimaced. They'd have to carry him down four floors. "Do you even have a car?" he asked. "I should have had my Uber wait."

"I've got a car."

"Thank god for that."

"I'm not feeling all that grateful at the moment," she said. "You grab Abaddon's shoulders; I've got his feet."

They carefully lifted Abaddon's heavy body and shuffled out of the apartment. When they reached the stairs, Marek pulled him onto his shoulders and carried him on his back. Although it was quite a burden, it was much faster than balancing the dead weight between them. In his anxious fear, he felt a rush of adrenaline, which helped him push forward. He'd feel the strain on his shoulders the next day, but now all he felt was the overwhelming need to get Abaddon to safety.

Several grueling minutes later, he hefted his friend into the backseat of Nyx's car. Abaddon fell like a sack of potatoes over the seat, crumpling in a way that would be comedic under better circumstances. Nyx slid behind the wheel, and Marek took shotgun. They sped and likely broke a few traffic laws on the way to the hospital a few blocks away. While Nyx left the car idling, Marek ran inside.

The receptionist picked at her fingernails, looking up lazily at him. "I have a friend that needs help."

"Well, where is he?" she asked. "Wait, don't tell me. Is he imaginary?"

Marek scowled down at her. "No, he's passed out in the backseat of a car. I think he ODed."

Her face shifted from one of utter boredom to instant worry. "Let me page someone right away for you." She called the code over the intercom, and three paramedics descended on the desk. Marek led the way outside, and between them, they hefted Abaddon onto a gurney and swiftly wheeled him into the emergency room. Nyx parked the car and then came running back in. From there, it was a flurry of activity.

As soon as the paramedics laid Abaddon into the bed, they injected something into his arm. Marek hadn't even answered questions or filled out any paperwork, so he worried things were serious. Eventually, one of them turned to him to explain.

"It's naloxone," he said. It was a statement of fact, cold and unfeeling. "Helps fight a fentanyl overdose."

"How did you know?" asked Marek.

"Happens more often than you'd think. Come on, let's get out of here." The paramedic directed Marek out into the hallway. "You too, miss," he said to Nyx. "Give my men some room to work."

They stood awkwardly in the hallway, nearly shaking with anxiety and relief. Anxious for the future, relieved that they had made it in time.

"It may take some time for us to get your friend regulated and back to normal. After the naloxone, though, he is going to be okay. Does he have a history of opioid use?"

Marek nodded dumbly, allowing Nyx to do the talking.

She replied that yes, he had, in years past. She thought he had kicked the habit, but as evidenced by this evening, that was no longer true.

"It tends to be a slippery slope," said the paramedic. "Even when you think they're free of it, the smallest thing can send them down that path again. Anything particularly stressful in his life lately?"

"Not that I know of," said Nyx. "Then again, Abaddon doesn't tell me everything." She glanced over at Marek, urging him to give some input.

"He seemed fine a few days ago," said Marek. "Nothing out of sorts. He was helping me through a slump."

"You use as well?" asked the paramedic.

"No, no. That's not what I meant. I've been down in the dumps, depressed. Abaddon helped get me out of the house."

"Do you know if he's ever been in rehab before?"

They both shrugged, not knowing the answer.

"We'll get him through this, and then we can look at the next steps. I recommend sitting out here or in the waiting room just down the hall. Don't worry; we'll come to get you once we've got him awake and aware. It will be much easier if you just give us the room now."

Marek and Nyx reluctantly made their way down to the waiting room. It was difficult to walk away, knowing their friend was in need, but they also recognized there was little they could do to contribute now. Marek found himself wanting a beer, but coffee would have to suffice. He also brought one for Nyx, and they sat silently sipping from styrofoam cups.

Eventually, Marek broke the tension with a question.

"How long have you known Abaddon?" he asked.

"Since before my son. He knew me even before Joshua."

"Joshua?"

"My ex-husband."

"Sorry, I never knew his name."

"No worries." She took a huge swallow from her cup, gulping the coffee down. "He didn't stick around long."

"Did you meet Abaddon at the Royal Club?"

"Yeah. But he used to be a bit wilder back in the day."

"Really?" asked Marek. He tried to picture a wilder Abaddon. His friend pulled him so far out of his comfort zone that he couldn't imagine what "wilder" would look like.

"I see those gears turning," said Nyx. "Think about Abaddon at his most wild, then turn it up a notch. You probably wouldn't be able to imagine it. You're too straight-laced."

"What - more drinking, more drugs? I gather that much."

"Near-nightly orgies."

Marek raised an eyebrow. "Are you saying you were involved?"

Nyx laughed. "We were all young and dumb once."

He looked her up and down. "Who are you kidding? You're still young."

She sighed heavily. "Not as young as I used to be."

Marek let out a breath he didn't realize he was holding. The wind rushed out of him, and he took another deep breath to replace it. Who knew these breathing exercises would come in handy? He glanced back at Nyx, but there was nothing left to say. He couldn't get his mind off Abaddon, and the anxiety and worry grew heavier in his chest. "I'm so tired," he said eventually.

"You and me both," said Nyx.

The emergency room doors opened with a great gust of wind, and a tall woman wearing a trench coat rushed in. Her wild, wavy hair cascaded down her shoulders, and her green eyes searched for a friendly face. Marek rushed to her side.

"Olive! What are you doing here?!"

She turned to him, and they embraced.

Pulling away, she examined his face. "How's Abaddon?"

Nyx walked up to join them and answered for Marek. "He'll be fine. It'll just take some time."

Olive turned to Nyx, and they hugged as well. "My friends need to stop winding up in the emergency room," she said. "Soon enough, I'll be admitted with a heart attack from all the worry."

Marek struggled to remember who else had been in the emergency room, and weeks had passed since the incident at the wedding. It all seemed like a nightmare now, and he hadn't even seen or talked to Olive since then. He wanted to ask about her cousin but figured now wouldn't be the time.

"Did someone from the club tell you?" asked Nyx.

"Yeah." Olive nodded as if in accompaniment to her words. The image on a child's flashcards is "yes," with the downward-tilted head. "Ronnie let me know as soon as I got there. I left and came straight here. It made more sense than stopping at Abaddon's place when he would most likely end up here if something had happened. You need to answer your phone, girl."

Nyx looked down, "Oh shit. It looks like it's been dead for a while."

"And you." Olive advanced on Marek. "How is it that I still don't have your phone number?"

Marek shrugged. "Beats me."

Before they could settle in for what seemed to be an interminable wait, one of the nurses came to find them. "Family for Abaddon Navarro?" she called out.

Nyx approached first. "Friends. But yes, family, too."

"You can come and see him now," the nurse said. "He's just up this hall, to the right. Room 121."

"Thank you so much," said Nyx. She grabbed Olive's arm, and they walked down the hallway, Marek following behind.

Turning the corner, they saw their friend shuffling down the hallway, wearing blue slipper socks, carrying a large paper cup, and sipping water from a bent straw. He smiled mischievously. "Hey, bitches. Where's the party? Let's blow this joint."

IO

The King of Wands

Madame Rosivda turned the card. A large, black crow sat atop a crown, its claws wrapped around the encrusted jewels. It held its head high and proud, gazing at the flourishing garden below. Fat, red roses spiraled toward the sky, but they were soft and welcoming, without a single thorn. The moon and the sun rose above the horizon, a halo of light radiating from each, creating an otherworldly aura. It was the King of Wands.

"There once was a well-loved king," she said, "who took a crow as his only advisor. No one else could tell the king what to pay attention to, what laws to enact, or who to give his blessing to.

"The crow, you see, could speak. It spoke not just nonsense or words it had heard others say but rather a certain truth unknown to the other royal court members. Some wise men even held it in contempt because the king did not listen to their words, only the crow.

"There was some debate regarding where the crow had come from. After all, what if it had been raised in a foreign land or by one of the kingdom's enemies and taught to whisper sedition to the king? If this were the case, it could prove a traitor and inspire the king to act in ways not in the best interest of his people. After all, the crow often flew out from the castle and, at times, did not return for days. When it came, it brought news of distant lands, but could someone twist its supposed observations?

"A young page tasked by his master with following the crow observed to see where it flew. He noticed that it often alighted on a flight to the northeast, seemingly flying directly into the sun on a hot afternoon. The page brought the fastest steed he could find to chase after it but soon encountered a great ravine he could not cross. On the other side, he saw a small hut in the distance, built into the roots of a great oak tree. He saw more crows roosting in the tree's expansive branches than he could count. He surmised there must be hundreds of them, each cawing and chattering, and as he listened, he realized that there was not just one crow who could speak but dozens. He listened as they exchanged greetings, like a large family reuniting, and he also noticed that the king's crow, who had landed on one of the top branches, was not the same crow that flew up into the air to return to the castle.

"It seemed that the king had not just one crow advisor but many. Far too many to even count."

Marek sipped his tea. He enjoyed this story. Though odd, like most of the stories Madame Rosivda told him, it wasn't directly sad or dangerous. He found himself searching for a moral, though. Her stories did not always come with clear endings.

"That's it?" he asked.

"Yes," she said. "The next thing you'll ask me is who is the king and who are the crows. Oh, and better yet, who is the spying page and his master?" She grinned at him across the table as she started to put away the tools of her trade.

"You're getting to know me too well," he said.

"You always look for something so literal."

"I am a practical man."

"Are you?" she asked. "What was it like seeing Olive again?"

Marek started to answer, then realized he hadn't mentioned Olive, at least not on this visit. "How did you know?"

"I should tell you it's my psychic abilities, but I saw her this morning."

"You did? She mentioned me?" Marek unconsciously puffed his chest out. "What did she say?"

Madame Rosivda laughed a deep chuckle that rose from her chest like bubbles in a stream. "Look at you, preening like a peacock."

He shrunk back into his chair, deflating. "Nothing good, then."

"Nothing bad, either. You worry too much, Marek."

"I just want to be someone she thinks about. Unexpectedly, like I'm always there in the back of her mind, the way she is in my mind. She's always with me."

"That's a tall order, but give it time. Unlike a fairy tale, it doesn't happen overnight, at midnight, with a glass slipper. There's magic there, but the slow, gradual kind."

"If it's slow and gradual, is it magic?"

"I think so. That kind of magic is more powerful, too. Would you be interested in dabbling?" she asked.

Marek's eyes grew wide. Some would accuse him of accepting the occult simply for getting these readings, but he never considered himself a practitioner. He wasn't quite ready to take responsibility for it yet, but he did have questions. "I'm not sure, but I did want to know something."

"Anything."

"Why do you do your readings the way that you do? I did a little research, and it sounds like most tarot readings involve a full spread, several cards interacting with one another, and no one tells stories about the cards, at least not as in-depth as yours. And what about the tea, the candles? You use so many things."

"That's quite a few questions there. And it took you this long to ask them? Weren't you curious before?"

"Honestly, I didn't believe in any of it for the longest time. You convinced me it was mostly coincidence that events mirrored the stories you told, not that you were telling my future."

"Why did you keep coming back then?"

"Partially curiosity. Partially because it was nice to have someone to talk to." He motioned toward his now-empty mug. "And the tea is better than anything I've ever made for myself or found at any shops around town. Where do you get it?"

She slid his mug toward herself, picking it up in both hands. "It's my special blend. Some of these leaves and herbs I've been collecting for decades. Once I dry them, they keep for a long time."

"Do you serve the same blend to everyone?"

"I tailor it to the individual as we go along. For instance, Olive's blend has more rosehips and bergamot. Yours is more lavender and chamomile."

"Do you do magic with tea?"

She looked up at him, her eyes sparkling. "I do magic with everything."

He nodded. He knew Madame Rosivda wouldn't answer all his questions. Why would she when she served as the conduit for the magic other people performed? She would lose her livelihood if she gave all her secrets away. But he remembered the offer she had made to him. Could he perform his magic with her help? "What was that you mentioned about dabbling?"

"Now, I offer this with a few caveats," she began. "There is no such thing as a love potion, and you can't change someone else's feelings toward you; only make yourself more receptive, more ready to welcome a new relationship."

Marek had a general idea of where this might be going, but his heart still leaped at the thought of making Olive fall in love with him. So many things in his life were starting to look up, and if he could only have her, he felt he would be complete. "What do you have then?" he asked.

"I have a candle with runes carved into it with an athame or ritual blade. I also anointed the candle with jojoba oil. In other words, I have the ingredients for a spell with their intentions baked in, but you must also set your intentions."

"Understood."

"I want you to spend some time thinking about the aspects of Olive that you find attractive. What about her would make her a good mate for you? Then, likewise, you need to focus on what aspects of yourself make you a desirable mate."

Marek tried not to laugh. "One of those lists will be decidedly longer."

Madame Rosivda smiled but did not join in his brevity. "Ideally, you should both fit together. It cannot be one-sided. If your list is not long enough, you must work toward making it longer. Make yourself a suitable partner. Think carefully about what that means to you and what it might mean to her."

"That might take a while."

"That's what I mean by slow magic," said Madame Rosivda. "Keep these lists somewhere where you can see them every day. Maybe on top of your dresser or beside a bathroom mirror so you can reflect on them often. Do you have any roommates?"

"No."

"Good. That will make it easier. You should not hide these lists away. You should strive to add to them every day. Start small. Think of three reasons why Olive is a good match for you, and try to think of three reasons why you are a good match for her."

"Where does the candle come in?"

"Each day, after you have added to your list, burn the candle and meditate on it. Focus on what you are trying to achieve and envision the result. This meditation is best done at the beginning of each day to continue to work on yourself throughout the day. When you run out of things to add to your list of attributes, write down things you do not yet exemplify but wish to embody."

"Like what?"

"Say you are easy to anger, and you want to work o that. Try writing down 'patient' and then focusing on that for the next few days. If you write something down and still do not embody it fully after three days, erase it from the list. You can add it back once you can truly claim that attribute."

"This sounds pretty challenging."

"It should be," she said. "This kind of magic, to be lasting, should never be quick and easy. It is slow and gradual, like growing a plant. You tend to it daily; eventually, it will bloom for you."

"So, where is this magic candle?" Marek asked.

"Not so fast. There's more."

"More? I thought that was plenty."

Madame Rosivda lowered her voice to a whisper. "You must also remember that As Above, So Below."

"What does that mean?"

"While putting your intentions out into the Universe, all your hopes and dreams, you must work in the real world to make them happen actively. You can't just sit at home making lists and lighting your candle and expect Olive to fall in love with you."

"But that sounded so reasonable." This time, Marek let his laugh escape.

Madame Rosivda fixed him with a stern glare. "I won't pass this along to you if you think it is a joke. This spell is magic and will take real work to enact."

Marek sobered a bit. "I understand. I'm sorry for joking about it."

"You better be." She paused for dramatic effect. "So what kind of real-world action do you think this would require?"

"Taking Olive out on dates?"

"Not necessarily. But you must find ways to demonstrate that you have the qualities on your list. You need to get closer to Olive. If she doesn't see you how you see yourself, you'll never be able to make the connection you need to maintain a relationship."

"Sounds easy enough."

"It isn't." She leaned in to impart one last bit of wisdom. "And there's one more thing."

"What's that?"

"You need to believe in it. If you think this is some silly game and just go through the motions without believing it can work, you might as well not do it at all."

"This magic doesn't sound much like magic to me."

"Believe me, it is. Just not the kind you see on TV."

Marek cleared his throat, even though she'd fully convinced him several minutes ago. "I'm in."

When he got home, Marek set up a small altar around his bathroom mirror. He had heard of people using positive affirmations, saying things to themselves while staring at their reflection, but it made him think more of a Saturday Night Live skit than a thing real people did. He tried to push that idea from his mind, knowing it was precisely what Madame Rosivda had warned against. The dresser in the bedroom may serve as a better space.

He moved everything into the other room: the enchanted candle, a tall red taper set into its holder, two rolled sheets of parchment, and a calligraphy pen. He immediately started on Olive's list, knowing it would be easy to complete. Still, as he scribbled out why he was so attracted to her, those attributes started to sound superficial. "Beautiful" and "sexy" were nearly the same. "Kind" or "friendly" could apply to almost anyone. What was it about Olive that made her so irresistible? "Wonderful singing voice" was up there.

He paused, turning to his list, and drew a blank. What did he possibly have to offer? He felt like he couldn't even put "pianist" on the list because there were no adjectives to add. He wasn't particularly well-known or heralded, and how did he know if it was something that Olive even admired? He could use some input and knew who to ask: Abaddon.

Abaddon had been staying with Nyx since what they now called "the incident." His friend claimed his OD wasn't intentional, just a bad batch from a cheap dealer. Despite this, they still worried, mainly because he refused to go to rehab, which would have been a move in the right direction. He also refused to attend meetings, claiming, "Only addicts go to meetings, and I'm not an addict."

Marek was glad Nyx had taken Abaddon in, though. It made him feel a little better about the situation. Plus, it had the bonus of gathering two of his friends together in one place. He texted ahead to let them know he was coming, then ordered a car.

Nyx's apartment was gorgeous - a three-bedroom flat decorated in a black-and-white minimalist style, and she did not rent but owned the space. That was part of the reason she hadn't given it up in the divorce. She and her ex Joshua hadn't had much, but she walked away from the marriage with the apartment, and he left with all the electronics – the big-screen TV, the gaming systems, the computer. She couldn't care less about that, and if it got him out of her hair faster, she would gladly oblige. It did leave her without any form of at-home entertainment for a few months, though.

Abaddon had settled into the back bedroom with a futon, which he laid on almost all hours of the day. He wasn't going out and busking on the corner but wasn't using, which was the primary goal. She'd allow him to be a sloth if he just stayed clean. They occasionally shared a bottle of wine and some weed but nothing else. It was an improvement, at least, until he could get back on his feet.

When Marek arrived, however, he caught his friends in an argument. He heard their shouts from behind the door before he even entered.

"The least you could do is run the dishwasher," said Nyx. "You don't need to handwash anything, just put the dishes in."

"But the dishwasher is always full," said Abaddon.

"Of clean dishes. Put them away first."

"I don't know where anything goes."

Nyx started opening cabinets, flinging the doors open. She announced what was where as she went through the entire kitchen. "Plates. Glasses. Bowls." She turned back to Abaddon. "Just look. It's not that hard."

Marek interrupted before Abaddon could respond. "Am I interrupting something?" he asked.

Nyx sighed and motioned at Abaddon, who sat sprawled across the couch. "Our little friend here is a fucking child."

Abaddon sheepishly grinned as if to say, "Who, me?" and tried to change the subject. "How's it going, Marek?"

Marek made a noncommittal grunt and sat on a recliner beside the couch.

Nyx pushed up against Abaddon's shoulder, forcing him to sit up so she could sit beside him. "I guess the kitchen can wait," she said. "For now. What brings you by?"

"Just need to get out of my apartment for a bit."

"You ever clean that place up?" asked Abaddon.

"Yeah. It's not sparkling, but better than the last time you were by."

"You should have seen this guy," said Abaddon, turning to Nyx. "He had a tower of empty beer boxes piled up. Looked like a frat house."

"Remind me not to come to your place," she told Marek. "So. What would you boys like to do this evening?"

"Remember, no partying for me," said Abaddon. "New house rules." He said they were rules he had imposed on himself when everyone knew they were Nyx's rules. But either way, they accomplished the same goal. He might not be entirely sober, but he had toned things down a bit.

"Maybe we could play a game," said Marek.

"A game? Like what?" asked Nyx.

"I don't know, a board game?"

"Like Monopoly?" said Abaddon. "Candy Land?"

"I've got some cards," said Nyx. She disappeared into the other room and returned with a pack of playing cards. They had naked ladies on them posed in pornographic positions.

"Where on earth did you get these from?" Marek asked.

"Porn shop," she replied. "Where do you think?"

"Somehow, I always forget women go to porn shops."

"Where else do you think we get all our toys?"

"I don't know. Online?"

"You never really know what you're getting when you order online. You might want an eight-incher and get a three-incher instead."

"Sounds like online dating," said Abaddon, laughing.

"Regardless," said Nyx. "What do you want to play?"

"Texas Hold 'em sounds good," said Marek.

They decided not to play for money, but eventually, Nyx brought out some pretzels so they could visually see who was winning. Between rounds, Abaddon started popping pretzels in his mouth and stealing from all the piles, so even that devolved into folly. Eventually, they even subverted the rules so that the card's actual values didn't matter, but they judged instead based on the images printed on them. Whose card was the most lewd, the most inappropriate? Marek claimed to be the expert or final judge in this regard.

"I'm the only one here that's even attracted to women," he said.

Nyx gave him a sly glance and interrupted. "I like women," she said.

"But you were married."

Abaddon butted in. "A girl can convert."

"Or there's such a thing as bisexuality," she said.

"Oh, really. So that's what you're into," said Marek.

"That doesn't necessarily mean three-ways."

Abaddon shoved her shoulder with one hand. "But it doesn't rule them out either."

Marek didn't comment. He suddenly felt a little awkward. Were they implying what he thought they were suggesting? Nyx's offhanded comment about orgies the other day made him wonder. But they were friends, and that would be weird. Not just odd; it would be ridiculous. He tried to turn his mind toward his original reason for coming over in the first place.

"You know," he began. "I wanted to get your opinion on something."

"Whose opinion?" asked Abaddon. "Mine?"

"Both of you.

"So why the preamble? What's up?" asked Nyx. She set her cards down on the table between them. It was clear they weren't playing anymore anyway. She crossed her legs and leaned back.

Marek wasn't sure if he wanted to tell them about the spell. He could bring it up without that detail, couldn't he? It was worth a try. "What do you think is most attractive about me?" he asked.

Abaddon leaned in, pressing his lips to Marek's cheek before he could pull away. "About you?" he asked. "Everything, baby."

Marek laughed. "No, really. I want to know."

"What's this really about?" asked Nyx.

"Well, you know Olive..."

Nyx scoffed. "What is it with you and Olive? You barely know her."

"I know enough to know I like her."

"Ugh. You just think you like Olive. You've got that instinctive attraction, but have you ever spent real time with her?"

"Enough time."

"You know, that's what I hate about guys. You see a girl across the room, you walk up and have one conversation with her, and suddenly, you're *in love*. That's not love. That's lust. That's the animalistic part of you. That's pheromones, maybe not love. And then, you'll talk about love and all these obsessions with your friends, but meanwhile, the object of your affection doesn't have a fucking clue. Have you even asked her out yet?"

"I haven't had the opportunity."

"Haven't had the opportunity? You see her almost every week."

"It's not that easy. Do you have any idea how hard it is to take rejection? What if she says 'no'? You have no idea how hard that is. Why do I always have to be the one to initiate? Even a conversation? Women have it so easy. They just sit there looking pretty and wait for a man to approach them."

Abaddon grunted. "Calm it down, my heteros."

"Wait," said Nyx. "Who're you calling hetero? Didn't I just say I was bisexual?"

"That doesn't count," said Abaddon.

"What do you mean, 'doesn't count?'"

"Until you're shacking up with a lesbian, I call shenanigans."

"I've been with a woman before."

"Have you? In a relationship?"

"Well, no."

"I bet you haven't even been muff diving."

"That's such a crude way to say it. That's not the only way women have sex."

"Well, have you?"

"Have I what?"

"Gone down on a woman?"

She hesitated. "Well, no. Not exactly..."

"What does that mean?"

"Abaddon."

"No, really, I want to know."

Nyx turned away from Abaddon. "I thought we were talking about Marek here."

"You're just trying to change the subject."

Nyx released an exasperated sigh, stood, and left the room. "I gotta pee," she said as she walked down the hallway.

As soon as she left, Abaddon turned back to Marek. "I could tell you about a million ways you're attractive, man."

"But I don't want to be attractive to dudes. No offense, man," said Marek.

"None taken. But really, what is this all about? You just need a pep talk or something?"

"Kind of. I mean, I guess so."

"You don't need to hedge your needs. Do you want an ego boost? Come with me into any gay club, and you'll have all the attention you want. You are a handsome man."

"Like I said. That's the wrong audience."

"Fine, I can do you one better. I hear there's an amateur night at The Dirty Martini. We should check it out. It's a female audience, scouts honor." Marek held up three fingers as if he were swearing an oath.

Nyx walked into the room, letting a loud laugh escape her lips. "You were never a Boy Scout," she said.

"Of course I was," said Abaddon. "How do you think I figured out I liked boys so much? They even kicked me out."

"Regardless," said Marek. "I don't think that's what I'm looking for, just a little pep talk."

"Are you sure?" asked Abaddon.

"Besides, how do you even know about this place?"

"What place?" asked Nyx.

"Dirty Martini," said Abaddon.

"And why are we going there? Strip clubs are boring as shit. I don't want to pay to see something I can't touch. It's worse than porn," said Nyx.

"They have an amateur night," said Abaddon.

"You think I'm going to get up on stage? Is that what you've been plotting while I was in the bathroom? You fucking perverts." She looked off into the corner of the room. "I mean, really?"
"No, no, no. That's not it." Marek stood up and started pacing.

"Marek's going to strip," said Abaddon.

"Marek's going to what?!"

"I'm not doing anything like that," said Marek.

"Maybe you should," said Nyx, teasing. "It would be a great confidence boost."

"Could we maybe start with something more tame? Like performing solo at Open Jam?"

"Haven't you done that already?" she asked.

"Actually, no. I usually accompany someone."

"Really? I swear you've soloed before. Besides, I feel that isn't high stakes enough. It needs to be something big. Or bigger. A bigger step for you, something to aim for," she said. "Abaddon and I can tell you how awesome we think you are all day, but that doesn't mean you'll believe it. You have to prove it to yourself. We should book you a show."

"A whole show? Maybe just a song or two," Marek said. "Like not even half a set. I don't have that much material prepared."

"Then you'll have to prepare it."

"Hey, Marek," said Abaddon. He sounded like a small child, feeling left out of the conversation. "I still think you'd make a great stripper. But - I know you'd never do it. Not sober anyway."

Marek nodded. The stripping idea sounded ridiculous. He had a decent body but had no desire to show it off to everyone. That would be so embarrassing, like that nightmare where you show up to school with no pants, but in real life.

"I triple-dog dare you to perform a whole show at The Royal Club. Nyx and I can arrange it. You just have to play it. What do you say?"

Marek didn't respond.

"Hey, speaking of daring, we should play Truth or Dare. Nyx, are you in?"

"What is this, a sleepover?"

"It could be."

"I don't think so."

As Nyx and Abaddon began bickering back and forth, play fighting. Marek heard a tapping at the window. It was probably just a branch rustling against the side of the building, but then he heard it again, and it sounded just like someone tapping on the window, like with fingernails. But no one could do that this high up unless they climbed the fire escape.

He interrupted his friends. "Do you hear that?"

"Hear what?" asked Nyx, turning his way.

The tapping returned. This time, Marek envisioned a teenager tossing small rocks at their friend's bedroom window, trying to catch their attention.

"There's something at the window," he said.

"It's probably just the wind," said Abaddon.

Then, they all heard the tapping again. Marek moved closer to the window and pulled the curtains aside. Sitting on the sill was a large crow, and as it tapped its beak against the pane of glass, a tinny echo reverberated through the room.

Nyx moved closer, and the crow flew away, soaring into the clouds. "What the hell?" she said.

"That decides it," said Marek. "I guess I have to do that show now."

"Because of a crow?" asked Abaddon.

"Because I need to start making some decisions," said Marek. He didn't explain about the crow, but yes, also because of the crow. There had been a knowing look in the bird's eyes. He needed to show Olive he was a great musician and assertive. That would be something he could add to the list.

The Seven of Wands

Madame Rosivda turned the card, revealing a golden sky brightened by a large summer sun. In the foreground stood a young man, his short, rakish hair blowing in all directions with a gust of wind. He stood astride a pathway, not guarding it or defending it but claiming it as his own. He wore a short tunic belted at the waist, golden tights, and leather boots which stopped at his ankles. He wore a sharp dagger at his side but held a star-topped wand. Six other wands marked the land around him, and a small butterfly fluttered above him. It was the Seven of Wands.

Marek gazed into his teacup with determination. Now that he had goals, namely winning Olive's affection, these meetings with the tarot reader had grown more urgent. He wanted to know if he was on the right path and if what he was striving for was even achievable. It felt so good to have something, someone worth seeking.

"There once was a mercenary tasked with clearing a path from one town to the next, marking the way so that others could safely travel along it," began Madame Rosivda. "He was young and inexperienced but foolhardy enough to take on the task. Other more experienced adventurers knew there was much danger along this pathway: fantastic beasts who would attack anyone they encountered, even flesh-eating plants that could strike at a moment's notice. But the young mercenary set forth, alone, with only a tiny dagger to defend himself.

"As he traveled, he, surprisingly, didn't come across any challenges. There was some brush covering the pathway, which he hacked away, but he did not encounter any predicted violence. Instead, a small white butterfly flitted ahead of him as if leading him on the way. Little did he know that butterfly was, in fact, a fairy in its most diminutive form, protecting him as it warded away the flora and fauna that would have consumed him given the opportunity.

"Not only did the fairy protect him, but the mercenary found several wands. He picked each up in turn, attempting to perform magic he knew nothing about. Each wand possessed the power of a different element: Earth, Air, Water, Fire, and Spirit. He grasped them in his hands, casting the most basic spells held in the essence of the wands, not through any magic of his own. He collected them in a pouch he wore across his back, knowing they may prove helpful in future adventures, even if he didn't properly know how to use them. However, the last two wands he approached were those of Life and Death, which no mortal should have the power to wield.

"When he encountered Life and cast a small spell with it, he caused a great oak to grow, stretching ever higher toward the sky, creating a million perches for birds in its branches. The fairy watched silently but saw that it was good. The growth of nature is always a positive thing, especially for fairies who watch over the natural world, acting as guardians over every living thing, plant or animal, and protecting it.

"But when the young mercenary found the wand of Death, the fairy wished he could make himself known. This wand withered the grass, wilted the flowers, and sent a dark streak across the sky. It was not a storm but a chasm, a rip in the entire universe. This wand was too powerful for anyone to wield. Only the gods should have the ability to destroy on a massive scale. The mercenary had no idea what he had done; he thought it was only dark weather in the sky. He placed this wand alongside the others in his pouch and continued."

Marek drank the rest of his tea as Madame Rosivda put away the tools of her trade. "So, you're saying I'm going to be all-powerful now?" he asked.

"Am I?" she asked back.

"You just like toying with my thoughts and emotions, I think."

"By the way," she said. "How is your spell going?"

"Well. I think." Marek pictured the half-burned candle standing on his chest of drawers at home. Both lists had grown substantially. The more he interacted with Olive, the more he loved her. He placed her on a pedestal she couldn't possibly fall from. It was easy to love from a distance without seeing the messy humanity of a person. But he felt like he was putting himself out there with every glance exchanged, each conversation, even those as simple as asking how her day had gone, her favorite songs to sing, and they could continue collaborating. They hadn't been on a proper date yet, but he felt they were building a solid friendship. He was already rehearsing for the planned feature performance, which would come by the end of the month.

"Anything to report yet?" she asked, breaking his reverie.

"Nothing worth noting, but I think I've progressed at least."

"Good," she said. "Anything else?"

"Since my last time here, I saw a crow."

"There are crows all over the city."

She said it like a passing observation, like it couldn't possibly be of any importance. Maybe Marek was reading into things too much. After all, perhaps a crow is just a crow.

"But this was different," he said. "It was at the window, tapping like it wanted to get in."

"What did it say to you?" she asked.

"Say to me?"

"It might have been a talking crow."

Marek blanched. "I shooed it away."

"Next time, you should let it in. See what it has to say."

* * *

With that conversation running through his mind, Marek returned to his apartment. The electronic keyboard felt more and more like a sad simulation compared to the baby grand at The Royal Club. He wished he could afford (and had the room for) a real piano. Feeling inspired and a bit lucky, he rang up Ronnie, the bartender at the club.

"Hey, Ronnie, how's it going?"

Ronnie sounded like he had just rolled out of bed. "What are you doing so early in the morning?" he asked. "I thought musicians were supposed to be night owls."

"Sorry if I woke you."

The conversation lagged momentarily and hung there in the air like a half-built spider's web. "You did. But now that I'm up, what do you want?"

"I was wondering if I might be able to get into the club this after-noon," said Marek.

"You know we don't open until 5."

"Any chance I could come in around 3?"

"For what? The ambiance?" Ronnie sounded a bit irritated at Marek's persistence.

"I was hoping to get in there to use the piano."

"Ugh. Can't you just play a portable instrument like everyone else?"

"I would, but my immigrant father insisted that the piano was the perfect instrument."

"Don't pull that woe-is-me shit on me today."

"Somebody woke up on the wrong side of the bed."

"Tell you what, I'll let you in an hour early to tickle the ivories, but what's in it for me?"

"I could throw a fifty your way."

"Fine. I'll see you in a few hours. I'm going back to sleep."

Marek flipped through his sheet music to select the best pieces for his showcase. He still hadn't written anything, though, nothing of his own. It would be a few hours before Ronnie let him into the club. He tried playing absent-mindedly but kept slipping into other songs he knew. It was hard to start with something original. He tried out a few chords, a major, a minor. He tried closing his eyes, and the first thing he envisioned was Olive, her perfect honey-hued skin. He still hadn't taken her on a date, even a coffee. What was he waiting for?

He wandered back to his bedroom to look over the lists again. Olive's list overflowed with kind words, compliments he would willingly give if he could just drum up the courage—beautiful, excellent singer, articulate, kind, contagious laugh. The list went on and on and on. His list, by comparison, contained only a few things, some of them copied from compliments he had received. He wasn't confident that he believed in all of them. Kind, concerned for others, beautiful blue eyes, fine piano player, a good friend. What else could he add? He hoped to add "composer," but what else could be considered attractive? As he contemplated, he lit the candle. He looked into its wavering flame and allowed his mind to drift back to the mercenary surrounded by wands he toyed with but did not understand the power of. What ability did he possess that he had not yet utilized to its full extent?

His phone rang, and he blew the candle out. It was Olive. His heart leaped into his throat before he could answer.

"Marek, what are you up to?" she asked.

"Nothing at the moment."

"How would you like to grab that cup of coffee you owe me?"

"Where would you like to go?"

"There's a new cafe near the club we could check out."

"Sure. Sounds great."

"I work after, but we could catch up. We haven't talked much since Abaddon was in the hospital."

"We've talked."

"Just in passing."

"When do you want to go?" he asked.

"Right now?"

"Sure. I'll see you there."

Like most men, Marek hated the words 'we need to talk.' Was this the coming-to-Jesus moment when she told him she wanted to be friends? He tried to push past the negative assumptions and flip them. Maybe it was the opposite, and she was interested in dating. It could be one of a million different things. It was so noncommittal, getting coffee. It could be a five-minute conversation, or it could last for hours. Actually, at this moment, it couldn't last for hours; it would have to be shorter than that because he had promised Ronnie money to get into the club early. Maybe he could drag her along, have an audience, and stay for her show.

When Marek arrived, the cafe was brimming with people, locals who no doubt wanted to check out the new space. Brewed Awakening was not only cute but kitschy to the max. Vintage coffee pots and cups, some of them seemingly rusted together, covered every available surface. Paintings and photographs from local artists hung from the walls, many of them so abstract Marek couldn't determine what they represented or if they meant anything. Unfortunately, there was no room for them to sit in the small space, even out on the patio, packed with young people drawing on their e-cigarettes, leaving a pinkish-purple cloud of blueberry, peach, and other fruit-scented nicotine.

They opted, instead, to walk. Thankfully, the weather was much calmer than in the past few weeks. The wind didn't rip through their clothes, freezing them to the bone. Instead, the sun shone down upon them, creating a warmth that felt much more comforting. Marek had ordered his Brazilian blend black, and Olive had mixed in so much cream and syrup that her drink could hardly be called coffee.

As they began their walk, he glanced at her again and grew suddenly overwhelmed. She was so perfect in every way. How could he even start this conversation?

"I've seen you looking at me," she said.

His tongue caught in his mouth.

"I didn't say I didn't like it," she added.

What could he say to that? He stumbled over the words. "Um. I'm sorry."

"What did I just say? Were you listening?"

He nodded. Words failed him horribly.

"I said that I liked it."

"Okay, but what does that mean?" he asked.

She paused to sip her coffee.

"Do you want to..."

"Want to what?"

"I don't know," he said. Why was this so difficult? "Spend more time together?"

"What do you think we're doing now?"

Marek choked back some coffee. Walking and drinking, and talking felt suddenly impossible. Add thinking to that, and he was immobilized. "Is there any place we could sit?" he asked.

"Tired already?"

"No, I'm just having a hard time walking and talking and... I'm not very coordinated."

As if responding to his wish, rounding the corner revealed a bench where they could sit. As Marek settled himself, she sat beside him, so close that he could feel her warmth, her leg rubbing up against his thigh. Oh, God, what exquisite torture. At least now he could focus on the conversation if he could only form the words in his mouth. He caught himself staring at her lips, deep crimson in the afternoon light.

"I like you, Marek. You're quiet and a little awkward, but you're honest. I could use someone who can be honest with me."

Marek thought over these qualities for a moment. He considered how they would sit on the list he had been building. They sounded authentic, but were they what she was looking for? He focused on what he considered the best of them. "I'm not much for lying," he said, then shifted gears, trying to add "caring" to the list. "Is that something you've struggled with in the past? Did someone lie to you?"

She looked suddenly vulnerable, like a baby bird thrown from the nest. Why did he find that helplessness attractive? Maybe it was the desire to swoop in and save the day. She began a story about a sordid affair that was incredibly one-sided. She had fallen in love with a cheat and wife-beater who lied about his marriage, job, and everything. It seemed that the man's entire existence was a fabrication, and when she found out, she was utterly devastated, as any sane woman would be.

"When did this happen?" he asked.

"It was about a year ago. I can't believe I fell for all that," Olive said.

"It could have happened to anyone."

"But it happened to me. I was weak. I was gullible. I believed all of it." She wiped an invading tear from her eye. "I hate that it still triggers me."

"We can talk about something else."

"Sometimes it helps to work through it, though."

"Does it?" He reached up to catch another of her tears. "There's a difference between working through it and dwelling. If thinking about it only upsets you, is it worth thinking about? Instead of looking back, your eyes always on the rearview, you can focus on what's in front of you."

She looked up at him, those shimmering eyes full of admiration and trust. He felt like he held her precious heart in his hands momentarily. Then she looked away, breaking the connection.

"Are you done with your coffee?" he asked.

She nodded.

"Let's walk then."

When they stood, he snatched her empty cup away and then reached to hold her fingers with his other hand.

"Are your hands always so cold?" he commented.

She let a shy giggle escape her lips. "Usually. You'll just have to get used to it."

Marek liked that idea.

They strolled for half a block before finding a trashcan. While Marek tossed the cups away, she glanced around. Looming above them was a purple and black canopy, the entrance to a Wiccan supply shop called Herb & Altar. Olive's eyes lit up with excitement.

"Want to go in?" she asked.

Marek checked his watch. It was nearing when he'd have to meet Ronnie at the club, but he still had a few minutes. "You're into this kind of stuff?" he asked.

Olive pushed through the door, bells ringing as they entered. "Aren't you?" she asked. "I think that's where I saw you first, at Madame Rosivda's."

"You noticed me?" he asked.

"I notice everything."

When they had gotten only a few feet into the shop, a stooped older man leaning on an ornately carved cane approached them. "Welcome!" he said. "To Herb & Altar, magic emporium, supplier of all your witchy needs!" His dark eyes sparkled. "I'm Jasper. What can I do you for?"

"We're just browsing," said Marek.

"Actually," said Olive. "Is there a crystal you would suggest for manifesting positive intentions?"

Marek felt himself making a face and tried to hide it. She was more into this stuff than she had let on. As Jasper led her into the shop's back corner, asking questions about her specific needs, Marek browsed some of the herbs at the front of the shop. He wondered if buying bay leaves and rosemary from a specialty shop was entirely necessary or if the much cheaper versions available at a grocery store would suffice.

"The best option is to grow your own," Jasper said, sneaking behind him. How the older man managed to be so stealthy, even with a cane, was beyond Marek's understanding. "I'm trying to make a buck but not a living here, so I won't steer you wrong."

Marek nodded.

"She's looking at rose quartz," the old man said as if that should mean something to Marek. "So you better watch out if she has plans for you. That stuff is wicked powerful."

Marek tried not to respond, but eventually, his curiosity overcame his hesitation. "What's rose quartz for?"

"Well, positive intentions, healing mostly. But also love."

Marek tried not to laugh. Wouldn't it be ridiculous if they were trying to cast love spells on one another? Madame Rosivda had already explained that it didn't quite work that way, but it seemed unnecessary if the intention existed. Couldn't they just talk their way through it like normal human beings?

"You think you don't need it?" asked Jasper, as if reading Marek's thoughts. "Any relationship needs all the help it can get. I, myself, have gone through three wives."

Marek wanted to comment that this said something more about Jasper than the nature of love, but he kept his mouth shut.

"Are you looking for anything in particular, or are you just here because the lady wanted to look at my wares?" Jasper asked.

"Just looking around," said Marek.

"I bet you'd be interested in my wands." Jasper gestured toward the front wall, where several crystal-laden rods nestled in heaps of purple velvet.

"Does each wand have a specific meaning?" asked Marek.

"The crystals correspond to specific intentions, but the wand selection should come from a personal connection. That could mean you feel particularly drawn to a certain one, or maybe you just like the look of it."

Olive returned from selecting her crystal, holding a pale pink stone that looked like rock candy. "I think this is the one," she said.

She turned to Marek as Jasper wrapped the crystal in tissue paper before placing it in a small bag. "Did you find anything?" she asked.

Marek glanced around, still running his eyes and fingers over the selection of wands. He could imagine some of them having specific elemental correspondences: blue for water (of course), red for fire, and brown for the earth. Some bore a combination of colors, a mottled blend of brown and black, or a rainbow kaleidoscope of shades. He picked up the brown and black wand, which felt heavy in his hand, awkward and unbalanced. He put it back. He stepped away from the display.

"What is the point of a wand, anyway?" he asked. "It's not like it's gonna shoot sparks when I cast a spell or something."

Olive raised her eyebrows. "Well, no, this isn't special effects in a movie or something," she said.

"Then what is a wand even for?"

Jasper appeared from behind the counter, approaching Marek again. The way the older man moved with such stealth was unsettling. "It helps focus your energy," he said. "You focus on the wand and the spell you are casting. I feel like some newbies just use it for window dressing, though."

"Window dressing?"

"So they feel like a real witch. They don't use it; they just keep it for decoration or to fill out their altar. Do you have an altar?"

Marek paused. "Not exactly."

Olive's eyes lit up. "So you do practice magick?" She nearly jumped up and down at the prospect.

"I dabble," he said, trying to remember the terminology Madame Rosivda had used. "I'm not exactly an avid practitioner."

"Tell you what," said Jasper. "How about you come back sometime when The Circle is gathering? We have several new members and would love to have you."

"When is this?" asked Olive.

"Tuesday night is our next meeting. We get together a few times a month. There is a more formal group that meets for the Moon Rituals. We call it the Inner Circle."

Olive gave Jasper a polite smile.

Marek frowned. "No, I don't think so," he said. "Like I said, just browsing."

"And dabbling?" asked Jasper.

"I guess," said Marek.

"Well, I might make an appearance," said Olive. "Thank you for the invitation."

They stepped back out onto the sidewalk, and Marek's phone rang. It was Ronnie. Marek hesitated to answer, knowing that he was already late and Ronnie was opening the club just for him to be able to practice. No doubt he would be pissed.

"I have to get to the club," said Marek. He grabbed Olive's free hand and touched it to his lips to kiss it. Her fingers felt so velvety soft; he couldn't help but wonder about her lips, which parted in surprise at his gesture.

"The club?" she asked absentmindedly.

"Is that where you work tonight?" he asked. "Why don't you join me? Ronnie is letting me in early to get some real piano time. I'm not making much progress with the keyboard at home."

"Sure."

As they walked hand-in-hand, Marek noticed a small white butterfly flittering toward them. As it approached, he caught a better glimpse of it. It landed on his forearm, and as he looked down, he could just make out the shape of it. It wasn't a butterfly but a small man with wings. His face was red, and he stomped against Marek's arm. Marek peered closer, trying to make the image make sense, but it didn't change. In a sudden panic, Marek shook his arm violently until the thing (the fairy?) flew away.

He looked to Olive, who didn't notice the exchange. Was he going crazy or just imagining things?

"What is it?" she asked.

"You didn't see that?"

"See what? The butterfly?"

"Yeah," he said, feeling dumb. "It was just a butterfly." He couldn't convince himself of that, but what else could it be? Maybe he needed to take a break from all this witchy stuff. It was starting to make reality feel fuzzy.

12

The Devil

Madame Rosivda turned the card, revealing a pink prison cell, a garden filled with roses and heavy iron chains. A fushia sun hung low in the sky, and a couple, one man and one woman struggled in the shadows, fighting against their restraints. In the foreground, a naked angel, a man with wild red hair and tiny pink wings that could barely support his weight, flew past. He bit his lip and fawned over his prisoners, satisfied with his catch. It was The Devil.

"Now, this looks interesting," said Marek. "A bit of bondage?" he asked.

"Not quite," said Madame Rosivda. "Remember that these cards are largely symbolic rather than grounded in reality."

Marek nodded. He had grown comfortable enough in these sessions to tease Madame Rosivda, but he still respected her judgment. At the same time, he was too nervous to mention what he had seen. The fairy butterfly, or whatever it had been, couldn't be real. His worldview did not have enough wiggle room to accept such things. Then again, he had almost believed in a talking crow, and there were so many other moments in the past few months that had felt not quite real, and the time he spent with Olive as of late seemed like an absolute dream.

"There once was a common man so desperate for the love of a

princess he would do anything," Madame Rosivda began. "He watched her from afar, and although they had never spoken, he knew she was the one for him. How could she not be when his heart fluttered whenever he saw her perfect skin, hair, and smile? Her voice made his knees feel weak, like he couldn't stand upright. Even listening to her speak, he could barely breathe.

"Unfortunately, he was a stable hand, and she was unaware of his existence. While he mucked stalls and brushed horses, she attended dainty tea parties with the political elite. There was no way he'd be able to arrange a personal audience with her unless she suddenly took an interest in horse riding. Most of the time, she rode in a fancy carriage whenever she traveled. He barely caught a glimpse of her, but that was enough to catch his attention. On a lucky day, he could hear her voice carrying, lilting from the balcony.

"On one rare occasion, he heard her singing to herself, talking as if to the moon before she retired to her chamber. He was just finishing his duties in the stables. Before she disappeared inside, he called out to her, his voice nearly wavering.

"'Oh please don't stop singing,' he said. 'I would give anything for you to sing for me.'

"She looked frantically around, unsure of where the voice came from. 'Who is there?' she asked. She shivered and wrapped her arms around herself. The young man struggled to find the words. The princess disappeared into the castle before he could implore her to stay.

"The next day, a stranger came to the stables, claiming he wanted to purchase the fastest steed for a trip to a neighboring town. At first, the stable hand resisted, not knowing the man's credentials. He was even more reluctant when the man claimed not to have the coin needed to purchase the horse.

"The stranger's hair was a brighter shade of red than the hand had ever seen in nature, deeper and more radiant than any flower. Where had he come from, and what did he want besides a fast horse? What was his intent? Instead of money, he offered a strange favor in exchange.

"'If you can lure your princess from her castle,' he said. 'I can provide a safe place for you to meet.'

"'What do you mean?' the stable hand asked. 'Have you been spying on me?'

"'I know everything that happens around here,' said the stranger. 'Tell me what you most desire, and it will be yours.'

"'Who are you?'

"'A friend.' The stranger promised to return the horse after his journey and help arrange a liaison between the servant and the princess if she would be willing.

"With this assurance, the servant let him leave with the swiftest horse. Newly emboldened, he found the courage to speak with his princess, even climb her trellis to meet her on the balcony secretly. She had never entertained a man's advances and found herself quite overwhelmed with the sudden attention of her new lover.

"On the appointed day of the stranger's return, the stable hand coaxed the princess down from her balcony, helping her carefully navigate the trellis. They escaped to a vast, meandering garden at the edge of the property. Rose bushes grew there, thorns tearing at their clothes as they collided excitedly.

"Once they had satisfied their desires, the red-haired stranger appeared from nowhere, striding into the garden with a mischievous grin. He had caught them red-handed, he claimed, and now they must pay for their sins. They looked up at him in terror, not understanding what they had stumbled into.

"The stranger stripped them naked and bound them in iron chains. They were now his to do with what he would, he claimed. His red hair shone brilliantly in the moonlight as he removed his clothing. Then they saw the wings on his back, but if this was an angel, it was surely a fallen one. It must be the Devil himself."

Marek sat in stunned silence for a moment. "So we've got angels, fairies, wizards, and mermaids, and now we've got Satan?" he asked.

"Again, tarot does not necessarily adhere to the Judeo-Christian tradition," said Madame Rosivda. Many devout Christians warn against anything supposedly linked with the occult." She smiled knowingly at him.

"You know I'm not all that religious."

"I just wanted to make sure you understood this accurately." She started to wrap up her tools.

"Is it like Death, where it is not a literal interpretation but rather an allegory?" he asked.

"Something like that."

"It doesn't look like it bodes well, though. I wonder what nonsense is coming into my life now."

"Only time will tell."

"Sometimes your readings feel like a fortune cookie."

"A fortune cookie?" She looked taken aback.

"Just very enigmatic," he said. "Sometimes it feels like you're right on the nose with what is happening, but other times things just seem to come out of the blue. I have no real context for the reading."

"If you just concentrated and opened yourself up to the possibilities, maybe you would get more out of it."

Marek grunted. He had been preoccupied as of late, preparing for his upcoming performance. Returning for his nearly weekly reading felt so grounding, though. It served as a benchmark to start each slight period as he moved toward his goals. It was like his church in that way, a waypoint to mark his way, to keep him on course. But he wouldn't admit that not even to himself.

At this point, Marek had bribed Ronnie a handful of times for access to the club outside of regular business hours. It allowed him to practice on a real piano and get the feel of playing more serious pieces that weren't just accompaniments to others. Olive occasionally came with him, and Ronnie suspected they were using the space for their private rendezvous there. In reality, that was far from the case. The two had barely kissed one another - just a soft peck on the cheek here and there, some handholding. For Marek, the incredible slowness of it was maddening.

He understood Olive had been hurt before, but that was due to someone else's lies. Why was he being held accountable for another man's faults? Her withholding wasn't fair to him. Hadn't he demonstrated his honesty, his devotion? In moments of weakness, he found himself fantasizing about taking what she hadn't offered, but he would never act on those impulses, would he?

Seemingly out of the blue, Marek received a call from Abaddon. He hadn't talked with his friend since the haphazard poker game at Nyx's place. Abaddon seemed to be laying low, spending most of his time at home instead of going out or partying. This call also came with a strange request. In addition to not going out, Abaddon wasn't buying his usual supply of illicit substances, and a particular drug dealer wasn't pleased with this development.

"So what?" asked Marek. "You want me to buy from him? You know I don't do that stuff. Besides, wasn't it enough that you nearly ODed on heroin? I don't think you owe this guy anything."

"You don't understand," said Abaddon. "This guy is crazy aggressive. He doesn't care why I'm no longer using it. He just wants his money."

"Or what?"

"I don't know. This dealer might get violent or something."

Marek found himself wishing he could defend his friend. Maybe just go to this guy's house and teach him a lesson with his fists. But Marek was so incredibly nonconfrontational that he had a hard time imagining a conversation with the dealer, much less a physical confrontation. "So what exactly do you want me to do about it?" he asked.

"I'll arrange an introduction, and you can buy something from him. It doesn't have to be the hard stuff. He has a lot of lesser stuff, party drugs and weed. You might have fun on some ecstasy with Olive."

"So now you want me to what, buy drugs from your dealer and share them with my girlfriend?"

"She's your girlfriend now?"

"Yeah. I think so."

"I mean, yeah. Is that too much to ask?"

Marek wanted to say yes, that this was just too much, but he kept his mouth shut. It couldn't be that bad. In theory, he could even buy something and not use it. But then what? Would he be on the hook to continue purchasing from this guy to keep up a reliable revenue stream? After all, Abaddon seemed to be on the hook. What would it take for him to end up in the same situation?

"So, how does this work?" Marek asked. "I've never bought it before. In fact, before you, I didn't consume either."

"You're so straight-laced. You don't even have the vocabulary down. Try not to be too awkward, or this guy will think you're busting him."

Marek sighed loudly. He already hated this idea.

"I'll call ahead, let him know you'll be stopping by, and give him an idea of what you might want. This guy is pretty high-class. He'll smoke you up and give you some other options. You'll give him the money. He might want to party with you. If he does, take him up on it. He's been lonely since his wife left."

"So not only am I giving this guy my money, but I'm also supposed to keep him company?"

"Come on, man. What else do you have going on? Need to rush back to selling your soul at that stupid hotel?"

"Fine. What's this guy's name anyway?"

"His real name? I'm not sure. He goes by Dante."

Against what should have been his better judgment, Marek convinced Olive to come with him. He figured safety in numbers, and besides, he liked the idea of getting high with her. Strangely, when his inhibitions were down, Marek could feel himself growing closer to those around him. After all, wasn't that how he and Abaddon had formed such a strong friendship? He'd shared a drink with Olive, but not a joint.

When they arrived at the address, Marek looked around in disbelief. It was a townhouse sandwiched between two other residences. It wasn't the smallness that surprised him - you could find homes crammed together like this in several parts of the city - but the fact that it was so close to each of its neighbors. Wouldn't you want more privacy if you were dealing drugs? Some semblance of secrecy? Or maybe the neighbors were in on it - or just well aware of what was happening.

A young man sat on a wooden rocking chair on the porch. He wore his baseball cap low over his eyes and smoked a cigarette. He glanced their way as they ascended the steps but didn't bother getting up. "You here to see Dante?" he asked.

"Yeah," said Marek.

"He's expecting you, but who's the girl?"

"I'm Olive," she said. She held her hand out in greeting, but the boy didn't take it. She let it fall slowly to her side.

"I don't care what your name is," the kid said. "Who are you, and why are you here?"

"She's my girlfriend." It felt so good to say it out loud, finally. Marek and Olive exchanged a meaningful glance, both of them smiling widely.

"Can she keep her mouth shut?" asked the kid.

"Yeah," said Marek. "She's cool."

"Cool?" The kid laughed cruelly. "How old are you, man?"

Marek was about to respond when the kid countered.

"Nevermind. Don't answer that. Go on in, but he's in a mood. Don't do anything to annoy him."

The kid had propped the front door open, but they pushed their way through a screen before entering. The place smelled unsurprisingly like dank weed, a wet, skunky smell that permeated everything. Besides that, Marek wouldn't peg it as a drug dealer's house. Then again, what did he know about how a drug dealer lived? The front room was little more than a long hallway. Marek paused. The carpeting was a pristine white, and he hesitated, wondering if he should take his shoes off before going any further. He turned to Olive, who was already slipping off her heels.

They made their way down the hallway into what appeared to be a large living room with a connected kitchen. A flatscreen TV covered almost the entire back wall, and various shapes of leather-clad furniture filled the space. There was a deep burgundy couch, a love seat, and two massive recliners. Their host was far from sight. Marek felt reluctant to sit down and stood there instead, trying not to stare, and wound up looking disconsolately at his bare feet. He wished he had worn socks, at least. Olive had a dainty pedicure and toes that could not have been cuter if she tried. Of course, he was biased in that regard. It felt equally disrespectful to stand on the carpet barefooted as it would have been to come in with their shoes on. A booming voice came from the kitchen before Marek could descend too far into his worries.

"So Abaddon sent you," said the voice. A huge, very round man soon joined it. He barrelled into the room, hand outstretched to greet him. "I hope Joey wasn't too rude to you."

"No, not at all," said Marek as he endured the man's tight grip. "Nice to meet you, Dante. I'm Marek."

The man laughed, his entire belly shaking like a middle-aged Santa Clause. "And who is this lovely creature?" he asked. He looked Olive up and down as if examining her for possible purchase. Marek resisted the urge to grab her waist and pull her away from him.

Olive introduced herself politely, ignoring the man's leer with a fantastic amount of grace that Marek wouldn't have been able to muster was he in her position.

"Well, don't just stand around," said Dante. "Sit. Sit." He directed them to the loveseat while he spread himself over two-thirds of the couch. Marek momentarily wondered if the man could even fit in the recliners. Maybe they were just for show, or more likely for guests.

"What brings you into my humble abode?" Dante asked, then laughed whole-heartedly when neither of his guests replied immediately. "Oh, who am I kidding? I know why you're here. We don't need the pretense. But I just got in something I'd like you to try with me."

Olive gave Marek a knowing glance. Just what had they gotten themselves into? They hesitated for a moment, then followed Dante into his kitchen. He pulled what looked like a connected series of glass tubes from the counter, setting it on the island's center. He retrieved a small glass jar containing a yellowed, waxy substance from the fridge.

"You know what this is?" asked Dante. He motioned toward the wax as he scooped it out with a specialized tool that seemed built for just this purpose. Looking at the wide eyes of his audience, he chuckled. "Abaddon did tell me you might be new to this, but I want to give you a quality experience." He placed a small amount of the wax into part of the glass tubing. "This is a dab," he said. "It's a marijuana concentrate. It will get you much higher, much faster. I've got a surplus, so we'll smoke this before we get down to business. I never want my guests coming and going too quickly. It might make my neighbors suspicious. I don't care if they know I'm smoking, but I don't want them to know I'm dealing. As far as they know, I have several excellent friends."

Marek looked back to Olive. She gave him a slight nod. They would do this if nothing to keep face. Besides, no one ever died from marijuana.

After returning the remaining wax to the fridge, Dante grabbed a small torch to heat the glass bowl holding the dab. The yellowish resin made Marek think of earwax, but as it melted, the smell mellowed into an earthy, herby odor, much more sophisticated than the not-so-subtle skunk smell of most buds. Dante lifted the entire rig and brought it into the living room while they followed.

Dante settled onto the couch, Marek into one of the recliners, and Olive perched at Marek's feet. She looked up at him like a mischievous cat, ready to pounce at any moment. Maybe this could be sexy, he thought momentarily, but their host would observe any contact they made, and he wasn't sure how he felt about that.

"Ladies first," said Dante as he handed the glass rig to Olive. "Lift the carb cap a little and slowly inhale. It's alright if you don't inhale it all. You can hand it to your buddy when you've got your fill. We'll do a few rounds, and I'll relight it for you."

Olive took a deep breath and held it for a moment before exhaling. She coughed violently, letting the smoke escape into a cloud around her.

Dante smiled. "I remember my first time," he said.

Olive struggled to reply between coughs. "It's not - my first - time," she said.

"Your first dab, though, am I right?"

She nodded, then passed the science experiment on to Marek. He inhaled more slowly, held it for barely a second, then exhaled. The taste, if it could be called that, was different, but he couldn't pinpoint the difference. He couldn't seem to get past the appearance of the liquified wax. He imagined a lump of earwax melting. At least bud looked natural, something like a plant. The wax looked like a chemical substance that you should hesitate before putting into your body.

He passed the rig back to Dante, who inhaled the rest of the smoke in one smooth movement, like a yogi doing breathing exercises. He didn't even cough, not even a little bit. With his small torch, he applied more heat. "I probably put too much in there," he mused. "But you said you're a musician, right? You ain't go nowhere to be."

In what felt like moments, the high hit them. Marek felt like he was melting into the chair, his body too heavy to move, but the glory was that he didn't need to move. He could just relax here, feeling his heartbeat slow, the edges of his world growing pleasantly fuzzy. After a few rounds, Dante stored the rig away, returning to put a record on. It was some experimental jazz from the '60s, just the right mix of odd sounds and melody to focus your thoughts without being too distracting. Olive stretched out on the floor, rolling onto her back and staring absent-mindedly at the ceiling.

"This is good stuff, huh?" asked Dante. He didn't seem to expect an answer. "And I appreciate that you brought some eye candy."

Olive smiled indulgently. Marek wasn't sure how he felt about Dante watching his lady, nearly writhing in delight on his carpeting, but he also didn't have the energy to worry. Everything was fine. Everything would be fine. He felt warm and welcomed, even in a stranger's house. As long as he could hold onto this feeling, everything would be just fine.

Marek must have dozed off because the next thing he knew, Olive was straddling him in the chair. Well, this was unexpected but not unwelcome. Her hungry kisses nearly made him gasp for air, though. He felt clumsy and uncoordinated, even more than usual. She leaned back, her hair cascading in a waterfall down her back, and smiled widely at him.

"Well, look who's come back to the land of the living," said Dante. "Would either of you love birds like a drink?" he asked but didn't wait for a response. Instead, the drug dealer wandered into the kitchen, returning moments later with two nearly overflowing glasses. He set them on the end table alongside Marek's chair.

Olive folded her legs over him, sitting sideways across his lap. Her skirt had ridden up so high he could nearly see her panties, but no one seemed to be complaining. She took a long swig of her drink while Marek took a few tentative sips.

"What is this?" he asked. It was sweet, not unwelcome, but he felt strangely nervous about it.

"Rum and juice. Nothing too complicated," said Dante. "The lady seems to like it."

Marek didn't like the way Dante kept referring to Olive as if she were an object. It was tempting to allow himself to view her the same way, but it didn't feel quite right. She was so much more than that; he despised Dante's roving eyes. He would take her away somewhere private and have his way with her without the audience. At the same time, she didn't seem to mind and had returned to planting wet kisses into the crevice of his neck. It was everything he could do not to let a moan escape his lips. He wanted her so much at this moment that he could barely hold back. Yet, Dante was watching and didn't try to hide his interest in what was happening just feet from him. If given the opportunity, Marek was sure the man would join in. Instead, Dante just stared, unabashedly following Olive's every movement as if it were a show she was putting on for his enjoyment.

It might be a surreal moment for Marek, but instead of shying away, he decided to take the opportunity to give Olive what she wanted. While she straddled him, he wrapped his arms around her lower back and pulled her closer. Lifting her, he stood from the chair and pulled her roughly down to the carpet. He looked down into her face, her eyes wide with feigned surprise. With one hand, he swept a few stray hairs from her face, and with the other, he hiked her skirt higher, hooking one thumb into the waistband of her lace panties. If Dante wanted a show, he'd give him a show.

Between the pulsing music, the fuzzy reality of his perception, and their rocking bodies, he lost all sense of self. Everything was part of an aching tableau, an urgent movement he could no longer resist. When he finally felt the necessary release pulling his energy from him, he glanced up to see Dante watching them and felt suddenly broken and ashamed. He stared down into Olive's face and couldn't read what he saw there. Her eyes looked empty and depleted like he had stolen her soul and left her a mere shell, a cracked porcelain doll. He rolled away, sated but also terrified. What had he done?

13

The Queen of Swords

Madame Rosivda turned the card, revealing a rose garden filled with blue shadow, where a beautiful princess sat. She wore a crown and a maang tikka, a central jewel resting over her Third Eye. Around her neck wound an albino snake, coiling its pale white body around her waist and stretching out on the ground. She held a red and white bouquet of roses in her hands, and as the snake slowly strangled her, she bent her head to peel off the petals with her mouth. She gripped a bright gash of red with her teeth. It was the Queen of Swords.

Marek hung his head over his tea. This card could mean only one thing, and he was ashamed to admit his misdeeds. After their sordid display at Dante's, Marek had been quick to whisk Olive away, calling her a car and making sure she made it home safe. Marek bought some weed from Dante, even though the man seemed pleased to have gotten a free show. The dealer had given him a far too knowing look during the exchange. For the past few days, Marek had hung low, hunkered down in his apartment, barely able to leave his bed. There was no way of fixing this. Even the queen in the tarot seemed to be judging him, as he had given in to animalistic tendencies.

"You're quiet today," Madame Rosivda said, trying to catch his eye. "Is there something bothering you?"

"What is this, therapy?" he asked. "Just do the reading. I need guidance, but I don't want to discuss it."

"It might help to talk."

"Just tell me what it means. I already have an idea, but go ahead."

"Are you starting to attune to the cards? Do they speak to you?" she asked.

Marek gave a slight nod but didn't look up. He shut his eyes to listen as she began the story.

"There once was a princess who was distraught at the loss of her lover. It had been a sordid affair, one not approved by royalty. Her father had arranged to have her young lover killed in battle. It was not a direct assassination, but it might as well have been. When the nation went to war, the young man was drafted to serve on the front lines and died there, gun in hand, bleeding out a deep red on the pale white rocks surrounding them.

"The princess was heartbroken and fell into great despair, and understandably so. With her lover now dead, she could no longer object to the arranged marriage which her father decreed. She felt no love for anyone but him, and what remained of her after his death felt like a shell. She was empty and despondent. Every day, the face she wore for others felt like a mask, and any hint of happiness was an act she performed.

"When night came, she could not sleep, so she would wander in the gardens below, a massive twisting maze filled with tall hedges and roses, her late mother's favorite flower. When she was a child, before her mother had passed through the veil between this life and the next, she had asked her why the rose was her favorite flower. Her mother replied that it was both beautiful and dangerous, for along with its velvet petals, it also bore thorns to protect itself.

"On one of her nightly sojourns through the garden, she heard a deep, whispering voice and felt the presence of another person with her. When she looked around, though, no one was there beside her. She continued walking but paused when the voice returned. This time she could hear what it had to say.

"'My child,' it said. 'Why do you wander when you should be sleeping?'

"The princess couldn't explain the depths of her sorrow, but tears began streaming down her cheeks. Her breath became quick and labored as she sobbed and crumpled to the ground.

"'What has destroyed you?' the voice asked, closer. The princess could feel a warm breath on her neck. She looked around frantically but still could see no one.

"The next night, the princess found herself at the garden's center, where a small pond rippled with the cool breeze. A wind whipped up around her, scattering leaves and darkening the pond. She looked into it and saw a shadowy figure. It was not a reflection but an image stretched across the water's surface.

"'My child,' it said in a desperate whisper. 'Who has done this to you?'

"This time, the princess got up the nerve to answer. 'My father sent my lover to die in war, and now I am expected to marry another. But my love belongs only to he who is dead, and I will never be with him again.'"

"'That is where you are wrong,' said the voice. The water shimmered, and the princess recognized the form of her mother. Her words sounded familiar and comforting.

"'What do you mean?' the princess asked.

"'You can be joined together again.'

"The princess stared in awe as her mother stepped from the water, a fully formed being, and wrapped her daughter in her arms. She did not feel wet, as the princess had expected, but relatively warm and comforting. The two women embraced and then stepped apart, examining each other.

"'You have grown,' the mother said. 'Beautiful and dangerous.'

"When they embraced again, the mother's arms transformed into a great white snake, and her human form faded. The princess squirmed and tried to pull away, but the snake wound around her neck, hissing in her ear.

"'Do not struggle,' it said. 'I will take you to your lover.'

"'But how?' she asked.

"'Just relax,' the snake said. It tightened its grip around the princess, wrapping the length of its body around not just her neck but also her waist. She could feel it starting to constrict and strangle her.

"She bent to grab some roses from a nearby bush as she collapsed. Her hands were full of thorns, pricking and drawing blood from her shaking fingers. As she gasped her final breaths, she plucked a few petals with her teeth, trying to cling to the last real thing that made her feel alive. What trick was this?

"Then the snake whispered one last promise. 'You will be together again,' it said. 'In death.'"

Marek shivered. "So it's over then," he said. "There will be no chance of reconciliation."

Madame Rosivda covered the cards with their black scarf, storing them away. "Would you like to talk now?" she asked. "You realize each reading can have multiple interpretations, right? This version is only one possible outcome. You can still work to change it."

"How?" he asked.

"Well, first," she said. "You might need to give me some more specific information."

"I don't know if I'm ready to do that."

"How can I help you then?"

"Don't worry," he said. "You already have."

* * *

After about the third or fourth ring, Marek finally answered his phone. Who was being so persistent at this time of the morning? He glanced at the caller ID. Why was Nyx calling him?

Rolling out of bed, he grunted into the receiver.

"Why aren't you answering your phone?" she asked. Her voice was shrill and demanding.

Marek didn't bother responding.

"And what did you do to Olive? She called me in a fit of hysterics the other night, claiming that you raped her. I know they tell you always to believe the victim, but that didn't sound like you. What happened?"

A sudden heat rose in Marek's throat. "That's what she said?" he asked. "That I raped her?"

"Something like that. Olive was a complete mess. When she called, I rushed to her place to get the whole story, but it was hard to understand what was happening."

"And you're just now calling me?"

"I've been calling you, but you haven't answered. Why haven't you answered your phone?"

"It was... weird."

"What was weird? You don't know how to ask for consent?"

"She was all over me. She wanted it, and then, I guess, she didn't? I don't know what happened."

"If there was a point where she said no or pushed you away, that's a no. We joke about it like it's no big deal, but it's a big deal. No means no, no matter what else is going on."

"She never said no."

"Did she say yes?"

"What do you mean?"

"Did she say yes? There's such a thing as enthusiastic consent. That's what guys don't seem to understand. She doesn't even have to say no. If she isn't saying yes, that isn't consent. If she's drunk or on other substances, that isn't consent. Wait, had she been drinking?"

"We both had."

"Anything else?"

"We were at Abaddon's dealer's place."

"Wait. You were at the drug dealer's house when it happened?"

"Yeah."

"I'm just trying to put together the pieces here. It's a 'he said', 'she said' situation. Some parts of your stories line up, but other parts don't. She didn't say you were at the drug dealer's place. Why did Abaddon even send you there? He knows you're pretty straight-laced."

"Am I?" The heat rose from Marek's throat into his face, making him feel suffocated. "You think you know me so well. You don't know shit."

"Christ, Marek, I'm just trying to help."

"Are you? It sounds like you're accusing me of things I didn't do."

"I'm just trying to understand what happened. Something went south if Olive called me crying in the night. Have you even talked to her?"

"Not since that night, no."

"Well, why the hell not? You know, the key to any good relationship is communication. If you're ever going to hold onto her, you need to talk to her. Especially when shit like this happens."

Marek made a low growling sound deep in his throat. She was right, but he didn't want to admit it.

"So now what? Are you just not going to talk to each other and let this fester and ruin everything? I had high hopes for you two. You're going just to throw everything away?"

"No, of course not."

"That's what you seem to be doing."

"What can I do? If you have the answers, Nyx, I'd love to have them. Right now, I haven't got a clue how to fix this. I'd like to work things out, but will she talk to me? If she's claiming I raped her, I'm guessing she wants nothing to do with me."

"Tell you what. Why don't I arrange a meeting? You can talk, but I'll be available if you need anything. I won't interfere, but I'll mediate if you need it."

"What, like couple's therapy? That sounds like a bad idea."

"Do you have any better ideas? I won't hover, I promise; just be there. If you need me."

Marek thought about it, then nodded, forgetting that Nyx couldn't see him through the phone.

"Marek?"

"Fine, I'll do it. When and where can we make this happen?"

"Well, you should do it as soon as possible. It's already been a few days. I can't believe you two haven't talked yet."

"I said I'd do it. I'm trying."

"Not hard enough. I've got a shift at the club that should be neutral-ish ground as long as Olive isn't working tonight. You too could meet there. It won't be too busy. The weather's shitty, and I can check in if you need it."

"Fine."

"I'll talk to Olive, too, and make sure she comes. Plan for seven. I'll let you know if anything changes."

"Sure."

"Don't fuck this up."

As he hung up, Marek ran one hand over his stubbly chin. He desperately needed a shower and a shave. He'd dress nice, too, he decided. His heart beat out a quick, chaotic rhythm in his chest. As he rifled through his closet, trying to decide what to wear, he glanced at the stub of a candle still sitting on the top of his dresser. The two lists curled like discarded receipts. He looked at the list he had curated for himself. "trustworthy" and "reliable" now sounded hollow and untrue. With one violent sweep, he sent everything flying to the floor. What kind of sick joke had this been? He could never be good enough for a woman like Olive. What false hope made him believe that? Of course, Madame Rosivda encouraged his delusions. She didn't care about his well-being. She just wanted his money.

At the back of his thoughts, he knew that wasn't true, but he couldn't stop himself from starting the downward spiral of self-doubt. He fought back the hot tears that threatened to fall. Then he heard a loud tapping at the window. In his grief, he pushed the sound to the back of his mind, ignoring it entirely. Trying to win Olive back was a fool's errand, and he knew it. Sure, she hadn't officially ended it, but if she talked to Nyx and said horrible things about him, making such accusations, maybe she was too scared to confront him. It sounded like she had already made her mind up about him, though. Who would continue to date a rapist? Was that what had happened? Is that why she looked so empty and broken afterward? Was he that degree of monster?

The tapping returned, and this time Marek listened. He walked toward the window to investigate, pulling the curtains aside. A large crow sat on his windowsill, staring at him intently, cocking its head first to one side, then the other. It tapped its sharp black beak against the glass, tapping rapidly. What was it that Madame Rosivda had said about crows? That he should open the window, that they would speak to him. Even now, in his desperation, that sounded ridiculous. But as Marek hesitated, he heard his name in a low, gravelly voice. Was this happening? He stared down at the crow.

"Marek, open the window," it said.

It was still the beginning of spring, and storm windows were still up. Marek struggled with the latch, then lifted the outer pane of glass. The crow was impatient and hopped from one foot to the other, waiting for him, but it didn't fly away. When Marek finally pried the window open enough for the crow to fit through the crack, it scrambled into the apartment, flew in frantic circles around the ceiling, and then flapped from the bedroom into the kitchen, landing on the small table. Marek, dumbfounded, followed it.

He spent a good minute or two just staring at the crow from across the room. It tilted its head at him and stared but didn't say anything. He must have imagined things, and now he had let a bird into the apartment. How was he going to get it out? He walked back down the hall toward the bathroom, where he was sure he had a broom in the closet.

"Where are you going?" asked a voice.

Okay, maybe he was just going crazy. He returned to the kitchen and stared at the crow. It stared back, then paced back and forth across the length of the table.

"You're not going crazy," the crow said. "Just listen."

"You're a talking crow," said Marek. "I must be going crazy."

As the crow continued to speak, Marek wondered if it was possible to have an after-effect trip, but it seemed too natural to be a hallucination. Besides, it spoke like a human, but he wasn't sure if that was more evidence of it being real or less.

"People used to be so much more understanding of talking crows. Do I have to explain everything?"

A few words here and there, Marek could have brushed aside. If the crow talked like a parrot, mindlessly repeating the exact phrase repeatedly, but this thing was talking to him. Instead, Marek felt like the dumb bird. "You're a talking crow," he said again. "You're talking to me."

The crow flitted into the air momentarily and came back down to land on Marek's shoulder. It squawked into his ear, then bit his earlobe.

"Ow!" Marek pushed the bird away from him. "What was that for?"

The crow flew a few feet away and perched on the back of one of the chairs, wrapping its claws around the top wooden rung. "What's that thing humans always say? I must be dreaming. Pinch me?" It stretched one of its claws out, flexing each toe in turn.

"I never said that."

"Well, you were acting like it, and I haven't exactly got fingers to pinch you with."

"Fine. Fine. I'll accept that you're a talking crow, and I seem to be awake and not hallucinating. What is this message you have for me?"

"Don't be a dumbass."

"Really? That's it?" Marek took the other chair across from the one the crow perched on.

"What, you wanted something deep and insightful? Something dark and mysterious?"

"I mean, you are a crow."

"I'm a familiar."

"What, like witches? Who's the witch?"

"That's none of your business," said the crow.

"I see. So what is it I'm not supposed to be a dumbass about? I'm usually not a dumbass."

"Hard-headed then. I've been watching you, and you keep tripping over your feet. Thought you needed some guidance."

"From a crow?"

"Familiar."

"What does that even mean?" Marek might be awake and sober, but he could use a drink. He rummaged in the fridge as the crow began to explain.

"A familiar is a spirit or entity, usually taking the form of an animal, who assists a witch in the performance of spells, sometimes serving as protection against those who might wish their liege harm."

With beer in hand, Marek returned to the table and settled back into his seat. The pop and fizzing sound the carbonation made as he opened the tab was strangely satisfying. Normal, something understandable. He took a swig.

"That's not going to help you," said the crow.

"What right do you have to judge me? You're a talking crow."

"Familiar."

"Crow, familiar, whatever you are, you don't have any right to judge me."

"I was human once."

"Oh, were you?"

The crow bent its head down as if in a deep bow. "Nice to meet you, Marek," it said. "My name is Kevin."

"And you came here to tell me I'm a dumbass," said Marek. He took another long swig. "Alright, let's say you're a witch's familiar, you're trying to help me or warn me or whatever, and we've established you think I'm doing something wrong but won't say what. Are you just here to insult me?"

"Of course not. I'm here to help you."

"Why?"

"My master has great plans for you. We've been watching, but you need some help."

"Can you fix a romantic relationship I royally fucked up?"

"No, but you can."

"Then why do I need you?"

Marek and Kevin, the crow, exchanged stares for a long time. It was long enough that Marek began to believe he had made up the entire conversation in his head, that none of this was happening. Eventually, Kevin spoke again, in more measured words, as if he had rehearsed them.

"You choose your path. Others may guide you along the way, but only you can walk it. Do you know where you're going?"

"So now I get the cryptic message. I knew it was coming." Marek swallowed more beer and then belched loudly.

"That's the message from my master."

"And your master is?"

"I cannot divulge that information. I don't have permission."

"This is not helpful."

"Shut up. You're not helping."

"Back to the snark, then? Some help you are."

"Just get your shit together, Marek. That's all we're asking."

"Again, with the 'we,' like you're the feds, spying on me."

"I have been watching you."

"Was that you at the window before?"

"How many window-tapping crows do you know?"

Before Marek could question the crow further, the bird reeled back into the bedroom and scrambled out the window. Marek followed and watched as he pushed away from the window, free-falling into the alleyway and climbing back into the sky. The advice hadn't been beneficial, but Marek was awake now, wishing he could tell someone about it. No one would believe him.

He returned to the kitchen and collapsed back into the chair. He crushed the can and threw it into a wastebasket across the room. He felt his pocket vibrating. It was a text from Nyx. She wanted to know if he was still coming. It was time to right what he had wronged, or at least attempt to.

When Marek arrived at The Royal Club, Olive was already waiting for him. It looked like she was deep in her cups, and he wasn't sure how to approach the conversation. Wasn't this what had caused the trouble in the first place, that neither of them had been sober? She wasn't very responsive when he greeted her, staring down into her lap. Nyx finally came by to take his order.

"Can I borrow him for a minute?" she asked Olive.

Olive nodded.

Nyx grabbed him by the arm and pulled him toward the bar. "Don't you dare hurt her again."

"That was never my intention," said Marek, "but she's already been drinking. We should probably have this conversation sober, in the light of day."

Nyx stepped closer to him and sniffed deeply. "You're one to talk. It smells like you've been imbibing as well."

"Imbibing?"

"What? Is it my fault I have a vocabulary?"

Marek tried not to laugh at her incredulity.

"What are you laughing at?"

"I've just... had an exciting day. Some interesting conversations." Like one with a talking crow, he thought but did not say.

"Will you two just kiss and make up already?" Nyx poured him a whiskey and pushed him back toward the table.

"If only it were that easy," said Marek.

Olive slowly looked up at him as he approached. He could tell her eyes were glistening, just on the verge of tears. He wanted to reach for her, hold her close, and pretend everything would be okay, but he knew he couldn't undo his actions.

"Can I just say something?" he asked.

"Anything," she said. "I'm unsure if I'm ready to hear it, but go ahead."

"I'm so sorry." He wished he could just wrap his arms around her. As Nyx had said, kissing and making up were entirely impossible. "I don't... I don't have a good excuse or reason or anything." He paused, then added, "Nyx told me what you said."

"What I said?" Olive swirled her drink with one hand, staring at the thin film of liquid sloshing around in a circle. "What did she say I said?"

"I don't want to repeat it."

"Then why bring it up, then?"

"You said I raped you?"

"Isn't that what happened?"

Marek tried to remember, but the whole night was incredibly fuzzy, like a dream. He could barely remember how they got to Dante's house, much less what happened there. She had been nearly smothering him with kisses. She was in his lap, and then on the floor, and then they were having sex on the carpet, and Dante was watching. But as these images came back to him, it felt like he was watching a movie of someone else, that it wasn't him. It was just some guy who didn't know what he was doing, A dumbass, as the crow had said. That person couldn't be him.

Nyx returned to the table on the pretense of getting them new drinks. "How are things going over here?" she asked.

"This was a great idea," said Olive, but sarcasm dripped from her lips like thick honey.

"I just thought you two needed to talk it out," said Nyx.

"We do. But Mr. Stoic over here hasn't said much."

"I'm trying," said Marek, even though he wasn't sure it was true. He knew he had to do better. A blind apology for something barely remembered wasn't a sincere one. He was still putting together the pieces, but Olive seemed pretty sure. He didn't think she was lying about how she experienced the night, but could he be held accountable for something he didn't quite remember doing? Could he plead temporary insanity?

"I guess I'll leave you to it, then," said Nyx, strolling away.

The women in his life attacked him from all sides. No one seemed to want to hear his version of events. He was accountable for whatever these women said. He had to go along, but he didn't appreciate their accusations. It wasn't his intent, even if it had happened as Olive claimed.

"I never meant for any of this to happen," he said eventually.

"Just what were you thinking then? Do you think I wanted to put on a show for that sleazy dealer? You think I'm that kind of girl."

"Well, no. I didn't plan it. I was just going with the flow, you know? You seemed to be into it."

"Did I?" she asked. She was searching Marek's face now, but he didn't know what she expected to find there. "That's not how I remember it."

"Then tell me," he said. "Because apparently, I missed something."

Now their words were growing heated. The tears Olive had held back started to fall down her cheeks.

"You want me to relive that moment?" she asked.

"That's not what I meant. I just want to understand what happened."

"You were there. What don't you understand?"

"Can we just talk through it?"

"You raped me, Marek. That's what happened. No, I wasn't into it. I was pushing you away, but you kept on going. You were on top of me. I couldn't get away. And that - that man just watched it happen. Let it happen. And then you called me a car, sent me home, and haven't talked to me since. Who does that?"

Marek didn't have the words to improve the situation, but he tried to defend himself. He couldn't accept what she said, the claims she made. He wasn't that person.

"How can you remember everything in such vivid detail?" he asked. "We were both wasted, Olive. We had a good time. You were all over me like you wanted me then and there, so that's what I gave you. I gave you what you wanted."

"You think I wanted this? You think I wanted you to rape me?"

"Can you please stop using that word?"

"You want me to lie about it? You think you can just silence me?"

"Are you going to file charges or something?"

"Do I need to?"

She stared at him defiantly. She might be crying, but her tears came from a place of hurt and anger rather than sadness. Abruptly, she stood from her chair and started to walk away. Her heels hit the floor with a loud tap-tap-tap. Marek started to follow her but stayed a few feet behind her stride. He called out to her, but she wasn't listening. He watched as she moved, creating more and more distance between them. Then she disappeared backstage.

Marek returned to his seat and downed the last of his whiskey. Nyx arrived with a deep frown creasing her face. "Looks like my plan didn't work out that well," she said.

"Not really," said Marek.

She sat across from him momentarily, setting her tray on the table. "Maybe it will just take time."

"I don't know if we can fix this."

They sat in silence for a moment. Then, Nyx gathered up the empty glasses, placing them on her tray before standing to take them back to the bar.

"How's Abaddon doing?" he asked.

Nyx sat back down. "Alright. I think. He hasn't quite been himself."

"Well, he's been sober."

She chuckled, but a shadow fell over her face. "As far as I know, yes."

"Has he been getting out much?" Marek asked.

"Not really. Abaddon has been holing up in his room. Laying around watching old movies."

"Maybe it'll just take time."

"Maybe."

Ronnie approached the table then, with something large and white wrapped around his neck. It wasn't until the mustachioed man began speaking to them that Marek realized it was a snake. "Check out Penelope!"

"What the hell," said Nyx, backing away. "And what kind of name is that for a snake?"

Ronnie looked like a sideshow attraction, between his large, twisty mustache and the snake slithering across his shoulders. "I was thinking we could use her in one of the acts," he said. "Isn't she gorgeous?"

"One of the acts?" asked Marek.

"Yeah. Can't you just imagine Olive up there on the stage, all gorgeous and singing her heart out with a snake?!"

"This isn't Vegas," said Nyx. "Or the circus."

Marek could see it. He could see it all too well, like a desperate attempt to connect with his lover. Marek could win Olive back if she were still within his reach. He just wasn't sure how he would accomplish it.

14

The Four of Swords

Madame Rosivda turned the card, revealing a pale blue dais on which sat a sparkling glass coffin. In the coffin lay a beautiful woman in a white lace dress. She looked like she was merely sleeping rather than dead - her features so youthful and vibrant. Alongside the coffin, a cascade of white roses descended to a sword lying on the floor. Above her hovered three more swords, poised as if to strike her breast. Although the room lay in shadow, a yellow sun hung outside the window. It was the Four of Swords.

"When they found the princess in her garden, all life had left her," said Madame Rosivda. "She had joined her lover in death, but the body she left behind still looked alive. There was pink in her cheeks, red in her lips, and when the king looked down at his daughter, he expected her to wake at any moment.

"Because she was still so beautiful, he built a glass coffin to display her body. The wake lasted for an entire week, and when it was time to bury her, the king couldn't bring himself to let them lower her into the ground. Instead, he left her coffin at the front of a small chapel on the royal property.

"Years passed, but her body did not deteriorate. She remained just as fresh and pristine as the moment they had found her. It looked like she had just descended into an eternal sleep. As the king aged, she stayed the same, the young woman he had denied her love.

"A prince from another nation set his troops upon the kingdom and claimed it as his own, killing the elderly king and sitting on his throne. When he found the chapel, he walked in and looked in awe at the princess. He had his men lift the lid of the glass coffin and bent to kiss her perfect lips. As soon he connected with her in a kiss she could no longer resist, her body disintegrated into a million pieces of dust and blew away with the wind. If she could not have her lover, no one else could claim her either."

Marek had taken a step back from Olive, giving her the space she needed, but he also wasn't sure if he could win her back either. He had thrown away what remained of the spell, and the candle burned down to a stub, the lists written out so carefully. Instead, Marek turned his attention toward his debut concert at The Royal Club. If he could start making real money there, it might be more sustainable than the accompaniment gigs he played. There might be some future in it.

Ronnie, who had begrudgingly allowed him to use the space and piano outside of normal hours, now opened without complaints. He usually used the time to clean and restock the bar. For his part, Marek had picked a few more difficult pieces to master and had begun composing his song.

He started in a high-tempo major key, flying across the black and white keys in a jubilant dance of ascending glissandos. However, it evolved into a slower minor key with ponderous chords and lingering moments. Although he felt a bit burned out, the music proved therapeutic, a way to meditate on recent events. A great weight had descended on him, making him not only physically but mentally exhausted. He woke up feeling like a truck had run him over each morning. Each aching muscle strained against him and any forward movement. The universe wanted him to stay in bed, but he pushed through it somehow.

He would wake and sit slowly, drinking coffee, awakening to the world. Even before his fingers reached a piano, the music ran through his head like the soundtrack to his life. He would sketch out a few more bars and notes before his day began. Then he would spend all morning putzing with the keyboard at home before a quick cafe lunch and then an afternoon on the baby grand at the club. Eventually, he promised himself he'd have enough money to buy an apartment and his piano. He woke and slept early, talked to a few people, and spent his days in a peaceful fugue.

He would leave the club most days before regular business hours, so he didn't even run into Nyx or Abaddon or Olive, for that matter. It wasn't something he necessarily did on purpose, but his life felt much more peaceful with only himself in it. The other significant characters faded into the shadows for now, like whispering curtains in the eaves, pushed aside. He didn't forget them; he just set them aside for now. He wasn't sure he was ready to face Olive. He was just beginning to reconcile their latest interactions within himself, much less in the public sphere of what remained of their relationship. Did anything remain? He wasn't even sure of that, but he wasn't ready to face it.

One late afternoon, as he finished practicing and closed the piano's fallboard, she came to him like a barely there ghost from across the stage.

"Marek," Olive called to him.

He couldn't find the words to reply.

She placed one light hand on his shoulder, and he turned to face her. She was as beautiful as ever, but her eyes were dark and sorrowful.

"Olive," he finally said.

"Your music is amazing," she said, but it came as if in a dream, far, far away.

"Thank you. It's been - well, it's something I'm working on."

"Did you write it?" She sat on the bench beside him, and he could feel her warmth. But instead of exciting him, making him want her, it felt like torture.

"I did. It's the first song I've ever written."

"Really? Haven't you been playing since you were a child? You've never composed before?"

"I've never had the inspiration." He looked deep into her eyes and broke the gaze when it became too intense.

"I think it's wonderful," she said, repeating the compliment but putting more emphasis on it. "When is your show again?" she asked.

"Soon. Next weekend."

"I'm looking forward to it," she said.

"Really?" He tried not to sound too eager.

"I've always thought you were a talented player," she said. "I think we both needed some time to rest and recuperate."

He nodded. That sounded hopeful, but he wasn't sure how to respond. "So you plan to come?" he asked.

She stood from the bench. "I wouldn't miss it for the world."

Then she walked off the stage, leaving him wondering if it had been her or a ghost of his imagination. He had expected their interaction to be fraught with emotion, but this was so matter-of-course, so natural. At the same time, his heart ached for her in a way he could not describe in any other way than music.

15

The Hermit

Madame Rosivda turned the card, revealing a deep blue night lit intermittently with pink cascades of illumination. A range of mountains rose on the horizon, but a bald monk wearing a shapeless robe and a red sash stood in the foreground. The monk traveled barefoot with an ornate lantern held aloft in one hand. In the other hand, he had a tall staff adorned with six golden rings attached to a metal hoop. As he slowly made his way down the path, he raised the rod and brought it down again, pounding against the earth and sending the rings cascading and ringing against one another, warning any who came near that he was mourning. It was The Hermit.

"There once was a monk who lived alone in a cave at the top of a cliff overlooking the sea. He had left the monastery in a fit of rage when he realized that what the monks sought was not the betterment of themselves but rather a separation from the physical needs of life. For instance, they spent days fasting, taking vows of silence, and depriving themselves of sleep, all to become closer to God. The hermit monk did not accept that these things would make them closer to God but served as distractions from the true purpose of elevating themselves to god-like beings who could approach the deity as equals rather than lowly servants. He pursued this newer, higher cause and left the others behind.

"He did not entirely give up what he had learned as a monk. He lived simply in the warm, dry cave he found, but he did not deprive himself either. When the man was hungry, he ate; when he was tired, he slept; and spent time in quiet meditation. Every day, he would walk to and fro along the great cliffs bordering the sea, partially for physical health and partly to attune himself to nature.

"Often, he took these walks in the early morning or late evening when he did not have the sun to guide him, so he carried a lantern. Others who saw his light approach would mistake him for a will o' the-wisp or another spirit, perhaps that of a sailor whose boat had crashed upon the rocks. Eventually, he crafted a sounding rod to warn others of his coming. The clanging also served as a sound to meditate upon, as he considered ways to emulate the ways of a god more closely - the clear understanding, the urge to create, the all-knowing instinct."

"I've never heard of a sounding rod before," said Marek. "Was this a common tool used by monks in the past?"

"Buddhist monks used the khakkhara to announce their presence and scare away animals. Eventually, they adapted it to serve both as an instrument for use during recitation and as a weapon. It was a multipurpose tool."

"Interesting."

"Just don't search for 'sounding rods' on the Internet. You'll find all kinds of unpleasant kink toys."

"Like what?"

"Urethral rods."

Marek shrugged. "To each their own, I guess." He paused to sip the last of his tea. "So now I'm supposed to become a hermit?"

"How often do I have to tell you this is one possible outcome you shouldn't take literally?"

"So many times, it has manifested literally, though. When you showed me a crow, I met a crow. A speaking crow, by the way."

"I told you to open your window."

"I finally did, and the thing wouldn't shut up, but he didn't make much sense. Said he was a familiar, and he used to be human."

"Stranger things have happened."

"Have they, though?"

"You are still a child, cosmically. There is much more to come."

"I just wish some of this would start making sense. Right now, it seems so incredibly random. My life, the people in it, none of it seems to follow any logic. That spell you gave me made so much sense until it didn't."

"What do you mean?" She leaned back in her chair, looking him over.

"I don't think it helped me get together with Olive, and either way, I've lost her already. I'm not sure I can reconcile what happened. She no longer hates me, but I don't think she can trust me again. It's all a great big mess."

"Despite all these spells and intentions, they are just tools, Marek. The real magick lies in you, not just your intentions but also your actions, which have consequences."

Marek groaned. "I know, and sometimes I wish I could undo what I have done."

"The flow of time is only in one direction," Madame Rosivda said. "Forward."

Marek had taken long walks of his own in the past few days. It kept his body occupied while his mind wandered. On one of these walks, he found himself passing Herb & Altar. As he entered, a bell rang above the door, and the strong scent of incense sent him into a sneezing fit.

Jasper, leaning heavily on the counter before Marek's entry, quickly approached him. "If you need something for a cold, I have plenty of herbal remedies."

Once Marek managed to stop violently sneezing, he responded. "I don't have a cold."

"Then what brings you in today?"

"Nothing specific."

"Still browsing?" Jasper arched one eyebrow.

"Something like that."

Jasper returned to his post, grumbling under his breath. "So many people browsing, taking up space. Nobody knows what they want."

Marek didn't remark on something he was most likely not supposed to hear. He gravitated back toward the wands he had been examining the last time he was there. Olive's shadow followed him. He still wasn't sure if he believed in any of this stuff, but Madame Rosivda's readings had been so insightful over the past that there must be something to it. Maybe he hadn't tapped into his potential yet or found what kind of magick worked for him. He ran his fingers along the length of a few wands, expecting to feel something, some sort of energetic jolt telling him which, if any, of them to choose. But he felt nothing, just an overwhelming numbness.

As Marek approached the front door empty-handed, Jasper smiled up at him. The older man looked strangely hopeful. "You know," he said. "You could come back tonight for Amateur Hour."

"That sounds so much like an open mic," replied Marek.

"An open what?"

"Nevermind."

Jasper handed Marek a bright yellow flyer. "I've told you about it, but you haven't come out. Yet."

Marek glanced at the flyer. It did, indeed, say "Amateur Hour," but the type of "amateur" it referred to were witches, those like himself who were "just dabbling."

"You might even meet someone new there."

Now it was Marek's turn to grumble. "I don't want to meet someone new."

"You might learn something, then. Find what it is you've been searching for."

Marek wanted to say he wasn't searching for anything, but the words caught in his throat. Was that true? Wasn't he on his journey, trying to make sense of his life? Weren't we all on that journey? "I'll have to think about it," he said.

As Marek made his way to The Royal Club for what had become

a nearly daily practice routine, he felt a sudden weight on his left shoulder, then a voice in his ear.

"Go to the fucking witch's night," it said. "You don't listen to the universe, do you?"

Marek balked, swatting at the crow. "Mind your own business," he said. Kevin flew up into the air momentarily, flapping after him, then landed back on his shoulder.

"Spying on you is my business."

"Don't you think I have enough to deal with without a talking crow pestering me?"

"Familiar," Kevin reminded him. "A crow is just the shape I take."

"Did you have a choice in the matter? Why would you choose a crow?"

"For your information, I did not have a choice, but even if I did, what would you prefer me to be a pigeon?"

"That might be more inconspicuous."

"A pigeon on your shoulder?"

"I mean, maybe?"

"Or would it be better for me to fly overhead or immediately behind you like a bad omen?"

Marek groaned and settled onto a bench advertising a local personal injury lawyer. "I was trying to take a walk."

Kevin hopped from Marek's shoulder to the back of the bench."I was pleased perched on your shoulder, you know."

"Well, I wasn't. What the hell do you want?"

"Go to the witch's gathering tonight."

Marek frowned. "Why would I do that?"

"My master will be there," said Kevin. "He'd like to meet you."

"Well, I don't give a rat's ass about him."

"You should. Solomon could do great things for you."

"Like what?"

Kevin balanced from one foot to the other, seemingly dancing on the back of the bench.

"What are you doing?" asked Marek.

"My feet get itchy, and I can't exactly scratch them. Could you maybe..."

"Scratch your foot? You've got to be kidding me."

"You have no idea what it's like to go from being a human to living as a crow. Sure, I can fly, which is cool, but I don't have opposable thumbs, and I still haven't gotten used to this beak. It's been decades, but I still manage to injure myself sometimes."

Marek reluctantly reached out to run his nails between the crow's toes, scratching the itch the bird couldn't quite reach. If a crow could smile, that was what Kevin did exactly, his beak open just a crack as he looked appreciatively back up at Marek.

"Thank you," said Kevin. "You have no idea how much I needed that."

Marek nodded but looked away as if some foul-smelling stranger had sat down next to him, trying to distance himself from this creature he didn't quite believe was real. "How can your master help me?" he asked.

"He can help you find your magick."

"I don't think I have any."

"Everyone has magick; they just haven't tapped into it. The magick is there, all around us, but only a few have truly attuned to it. Part of it is finding the right frequency."

"I thought the event was for amateurs only."

"My master is a generous man. He likes to help fledglings learn to fly."

"Like he helped you? How did you become a familiar anyway?"

"That, my friend, is a story for another time."

Before Marek could ask any more questions, Kevin flapped his way back into the sky, riding the wind until he rose high into the clouds, slowly disappearing into a black speck. Marek heard the crow's voice again, at the back of his mind, urging him to go to the event. After all, what did he have to lose? He might as well go and see what this was all about.

After practicing at the club for a few hours, Marek returned to Herb & Altar, hopeful but not expecting much. What he didn't anticipate was that Olive would be there. She sat on the other side of the circle, and they both struggled to avoid eye contact. Even after their conversation about Marek's show, they were still awkward around each other. It was even worse than when they had first met. At least then, Marek was just trying to get the courage to talk to her. Now it was a matter of avoidance, pretending she didn't exist, that his face didn't grow warm whenever she was near. Once the group had gathered, a motley collection of granola-eaters, mostly women wearing shapeless skirts and oversized jewelry, Jasper gave a short demonstration.

He explained how to cast a magick circle, acknowledging the four directions and using tools associated with each element. While it was an impressive ceremony performed by one well-versed in practice, Marek remembered what Madame Rosivda had told him, that the tools used didn't necessarily matter.

He held back a bout of laughter, imagining some alternative tools Jasper could hypothetically use. Instead of an eagle's feather representing air in the east, he imagined a dingy desk fan. The tall pillar candle in the south could become a Bic lighter. The gathered rainwater in the west morphs into a lower toilet bowl, and the garden soil in the north becomes a cat's litter box. Would these thoughts be considered blasphemous to a proper Wiccan or rather more practical? He had heard of kitchen witches, using wooden spoons rather than wands, drawing magic circles with a standard household broom. Maybe you just used what was available to you.

After the demonstration, the newbie witches thanked Jasper and broke into smaller groups to share their recent spell-related adventures. Marek turned to one of the few men there, a tall man with a shiny bald head, and explained the "love spell" he had concocted at Madame Rosivda's urging.

"The problem," claimed the man, "is that someone else built the spell for you."

"How would I begin to build a spell myself?" Marek asked. "I don't know the first thing about this stuff."

"Intention is important," said the man, "but so is correspondence. Certain colors, objects, and tools have specific correspondences, and it isn't even that you need to match up the accepted correspondences, either, but that you connect these two objects. For instance, what do you associate with love, the type of love you were trying to find?"

"I have no idea."

"Think about it for a moment. It will come to you."

As they sat in a moment of silence, Marek noticed Olive slipping out the front door. They hadn't even exchanged a single word. Is that how their relationship would be, just passing glances? If so, it would be more agonizing to be around her than not.

Jasper approached them, leaning on his ornate cane. "I thought I told you this was a beginner's group, Solomon," he said to Marek's new companion. "Why do you insist on coming to these things? Don't you have your own coven to lead?"

"Not quite," replied Solomon. "The coven has recently disbanded. Besides," he glanced at Marek. "I like to help out where I can. Fledglings need guidance sometimes."

Jasper nodded knowingly and then moved to the next group to check in on them.

Marek looked back at Solomon, feeling a bit deceived. "Sorry, I haven't properly introduced myself," he said. "My name is Marek." He reached out his hand.

Solomon gripped Marek's hand and shook it forcefully. "I know."

Then, Marek realized he was talking with Kevin's master, but he felt no desire to speak about the crow, not with so many other people around them. Maybe to them, familiars were ordinary, but Marek still wasn't sure. Perhaps he could talk about Kevin as if he were a person, just a personal assistant.

"Kevin told me you might be here this evening, but he didn't tell me much about you."

"No?" asked Solomon. "I find that surprising. Usually, he won't shut up."

"I mean, that was true," said Marek. "But he spent most of his words berating me."

"That sounds like Kevin."

"He also said something about you having a plan for me. What was that all about? He was kinda cryptic about that part."

"The universe has a plan for all of us, Marek. Some of us just need a little guidance to find it."

"What is that supposed to mean?"

"Tell me a little more about Madame Rosivda."

Marek shared how he had visited the divination shop nearly weekly for the past few months. He included how people and scenes from the cards manifested in his life. He appreciated the guidance but wasn't always sure whether the readings led him to stumble upon these things or if they would have happened independently.

"Divination is an interesting thing," Solomon said. "You're not necessarily creating the future or even reading the future, just taking a glimpse at what might be. That glimpse can influence the decisions you make, which in turn influences the future which manifests. Time can only move in one direction."

"She said that. Too bad we can't go back to fix our mistakes."

"Every magician also has a medium they work most effectively in, the same way artists work with a specific medium. For the artist, that medium might be paint, clay, or textiles. It might be a specific element or magickal tool for the magick user. Your Madame Rosivda works with tarot, but it sounds like she also uses story-telling and hydromancy."

"What's hydromancy?"

"How she manipulates the water in your tea to depict the images she describes. It involves the use of water for divination."

"Not reading tea leaves?"

"She isn't interpreting the leaves."

"What is your magickal medium?" Marek asked.

"I like to call it alchemy because that sounds cool, but it's chemistry."

"That sounds more like science than magick."

"Science can be a type of magick. It depends on how you use it."

"How do you use chemistry, then?"

"I make compounds and herbal remedies but can also concoct a wicked cocktail."

"Sounds like a bunch of mumbo jumbo."

"Does it? I could use more technical terminology, but you'd probably get lost with your eighth-grade level of organic chemistry."

"I know you've had Kevin spying on me, and I'm not sure how I feel about that, but you seem to know an awful lot about me," said Marek. "What do you think I should base my magic on?"

"Well, music, of course. I can't believe you can't see that."

"This sounds just as odd as the chemistry."

"Maybe, but I could help you tune into it. No pun intended."

Marek laughed politely but was incredibly skeptical. What could some strange witchy man teach him about a skill he had been honing his entire life?

"Believe me, there is plenty," said Solomon, answering Marek's un-asked question.

"Could you teach me to do that?" he asked.

"Do what?"

"Read minds?"

Solomon smiled, rubbing one hand over the top of his head. "Only if you have the cure for male-pattern baldness."

16

The Nine of Wands

Madame Rosivda turned the card, revealing a fairy dressed as a jester holding a star-topped wand. He cast his eyes downward, staring at the leaf he had landed on. Surrounding him were eight other wands, rising like plants toward the sun, but he paid them no attention. It was the Nine of Wands.

"There once was a fairy," said Madame Rosivda, "who protected a mercenary as he made his way from one town into the next, clearing a pathway for other travelers. However, that mercenary had gotten distracted by the magical wands he had found along the way. These wands held the powers of Earth, Air, Water, Fire, Spirit, Life, and Death. When the mercenary found the Death wand, he used it carelessly, cutting a great gash in the sky, releasing every dark and deadly thing.

"In the aftermath, the ghastly beings he had released led to the mercenary's demise, and a deathly pall stretched over the land. The fairy did his best to repair the tear in the sky, but he could not fix what had been broken even after returning the wands to their rightful places.

"He sought two more elemental wands, which could rectify the situation. These were the wands of Possibility and Imagination. Together these two wands would be able to make his hopeful dreams a reality and restore balance to the world. He gathered them together and cast a careful spell, hoping for the best but fearing the worst. Ultimately, he restored the sky but not the mercenary's life. He had failed his mission and felt a fool for attempting it. After all, a fairy can never effectively protect a human, only lead them on their path."

Marek looked across the table at Madame Rosivda. "So, now it will be fairies, too?"

She shrugged her shoulders without saying anything.

"This sounds like the continuation of a story you told me a few weeks ago."

"That's because it is. You have a good memory."

"Are all of your stories connected?" he asked.

"Not necessarily. But the stories intertwine sometimes."

"I see."

"What do you see, Marek?"

"I'm not sure yet, but the picture is clearer."

Solomon had promised to mentor Marek in his understanding of magick. Marek wasn't sure what all this entailed, but he was willing to learn. According to Solomon, it had something to do with his music. Now that his concert performance was rapidly approaching, Marek was willing to try anything. Olive felt ever further from his grasp, but his music seemed to be growing in a strange organic way it hadn't before. He made much better progress on the baby grand at the club, and he had added several bars to the song he was composing. His other songs for the show would be classical greats, but this would be his first foray into writing music. In a way, it amazed Marek it had taken him this long. Most young musicians ventured into writing music early on, but he had been much more obsessed with perfection.

Marek could remember the first tuxedo he had ever worn at the age of six. At that point, he had already been playing for two years, but it was the first recital he attended, where most students were much older than he had been. A four-year-old just starting might be able to get away with jeans and a t-shirt, but his instructor expected a young virtuoso to look the part. And he had all thirty-nine inches of him.

He wasn't tall enough to ride a roller coaster but could play Chopin like a pro.

He remembered sitting on the bench, his feet dangling off the end because they couldn't quite reach the floor yet. The keys felt like an extension of his fingers then, and when he played, it felt so natural that he heard the music echo back at him as if he were listening to a recording. It wasn't until after his entire set, when his hands and wrists began to grow sore that he would remember he was the catalyst for the piano's sounds. That, and the resounding applause. No recording, even a live one, could replicate that welcoming feeling, the overwhelming embrace of applause that surrounded you like a loud echo from all sides.

While practicing, that supporting embrace didn't exist. It was just you and the piano and the empty room. Now that space also included all the emotions and notes that had not yet materialized. Marek needed to arrange, capture and remember all the sounds and the feelings behind them. On the way to the club, he tried to describe that feeling to Solomon with little success.

The added fact that Kevin had claimed a spot on the alchemist's shoulder, like a pirate's parrot, didn't help him articulate either. The entire situation felt surreal.

"We warned you not to be a dumbass," said Kevin upon seeing Marek again. "And what did you do?"

Marek hung his head as he plodded along.

"Don't listen to him," said Solomon. "He's overly critical."

"What?" squawked Kevin. "He did. He fucked up. Now what? We're going to help him fix it?"

Marek continued walking, his eyes on the cracks in the sidewalk, counting the ants as he stepped on them.

"Will you be quiet?" Solomon said. "We're bound to come across someone during our walk. Why don't you fly above us?"

Kevin stayed where he was, digging his claws deeper into Solomon's shoulder but remaining silent.

"How does this work?" asked Marek eventually.

"As I told you, we each have our material to work with – the substance of our souls. For you, that comes from your music. You can imbue particular notes with specific intents."

"Is there a record of others doing this? A book I can read or something?"

Kevin cackled a strange chortle that sounded like choking. "Listen to this guy," he said before flying several feet above them. He followed at a bit of a distance but continued to listen.

"Once you grasp the basics, it will feel perfectly natural. You can use a medium you are already comfortable with to communicate a message, influence others, and create change and substance."

"Sounds kinda wishy-washy to me."

"More like wibbly-wobbly."

"What's the difference?"

"There's a pattern to it, but most people aren't aware of it. There's a pattern to everything; you just need to take the time to see it."

"Are you a musician?" asked Marek.

"Not exactly."

"So, how are you going to teach me anything?"

"It will be more how you use the music, not how you make it."

Solomon glanced up, watching Kevin find a ledge above them. It seemed the bird wouldn't be following them into the club. Marek was admittedly a bit relieved. It was bad enough he was bringing a guest, especially one Ronnie wasn't familiar with, much less a talking crow.

Marek had his key now, but Ronnie was already prepping the bar when they entered. Marek introduced Solomon as a friend who wanted to hear what he had been working on.

"Fine by me," said Ronnie. "But don't be giving free shows, now. You're on Sunday night, and we hope to make some money off you."

Marek nodded, then led Solomon up to the stage. The baby grand sat in the back corner, under a few dim lights. He wouldn't bother drawing the curtain back. Admittedly, he liked the privacy, but it suddenly felt strange and clandestine with Solomon by his side. The two men sat beside each other on the bench, and Solomon intently stared as Marek played the first few chords, then paused.

"Go ahead. Don't mind me," said Solomon.

"But you're hovering. I don't see how I'll be able to play this way."

Solomon sighed deeply, stood from the bench, and began to pace back and forth across the small space. "Alright. Try now."

"That's not much better," said Marek.

"Try closing your eyes."

"I'm still working out the kinks."

"Try it anyway."

Reluctantly, Marek allowed his lids to droop and then close. He tried to focus on the movement of his hands on the keys. The notes felt uncertain. Cautiously, he played ponderously and then allowed the sounds to glide together. The few areas he hadn't entirely worked out, or written down, suddenly became music rather than individual keys. Eventually, Solomon's slow steps faded behind the sound of the melody, and Marek could place himself in the center of it, surrounded by his own emotion. It was the aching need for comfort, love, and gentle, caressing touch.

Before opening his eyes, he felt a light pressure and a second set of hands lingering over his fingers, following his movements. He paused, uncertain and uncomfortable.

"Keep playing," said Solomon. "Don't open your eyes."

Marek wasn't sure what was happening. He felt a strange warmth against his back, the rasp of warm breath against his neck.

"Keep playing," repeated Solomon.

Marek continued, and the other hands followed him as he went. It was like these fingers were an echo of his own that they knew where he was going even before he moved an inch. As he played, his hands grew warm and throbbing. The heat slowly grew more and more intense. He heard a voice at his neck. "Keep playing," it said into his ear, and his hands began to ache from the pulsing heat like he had been out in the cold without gloves and then sat beside a blazing fire. Finally, when finished, he moved his hands to his lap and opened his eyes. Although Marek expected Solomon to be standing immediately behind him, his hands wrapped around him, the alchemist stood, unmoving, on the other side of the stage in the shadows.

Despite himself, Marek gasped aloud. "What did you do to me?" he asked.

"Me? I didn't do anything." Solomon returned to Marek's side. "You just found your focus. What did it feel like?"

Marek didn't want to say what it had felt like, the terror that had started to grow within him. He didn't want to admit any of this to a person he barely knew.

"What is it that you want to accomplish, my friend? How would you like to use your magick?"

"How *can* I use my magick?"

"That's up to you. To begin with, you may only be able to portray emotion and make your listeners feel something. Eventually, you should be able to influence them, to persuade them in your favor."

Marek thought for a moment of all the concerts he had ever attended, those he had played in, and those where he listened from the audience. He had always felt a sense of connection in that space, everyone in the theatre drawn together.

"Is it possible to use magick without even knowing it?" he asked.

Solomon's face broke into a smile that looked more like a sneer. "Yes, but the best magicians use intentionality to work their magick."

"You've got me mixed up on terminology here," said Marek. "Are you a witch, warlock, or a magician?"

"I told you, I consider myself an alchemist."

"What does that mean, though?"

"It means I create potions to influence and shape the world around me."

"Potions?"

Solomon opened his trench coat, displaying an array of tiny test tubes caught up in elastic loops, each stopped up with a cork. "What do you need?" he asked. "Calming essence, a drought of drowsiness? Maybe something to awaken your senses?"

Marek stared wide-eyed at Solomon's wares. "You keep those on you at all times?" he asked.

"You never know what you'll need when. It's best to prepare."

"What are they made of?"

"If I told you that, I'd give away all my secrets."

Solomon rebuttoned his jacket, and Marek was surprised he couldn't hear the potions clinking against each other as the man moved. Just knowing they were there, though, made him feel like he was in on a secret.

"So, back to the task at hand." Solomon sat down on the bench next to Marek. "What is it that you want to accomplish with your music? With this song in particular? Think of it like a spell or a potion. The song is only a vessel to carry your intent."

"It's a song about losing love, feeling loss. I want others to feel that ache, that emptiness that remains. I want that emptiness to take shape in them. Most of all, I want Olive to feel it."

"It takes a bit more work to direct the energy toward a particular individual, but you can bring that feeling to anyone who hears it. Play the first part of the song, focusing more on the emotion you wish to imbue it with."

Marek stared back blankly.

"Go ahead," said Solomon. "I won't bite. Not unless you want me to."

As soon as Marek's fingers felt the keys again, that same aching heat radiated through them, but this time it was also tinged with sadness. If it were possible for a body part to absorb a feeling, that is how he would describe it. In the same way, stress settles into a person's shoulders or midback, the sorrow of losing Olive seeped into his fingers, slowly leaving them with each note he played. He felt the transfer, moving from his hands into the piano and the music. At the same time, a second set of hands joined his, and he wasn't sure if he was controlling his movements or if the other hands were. They hovered lightly, just over his own, like a whisper or echo. Although Marek had felt connected to music before, it had never felt as intense as this. For so many years, he had learned the notes, memorized them, and then allowed himself to move mechanically through the motions - now it seemed to sap everything from him, and as he finished the last few stanzas, he felt completely drained and empty. He opened his eyes to see Solomon gazing at him, appraising his progress.

"Good, good," said the alchemist. "Now you can learn to work with your magick and shape it, make it do your bidding rather than haphazardly throwing it about. Now you can target it and use it to your advantage."

Just then, somebody pulled aside the edge of the red curtain, and a lithe silhouette joined them. "Who is your friend?" asked Olive. "I think I've seen him before."

"You have," said Marek, shocked back into reality.

Solomon stood, towering over Olive. He extended his hand in an introduction.

"Olive, this is Solomon. Solomon, Olive."

The two shook hands awkwardly. Olive looked a bit wary of the alchemist.

"Does Ronnie know he's here?" she asked Marek.

"Yes," said Marek.

"I'm just here for a sneak peek," said Solomon by way of explanation. "I understand Marek here has a concert in a few days."

"Yes," said Olive. "We just don't usually let people get a free show."

"I should probably leave then," said Solomon, backing away as Olive stared him down.

As soon as Solomon had exited stage left, Marek turned back to Olive. "What was that all about?" he asked.

"I don't know," she said, brushing the hair out of her face with one hand. "That guy just makes me uncomfortable. I'm not sure what it is." She paused, trying to find the words. "He was at the amateur night at Herb & Altar. Is that where you met him?" she asked.

Marek nodded.

"I don't know how much experience you have in the witchy community, but you must be careful, Marek. Some would take advantage of you. They leech off your need to believe, and then, before you know it, they're filling you up with empty promises and robbing you blind. Did you pay him anything?"

"No."

"Did he promise you anything?"

"No, Olive, nothing like that."

"What was he doing here, anyway?" She walked up to the piano, running a few fingers down the length of the lid prop.

Marek couldn't help wishing her hands were stroking him instead. He momentarily fell into a daydream trance, one where they were much closer, and she enclosed him in her warm embrace.

"I just needed another ear to hear a song I'm working on."

"Lots of people have ears. Why him?" She stepped closer to where Marek sat on the bench, his legs feeling weak and shaky.

"I don't think that's any of your business," he said.

"Fine." She turned her back to him and started walking away. "Be that way." She swayed her hips as she moved further and further away. Why couldn't he find the words to reach out to her? How could she be so close and yet still so distant? She wanted to poke, tease, and play with him like a helpless bug rather than interact with him.

"Olive," he whispered, not nearly loud enough for her to hear him. He might be unable to reach her with his words, but he was determined to get her with his music. In just a few days, he would see what his new grasp of magick could do and prayed that she would be much more receptive then. Until then, it felt like his whole world had a crack in it, and nothing he did could repair it. Despite this, he finally had the tools in hand, and he had a plan.

17

The King of Coins

Madame Rosivda turned the card, revealing a vibrant green garden surrounded by tall trees reaching up to the heavens. A giant, white rabbit sat at the center of the courtyard, gazing angrily at the golden crown surrounding him like a small magic circle. Woven with the circlet was a laurel of white roses. In the background, a castle rose, looming like a dark foreboding. It was the King of Coins.

"There once was a king," said Madame Rosivda, "Who thought his place in the kingdom was sure, and no one could challenge him. One day a traveling magician came to the castle, offering free entertainment. The magician claimed he would ask for no payment or accommodations unless the king deemed him worthy based on the magick he could perform. Expecting a few little tricks, the King welcomed him into the throneroom and invited him to conduct his magick.

"What he didn't expect was that this magician was a great sorcerer who had come from another land with evil on his mind. The first few tricks he performed were simplistic, disappearing brightly colored handkerchiefs and passing golden rings through each other. The king had witnessed these everyday things before, but he clapped politely. When the magician invited the king for a walk through the gardens, he grew more intrigued.

"Whatever will you do in the garden?" the king asked.

"I must use nature for my next trick," said the sorcerer. "And it is a special trick, my king, meant only for your eyes.'

"The king's guards were understandably wary about this new tactic and warned the king not to go into the gardens with this magician alone. The king pushed their worries aside and insisted, and he, being the king, got his way.

"As they walked into the walled gardens, the sorcerer asked the king if he had ever seen a magician pull a rabbit from a hat. The king admitted he had never seen this trick but had heard of it.

"The sorcerer smiled as he pulled a wand from his robes. 'For you, my king, I will pull a rabbit from a crown.'

"The king looked around, wondering what the sorcerer could mean. After all, he wore the crown and would not willingly hand it over to the magician, even for a trick. The sorcerer waved his wand, chanting words in a language the king had never heard before, an old and ancient language that sounded like a demon arising from the depths of hell. The king felt strange, like he was suddenly shrinking, and as he looked around, he saw his crown surrounding him like a golden circle around his feet, which were white and fuzzy. When the king opened his mouth to protest, nothing came out but a strange squeal.

"Smiling at his handiwork, the sorcerer reached down for the crown, placing it upon his head. He had taken on the likeness of the king's true form and left the king as a rabbit to roam his gardens unhappily for the rest of his days."

Marek stretched, lifting his arms above his head and waggling his fingers. "So I have become a powerful wizard," he said.

Madame Rosivda raised one of her eyebrows. "How do you know the sorcerer represents you in this situation?" she asked.

"Because I'm magick. I've got the touch. Anything is possible."

"What have you been smoking, and why aren't you sharing?"

Marek laughed, sobering. "Just in a good mood, is all," he said. He wasn't ready to tell her about Solomon, especially after what Olive had said. He didn't want to hear any more naysayers. He'd rather keep positive and keep moving in that direction. The concert was no longer approaching; it was upon him now.

"How do you know you aren't the hapless king?" Madame Rosivda asked.

"Because everything's been coming up roses lately."

"Roses still have thorns, Marek. Don't be foolhardy."

Her admonition reminded him of a particular crow named Kevin sitting on his kitchen table, telling him not to be a dumbass, but he brushed it aside. Everything was going to plan.

Solomon had come to his rehearsals several times, and they hadn't encountered Olive backstage again. She had been conspicuously absent as of late. Marek wondered if Olive was avoiding him or still uncomfortable with Solomon. He hoped she still planned to attend his concert; otherwise, all his efforts would be moot. As Marek practiced, he learned to manage the weight of the second set of hands, which he now thought of as a shadow of his own. The magic felt like a duet, balancing playing with the emotional intentions, and then he had to focus it further to target Olive. Marek had clipped an image of Olive from one of the club fliers and affixed it with blue painter's tape to the bottom of the piano's frame. It wasn't an easy task with only six inches from the bottom of the frame to the stage, but he had managed to snake one long-fingered hand far enough under to affix the paper securely. It was far enough back that he hoped no one would notice it, and after all, no one would be looking for it in the first place.

"Will you be here tonight?" Marek asked Solomon. The alchemist had been pacing back and forth across the stage.

"Do I need to be?" he asked.

Marek paused, uncertain. "Sometimes it feels like having you here helps me concentrate." He still didn't want to admit that sometimes he thought he heard Solomon's voice urging him on as well. Indeed, that wasn't what was happening. Most of the time, the man was many feet away when he felt the shadow hands, heard and felt the rasping breath.

"I think I've got a handle on it," said Marek.

"Then I won't come unless you need moral support."

Marek hesitated. Did he? He suddenly felt like a child, unsure if he wanted his parents to attend a concert. Would it be more comforting or more nerve-wracking to have Solomon there?

"After all this work, don't you want to hear the final product?"

Solomon smirked in that odd way of his. He never quite smiled or frowned. There always seemed to be a hidden meaning behind his facial expressions. Marek could just see the gears working in the man's head. He wondered who had influenced who - Solomon or Kevin - when it came to this level of snarkiness. Either way, the two made a fine pair.

Marek found himself missing Abaddon's antics. It had been far too long since he had seen his friend. While he knew sobriety was good for Abaddon, it made him a recluse who rarely left the house. They talked on the phone occasionally, and Nyx gave Marek regular updates, but it wasn't the same. Abaddon didn't randomly arrive at events, squeezing his arm and shamelessly flirting. Not that Marek necessarily wanted the flirting, but he didn't necessarily mind the attention, either.

"I think you've got this," said Solomon as he walked into the shadows. "You're on your own now."

By the time Marek finished playing through the last few songs another time, Solomon had vanished. It was just as well, though, especially if Olive still felt uncomfortable around him. After all, Marek was trying to foster positive vibes. He wanted Olive to feel the loss and ache he had harbored since their separation. He wanted her to understand how broken he felt without her, to know that he had only the best intention and never wanted to see her eyes look so dark and empty. He never wanted to be the source of her sorrow ever again. He might be unable to convince her with words, which he could never quite grasp, but he hoped to do so with music.

But as the evening came on and guests began to gather in the ballroom, there was one person who was still missing: Olive. Marek approached the bar for his regular whiskey and water and confronted Ronnie about it. The barman said she hadn't been feeling well the past few days and might not make it. As she came past, Nyx assured him that Abaddon planned on making an appearance, though. Too bad I don't want to seduce him, Marek thought and almost said aloud. Instead, he bit his lip hard enough to break the skin and send blood into his mouth. He grabbed a bar rag to dab at it.

Ronnie scowled at him. "What the hell do you think you're doing?" He snatched the rag back, looking at the splash of red smeared across it.

"Instinct," said Marek. "I wasn't thinking."

"Obviously."

Nyx sauntered back over. "What's going on?" She looked from Marek to Ronnie and then back again.

"This asshole is making a mess, spreading blood-borne pathogens for all I know."

"What are you trying to say?" asked Marek. He leaned over the bar toward Ronnie, ready to argue with his fists.

"Cool it," said Nyx, getting between them. "Aren't you supposed to be getting backstage, Marek?"

"I just wanted a drink."

Nyx glanced at the whiskey sitting in front of him. "You've got it," she said. "Now go."

As Marek grabbed his glass and began to walk away, he could hear her arguing with Ronnie.

"I don't understand why you even like that guy," Ronnie whispered harshly.

"He's one of Abaddon's friends," she said, not even taking ownership of him.

"Hence why I'm worried about his blood all over everything."

"It's just a little," she said. "Get a fresh rag. No biggie. What, you think Marek's diseased or something?"

"For all I know, he might be. He does nothing but cause trouble for me, and he's been bringing this other guy in several times a week. He says he's practicing, but I hear more talking than piano happening. Who knows what they get up to."

So now Ronnie was making accusations. Great. As much as Marek wanted to upend a table or break a bottle over the barman's head, he needed to keep his cool. He chuckled to himself, just imagining the scene he could cause. The old him wouldn't have dreamed of starting a fight or instigating an argument. He felt so much more in control of his actions now, in charge of his fate. If only he could regain Olive's trust, everything would be great. Everything would be golden. Right now, he needed to focus and concentrate. She'd have to show. Everything was falling into place.

Although Marek's main focus was drawing out Olive's emotions with his composed song, he also imbued several other songs with persuasive qualities. It almost became easy once he began to get the hang of it. Most of his musical spells compelled the listener to feel a specific emotion. Still, some connected him and the audience – an affinity or liking for him as a musician, a higher likelihood of earning more tips. While all of these were spells he had cast unintentionally in the past, he now used them to his advantage. At the same time, he didn't want to be too obvious. If the entire theatre gave him a standing ovation with every song, that just wouldn't be credible – someone might wonder what was happening. Even so, what would they suspect? That someone had spiked the audience's drinks, and they were just having too good of a time? There was nowhere to go but up from here in his musical career.

As Marek played each song, he felt the shadow hands following him, the heat rising in his fingers, the intense ache rising and falling like waves through his frame. Even knowing that he had fastened Olive's image below the piano made him consciously aware of her presence, even if she was nowhere among the crowd. Marek both feared and hoped she would come, that his grand experiment would prove successful. He hadn't seen her, but he didn't let his focus waver for a moment. Marek leaned in to speak into the microphone to introduce the tune before beginning. As he did so, he stared into the audience but couldn't see anything with the brilliant lights. He shielded his eyes with one hand, looking further out, but still saw nothing. Nevertheless, he introduced the song and began to play, haltingly at first and then with more and more confidence.

While the other songs had started draining him, this one required so much concentration and energy that he could feel the music sapping from his limbs, like a physical pull swiftly becoming a pain. It was as if he were burning. At first, the heat surprised him because it was much more significant than anything he had experienced. It pulled away at his fingers, which felt like they were blistering as they touched the black and white keys, then ate away at his arms, shoulders, chest, and core. The pain became unbearable, a raging, hungry thing consuming him one part at a time, tearing him to pieces. The further it dug into him, the more numb his extremities became, and he began to lose all feeling in his fingers, amazed by the miracle of their continuous movement. He fought the urge to speed up the piece. He played slowly, to be ponderous and sorrowful. He tried to focus on Olive's face, the black-and-white outline of her features taped to the piano's frame. He would endure this for her and sacrifice for her if only she would hear him out and his plea in the notes he struggled to play. When he finally finished, the heat faded, but the terrifying moment's shock remained like scars across his skin. He feared he'd never be able to play that way again without sobbing, without screaming from the agony. He stood to take his bow, plastered a smile on his face, and finally saw Olive approaching.

Even though she wore a long evening gown, she clambered onto the stage to join him. Her green eyes stared at him intently. Maybe this had worked too well, he mused for a moment. Then he saw the worry on her face. He hurried to join her, grabbing both her hands in his own. She sounded winded as if she had run down to greet him.

"Are you alright?" she asked.

Maybe she had read all the emotions intended for her. Perhaps she finally understood how much Marek's heart ached for her.

He pulled her into a long embrace, feeling the shape of her pressed against him. It filled him with a different kind of heat, no longer a fire but a slow smolder. He didn't pay any attention to the applause still surrounding him or the crowd milling about at the bottom of the stage. Instead, he had eyes and ears and lips for only her. He pulled back from her momentarily, looking into her face to see tears cascading down her cheeks.

"Olive? What's wrong?"

"I had no idea," she said. "I don't know why I do now. There was something about what you just played. It reached out to me."

He pulled the pocket square from his jacket and wiped her eyes with it. She was in earnest. His magick had worked. He shushed her and pulled her in for another hug. He understood that he had only wounded her again in another way. They found a table at the back of the club for some privacy, but on their walk back, a dozen hands reached out to Marek, well-wishers congratulating him, some asking when he would perform again. He brushed them aside, seeing Olive with tears streaming down her face. She seemed inconsolable, and while the audience's appreciation was excellent, it was not his primary concern.

Finally, they were alone, or at least as alone as they could be in such a place. They sat across from one another at the table, but Marek reached for her hands across the tabletop.

"I'm sorry I didn't understand," she said. "I think now..." she gulped loudly. "I think I get it now."

Marek wanted to confirm that the spell had succeeded but didn't want to burden her more by meditating on it. He tried to move forward and pretend nothing had gone awry with their relationship, but it was clear that wouldn't be possible.

"Olive, I need to tell you something," he said. "I want to be completely honest with you."

She looked at him with wet eyes.

Oh, God. What if she got more upset? If she felt manipulated? He didn't want to hurt her anymore. He tried to dry her tears and move on with their lives. He decided he wouldn't lie to her but might withhold the truth.

"I never wanted to hurt you," he said. That was the closest he could get right now. Maybe later, years later, when they were old and gray, Marek could tell Olive about how he dabbled with magick that night and won her back with a spell.

"I know," she said, nearly sobbing. "I know that now."

Nyx started to approach their table, but Marek waved her away.

He didn't need her meddling right now. He'd explain later. Maybe not everything, but he'd explain.

"I'm so sorry, Marek," Olive continued. "I shouldn't have pushed you away."

"You don't need to apologize. I shouldn't have put you in that situation. We never should have been there. I wouldn't have acted that way if I had been sober."

He expected pushback. Marek almost wanted Olive to harbor anger toward him because he still hadn't forgiven himself, but she was like putty now, soft, pliable. Almost too pliable. He hoped that the after-effects of the spell were only temporary, not a permanent change in her disposition. That was part of what had made her attractive in the first place, her defiance of him.

"No, Marek," she said. "This is all my fault. I was just uncomfortable, was all. I shouldn't have implied that you raped me."

Again, Marek wondered if this was her speaking. He worried just how strong of a hold the spell had taken. Marek was grateful for her submission but also concerned it wasn't genuine. As she leaned over to kiss him, he felt himself slowly shrinking, disappearing into himself. He wasn't the powerful wizard in this situation, but rather the bewildered rabbit king, trapped by the power of magick.

18

The World

Madame Rosivda turned the card, revealing a naked woman as round as a planet sitting on top of the Earth. Yellow clouds surrounded her, and the pale visages of four other women looked down upon her. They looked down in adoration because she was the center of her world and the entire universe. It was The World.

"There once was a goddess who was complete in herself," said Madame Rosivda. "She needed no person, nothing to support her. Even naked, she was comfortable in her skin. She did not demand worship but created only to have more to love. She had so much love to give.

"So she made worlds warm and comfortable, places where creatures could live in peace and harmony. There was no conflict between them. She had seen what the male god had done, how he punished those who did not mindlessly believe in him, so she shunned his ways and created her own instead. Even though he was rough and coarse at times, she loved even him, even if he did not understand her constant need for touch and affection.

"Her creations did not require the violence and cruelty of reproduction because once created, they never died but lived eternally like gods. When she made humans, all of them were women. They were each perfect in their own way, yet they were unique and varied in their

176

incredible beauty. From the four corners of the world, they offered her devotion."

This story had entranced Marek for a moment. A world filled with women sounded so peaceful, so wonderful. He imagined he'd like to visit but would most likely not be welcome.

Olive finally seemed to be returning to herself, but in the initial days after his performance, she broke in a way he couldn't understand. She was being so incredibly soft and pliant. He had taken extra care not to take advantage then, to let her regain her strength.

"You're quiet this morning," said Madame Rosivda. "What's on your mind?"

"That story was beautiful," he said.

"Thank you. The World is a bit different than other cards recently drawn. Much less conflict."

Marek nodded. That was the case. He could use more calm at the moment. He wasn't quite sure what to do with Olive, but he also missed his friends. He hadn't spoken to Nyx since that night and hadn't seen Abaddon even longer. He had focused on the concert, and now that it was over and he seemed to have won Olive back, he wasn't sure what to focus on. Maybe it was time for a brief rest to reflect on all he had accomplished.

* * *

On the walk home, however, he received a call. It was a number he didn't recognize.

"Is this Marek Dabrowski?" asked the caller. It was a woman's voice.

"Yes, can I ask who's calling?" He would return formality with formality. He was already regretting answering the phone.

"It is so great to hear your voice, Marek. My name is Lizzie Mae. I'm a talent agent here in Horizon Heights. One of my boys heard you play and said I must sign you immediately."

"Really?"

"No doubt," she said. "Are you available to meet this afternoon over a coffee?"

They made arrangements, and he dialed up Nyx as soon as the call ended. She put him on speakerphone so Abaddon could listen in.

"I might have a talent agent to represent me soon," said Marek.

"That's great, man," said Abaddon. It was so good to hear his voice. It had been too long.

"I might be jumping the gun, but I'd love to have you both for lunch. We can even go to the High Note if you want."

While Abaddon jumped to agree, Nyx sounded less enthusiastic. "I'm not sure that's the best idea," she said.

"Oh, come on, Auntie," said Abaddon. "We're celebrating. I can have one smoke."

"I suppose," she said. "When should we be there?"

"Noon works for me if it works for you two."

"Sounds like a plan. See you then."

The High Note was one of the few dispensaries that served food alongside their legal weed, and they were killing it. People packed the place most days, especially on the weekend, but they were a bit slower during the week. In the evenings, they occasionally hosted local bands, giving the joint (pun intended) a dual meaning to its name. It was casual and relaxing, and provided outdoor seating on this unseasonably warm day. Marek knew it was a false spring, too early for the sultry weather to be permanent, but he'd embrace it while it lasted.

He arrived before Abaddon and Nyx and began perusing the wide bud varieties available. He considered Sour Diesel, which would boost his energy rather than make him sleepy. Before meeting with Lizzie Mae, he didn't mind smoking but didn't want to get stoned. Maybe he'd wait for Abaddon's recommendation when he arrived.

What felt like just moments later, his absent friend's arms were around him. They held the embrace longer than usual, slapping each other's backs several times.

"I've missed you, man," said Abaddon. "Sorry, I haven't been out much."

Marek shrugged. "It's understandable, given the circumstances."

"Still, you're a rising star, and I haven't been around for it. Nyx tells me great things."

Nyx winked at Marek from the door.

"Now, what have we got here?" Abaddon peered into the glass display case, perusing the different strains. "Something else I haven't done in too long."

"Just don't overdo it," said Nyx. "You don't have a tolerance built up right now."

"True." Abaddon grinned back at Marek before purchasing his selection.

Marek momentarily debated if he wanted some, then decided it couldn't hurt. He went for the Sour Diesel while Abaddon picked up some Purple Haze. Nyx declined the opportunity, claiming it tired her and she still had an upcoming waitressing shift.

The food, on the other hand, was a stoner's fantasy. They had every unhealthy, cheesy, salty, crunchy thing with every sweet thing for dessert. Marek ordered the grilled cheese with bacon, potato chips, and onion rings all piled on the sandwich, Abaddon opted for birria tacos, and Nyx picked up a nacho plate with all the fixings. They would undoubtedly return for theatre-style candy or ice cream for dessert. Marek might regret all the dairy because sometimes his stomach was sensitive, but he'd survive.

They sat under an umbrella, and Abaddon produced a bowl to smoke. Marek had requested a few rolling papers and crafted himself a thin joint. It was so small that Abaddon mocked him.

"What?" asked Marek, defensive. "I told you I've still got to meet up with this Lizzie Mae chick."

"Wait -" interrupted Nyx. "Did you say Lizzie Mae?"

"Yeah." Marek lit his joint and took a quick puff. "You heard of her before?"

"You haven't?"

"Damn, Marek," said Abaddon, who had stopped packing his bowl. "Anybody who is anybody works with Lizzie Mae. She's big league.

She'll get you into all the best clubs. One of my buddies used to work with her."

"Yeah?" Marek took another drag on the joint. "Tell me about her, then."

"She's some kinda gorgeous," said Abaddon.

"I thought you weren't into the ladies?"

"I'm not. But damn, I can respect some beauty, and that bitch glows." Nyx nodded in agreement.

"Great." Marek pinched off the end of his joint, the smoke swirling and dissipating around him. "I probably shouldn't smoke this then."

"Oh, she's cool," said Abaddon. "She wouldn't care."

"Still," said Marek. "If she's the real deal, I probably shouldn't reek of weed." He glanced down at his ragged jeans. "I probably should treat this like an interview."

Nyx had returned to eating her nachos, nearly spilling some of the cheese on her shirt as it dribbled off the edge of her chip. She leaned in to catch it with her mouth, then wiped her face with a napkin. "Well, what did she say when she called?"

"That someone had told her to come to check me out after hearing me play."

"I didn't get to tell you," Nyx said. "But you were fantastic, by the way. Are you and Olive back together? What was happening between you two that night? She looked pretty upset."

Abaddon leaned in to hear the answer, blowing smoke in Marek's face. They both coughed, then laughed heartily.

"Easy, you two," said Marek. "I'm done breaking hearts." He paused. "I think we're back together."

"You think?" asked Nyx.

"It's a little tenuous, but she doesn't seem to be raving mad at me anymore."

"What did I tell you? You just needed time."

"Maybe," said Marek. He wanted to tell them but wasn't sure if they would be receptive if he told them what happened, that he had won her back by conjuring a musical kind of magick.

Instead, the three friends enjoyed their smoke and snacks, graduating from catching up to making plans. Abaddon promised to start busking again to get some more sunlight on his skin after spending most of the winter cooped up in the bedroom he had claimed at Nyx's place. He had let the lease run out on his place, so he'd be staying longer than originally planned. Nyx suggested he might want to pick up something more regular, like a bartending gig, and he admitted that warranted consideration, at least. Marek's future was still a bit more fluid. If the meeting with Lizzie Mae went well, he'd be much more busy playing various gigs, and obviously, with Olive no longer mad at him they'd be spending much more time together as well.

"We should plan to meet again for the open jam," Nyx proposed. "Looks like I won't be working Thursday nights for a while. Ronnie is training someone new and wants me on the busier shifts."

"I would like that," said Marek. "We all get so busy, and it's hard to plan just to hang out."

"You get busy," said Abaddon. "I don't do shit."

"Well, you should get active again. Maybe we can put together a few songs."

"Nyx mentioned that you're a composer now." Abaddon cleaned his bowl, scraping the back tar from the glass with a bent wire. He tapped it against the table and then dumped what remained onto a napkin. "I'm sorry I slept through your event, man. That wasn't very cool of me."

"I'll forgive you," said Marek. "Just don't do it again."

"Or what?"

Marek grinned, remembering the violence he nearly visited upon Ronnie the other night. Abaddon hadn't seen that side of him yet, but he also had no intentions of sparring with his friend. Abaddon undoubtedly had more experience scrapping, even if it was playful.

Marek's phone vibrated with a text message, and he pulled it from his pocket. It was Lizzie Mae asking if they could meet earlier. He paused, then, feeling a rush of confidence, texted her back. She agreed to meet them at the High Note. Marek didn't bother telling his friends. He thought, "Let it be a surprise, " he tried to take a few deep breaths before she arrived. He might not have smoked much, but being in the hazy space gave him a contact high.

The three friends were downing ice cream sundaes when a large black woman approached, wearing a tight yellow sundress and looking for all the world like the sun itself. Her walk was nothing less than a strut, her hips swaying with each step, her smile spreading like a gift she bestowed on her adoring public. She came upon them and, quickly assessing the situation, decided to make the best of it.

"You're throwing a party for me already?" she asked. "I know I'm fabulous, but you hardly know me, dear." Her voice sounded smooth and buttery, like supple leather worn to the level of comfort. Although most of her accent had faded with years in the city, she still maintained a hint of a southern drawl. She flicked her hair over her shoulder as she waited for a response.

Marek stood to greet her, wondering if a handshake was appropriate. He almost felt like he should bow down to her. Her dramatic presence elicited a surprising response. Abaddon and Nyx sat frozen, wide-eyed, in their chairs. Before he could hesitate any longer, Lizzie Mae pulled Marek into a big bear hug. It was short-lived but warm and welcoming.

She looked around then, realizing there was no chair for her. "Maybe I was wrong?" she asked. "Where is my throne?"

Marek hurried to pull another chair up for her and find a cushion for it as well. They were wrought iron patio furniture but could be slightly more comfortable with the extra padding. She settled herself and then demanded introductions. "Tell me, who are your friends, and where is my drink?"

"This is Abaddon and Nyx." They each nodded in turn. "And what would you like to drink?"

"Oh, honey," she laughed. "You don't need to serve me. Just grab a waitress or something." It was more of a self-serve restaurant, but after glancing at a paper menu, Nyx offered to grab her a strawberry lemonade.

Once she had settled in, Lizzie Mae began her spiel. "So, Marek, one of my boys told me you were up-and-coming. What kind of places have you played in the past?"

"The Royal Club," Marek said. "I used to play at The Den."

"That's a hotel, right?"

"Yes," said Marek.

"The bad old days," said Abaddon.

Marek shot him a glare.

"What? You hated it there." Abaddon leaned in to touch Lizzie Mae's arm lightly. "He hated it there."

Lizzie Mae smiled, not acknowledging Abaddon's touch. She had shifted into business mode, like Barbie dressed for whatever number of professions suitable for a woman. However, it still felt like a costume she wore only momentarily.

Nyx returned with the lemonade, and Lizzie Mae accepted it gratefully.

"How's about this," said Lizzie Mae. She sipped at her drink, pursing her lips around the straw to not ruin her deep purple lipstick. "I'll take you on for a trial run. Get you set up with a few shows, mostly openers, to start, and see how it goes."

Marek hesitated. "I've never had an agent before," he admitted. "How does this arrangement work?"

Abaddon sighed loudly, almost obnoxiously. Marek thought maybe having his friends around wasn't the best idea.

Thankfully, Lizzie Mae ignored the peanut gallery and continued without missing a beat. "I do the legwork. Book you for the shows, select suitable venues, and make all the arrangements. You just play the music."

"And what do you get out of it?"

"A small cut," she said. "I'd love to do this out of the kindness of my heart, hun, but a girl's gotta make money."

"How many other clients do you have?" asked Nyx. "Will you be making Marek a priority?"

Lizzie Mae glanced in Nyx's direction as she slurped down more of her drink. "It depends," she said. "I prioritize my most successful clients, but from what I've heard, he's a rare talent. We can start this right now, sign a contract, and get going. The more money you make for me, the more I'll make for you. It's a reciprocal arrangement."

"Sounds fair," said Nyx.

"What do you think, dear?" asked Lizzie Mae, turning back to Marek, who felt a bit like he was still in a haze but wasn't sure if it was from the weed or the prospect of having regular gigs.

"Who would I be opening for?" he asked.

"Anybody and everybody," she said. "Don't worry, and I won't try to cross genres. For example, you would do better opening for a jazz trio than a local punk band. I'm not an idiot."

"Where do I sign?"

Lizzie Mae bestowed a smile on him. Olive may have his heart, but he could also worship at this goddess' altar.

19

Temperance

Madame Rosivda turned the card, revealing a dark-skinned angel with red wings opened to a pale pink sky. He stood amid a field of wildflowers, wearing a loose toga belted at the waist. He wore gold cuffs on his wrists and slowly poured water from one cup to the next as his shaggy hair blew from his face. It was Temperance.

"There once was an angel," she began, "Who practiced balance in all things. He had many followers who listened to his wisdom. Unlike many of his brethren, he did not practice austerity or deprive himself of life's pleasures. Instead, he lived a careful balance between deprivation and hedonism, not leaning too far in either direction. Because of this, he gathered quite a congregation and preached a much more sustainable life to them than some of the stricter religions required.

"Yet, he was an angel, and the gods looked down on him with disdain because people had begun to worship him. He would gather with his followers in the wild prairie fields, surrounded by flowers. Rather than drinking wine, they shared water there, poured from one pitcher into many glasses, and listened carefully to the wind."

"So many people demand worship," said Marek. It sounded like something an oracle would say or a fortune cookie.

"And you, Marek?" Madame Rosivda asked. "What do you demand?"

Marek wouldn't mind adulations, praise, and applause, standing ovations. The embrace of an adoring audience was something he always appreciated, but in the past, it had felt automatic, as mechanical and heartless as his playing. Now, Marek felt so much more connected to the people he played for, and now that he was learning to incorporate magick into the mix, he felt so much more effective.

The next night, Olive sang at the Royal Club, and Marek opened for a string quartet of women called the String 'Em Alongs. According to the posters, each of them was gorgeous in her way, and, of course, they all played – viola, violin, cello, and bass. Marek quickly realized that he'd be at the mercy of the venue to provide his instrument, and each piano felt slightly different. He tried to get there early to test the keys, get a little liquid courage into him, and plan his intentions.

He had seen Solomon, but only briefly. The alchemist wasn't surprised Marek hadn't sought him out. "Things must have gone well," he mused. "No one says anything unless there's a problem. Did you get your girl back?"

"You could say that."

Solomon nudged him, winking. "Good, good. What's next?"

"I'm working with a talent agent."

"Great. So you don't even need me."

"Nobody needs you," Kevin chimed in, always full of snark.

"Don't forget who feeds and houses you, so you don't have to live in the wild," Solomon responded.

"I'm sure I'll need you," added Marek.

"That's a kind sentiment, but I know how it is. Just let me know your progress, maybe where you're playing. I'd love to hear you some time," said Solomon.

Of course, Marek hadn't kept up his end of the promise, but whenever he rehearsed, he thought of how to use magickal music to manipulate those around him. It could be advantageous if he wanted to gather more of a following. Look how far it had gotten him already. And now that he wasn't trying to focus that attention on one individual in such a direct way, it didn't cause him nearly as much pain. Instead, what had felt like an intense burning now felt like a gentle warmth, and the shadow hands were barely noticeable, just a whisper against his skin rather than a force pushing against him, pulling his movements as if he were a marionette.

The viola player from the quartet approached him with a broad smile when they broke in the middle of their set, but he barely noticed her. His thoughts had wandered elsewhere, his eyes landing on a tall, muscular man who had been eying him at the bar. Marek approached with trepidation. He didn't want the man to get the wrong intent but wanted to know what he wanted.

"Can I help you?" Marek asked.

The man looked up and tapped his drink on the bar, alerting the bartender that he needed a refill. "What are you drinking?" he asked Marek. "I saw you play, and you were magnificent. Let me buy you a drink."

Marek accepted and took the stool next to his new companion. The man offered his hand in greeting. "I'm Zads, by the way. I don't think I've seen you play before. Are you new to town or just visiting?"

Marek tried not to let out an exasperated sigh. He had lived in Horizon Heights for his entire adult life but had never made a name for himself as a musician, at least not yet. "I used to play at The Den. Lobby pianist, a real high-profile gig."

Zads picked up on the sarcasm. "Well, we've all got to start somewhere, right?"

Marek nodded, taking the first tentative sip of his whiskey. It was much better quality than what he usually bought for himself. Marek gave Zads a once over, noticing the man's impeccably tailored suit and stylish Oxfords. Was he, like Abaddon, a friend of Dorothy's? If so, he better squelch any notions before they developed.

"I also had a low-key show at The Royal Club last week. My girlfriend would be in the audience tonight, but she's working there tonight."

Zads didn't miss a beat. "Waitress?"

"Singer."

"Nice. A musical power couple, I'm sure." Zads waggled his eyebrows.

"Not quite," said Marek. "Do you play?"

"Me?" Zads pointed at himself and shook his head vigorously. "No, I just listen. I write for the entertainment column at The Peak. Trying to scout out some new talent to glom onto."

"Glom onto?"

"Who knows, if I find the next new thing, I might get to follow them, or him, on tour."

"I'm just an opener," said Marek.

"Don't limit yourself. You have played a few shows, so you're not a rookie. Have you got yourself an agent yet?"

As if on cue, Lizzie Mae approached them then. She wore a wide-brimmed black hat and rhinestone sunglasses. Marek wondered how Lizzie Mae could see anything in the dim light, but she looked fabulous. "What's kicking, kitten?" she asked. "Introduce me to your little friend."

Marek looked from one to the other and then stumbled over their names. "Lizzie Mae...um...this is my new friend Zack."

"Zads," the man corrected him. "Short for Zadkiel."

Lizzie Mae held out her hand, and Zads kissed it, sending her into a girlish giggle. "That's quite a moniker," she said.

"Took me ages to spell it when I was a kid," said Zads.

"Did you get to hear my boy play?" Lizzie Mae asked. "He's gonna be a big hit."

Zads raised his glass in a toast, and Marek raised his in unison. "I think he already is."

A few drinks in, Zads invited Marek outside for a cigarette. They stood together under the streetlamps, looking out into the town lit up for the night. Horizon Heights seemed to come alive after dark as if the entire city slept through the day just to venture out as soon as the sun went down.

"Do you have many friends, Marek? I'm surprised you don't have your groupies yet," said Zads. He passed his cigarette to Marek.

Marek laughed. "Imagine that. Groupies. Again, my girlfriend is busy, and I don't think she'd be a big fan of that." He took a quick puff and then passed the cigarette back. It was an intimate thing. Sharing a cigarette reminded him painfully of Abaddon. Despite seeing him earlier that day, Marek missed going out with his friend.

"Just friends then. What do you do when you're not working?" asked Zads. He gratefully accepted the cigarette back.

"Is this on the record?" Marek asked. "An interview, perhaps?"
"No, nothing like that. I'm not new to town, but a friend recently moved away. I was wondering if you'd like to hang out sometime."

Marek considered for a moment, but an entertainment writer in his pocket wouldn't be wrong. "I've got friends," he said. "But they just don't come out very often."

"That's a shame," said Zads.

"It is."

"You got a phone?"

"Sure." Marek fished it out of his back pocket, fumbled to unlock it, and then handed it to Zads, letting him enter his number into the contacts.

"Give me a call sometime," said Zads. "Just not before noon."

Zads passed the phone back, his hand brushing against Marek's. After Marek put it away, Zads handed him the remainder of the cigarette they had been sharing.

"I'm going back in," said Zads. "You can have the rest of that." He disappeared back into the bar.

Marek paused to taste the last few draws on the cigarette. It had an earthy tobacco flavor, but mostly it was just ash. Smoke curled around his fingers as he exhaled and looked up to where the stars would be if there wasn't so much light pollution from the city or clouds heavy with imminent rain. He could use another friend.

The Four of Wands

Madame Rosivda turned the card, revealing a brilliant dawn with a yellow sun climbing from the horizon. A castle rose in the far distance. In the foreground, two delicate fairies floated, their pink dresses looking for all the world like flower petals. They wore small blooms in their long tresses and carried a giant flower between them. One of them closed her eyes, meditating. Immediately behind them stood four star-topped wands reaching up to the sky. It was the Four of Wands.

"There once was a kingdom," said Madame Rosivda, "protected by fairies. Years ago, unbeknownst to the royalty, a member of their ancestry had performed a great deed, freeing the fairies from the imprisonment of a sorcerer. For that grace, the fairies had agreed to protect their family. However, they did so at a distance. If they revealed themselves, they feared they would be misunderstood and destroyed. Instead, they worked secretly, casting minor spells and performing rituals to protect the kingdom from outside harm.

"Two young fairies, maidens, did their work with flowers, choosing when and where they would bloom. The fragrant pollen of these blooms warded away those with ill intentions. Throughout the spring and summer, they protected the kingdom, but when the snow fell, they would need to resort to another form of magic.

"For the time being, though, they were at peace and could close their eyes, even sleep while floating lazily among the flowers. The pink dresses they wore easily camouflage them, and only if you looked closely could a human discern what they were looking at: fairies rather than flowers, a magickal beauty few behold."

"Are there such things as fairies?" Marek asked, briefly remembering the butterfly he had seen a few weeks ago, which looked oddly human.

"You tell me," said Madame Rosivda. She gave him a sly look, challenging him.

"You're more well-versed at this stuff than I am."

"Of course, I am, Marek. But you're the one going on a journey. I'm not going anywhere. I've already found my place, my role in this life. Have you found yours yet?"

Marek thought for a moment, contemplating. "I think so," he said eventually.

"You're young yet," she said.

Once again, Marek found himself wondering just how old she was but knew it was an impolite question to ask a woman. Instead, he chose another question. "Does Olive still come to visit you?"

"Sometimes," said Madame Rosivda. "She doesn't come as regularly as you do."

"What kind of questions does she ask? Does she talk about me?"

"This may not be a lawyer's office or a confessional, but I believe in protecting the privacy of my clients."

"You can't even give me a hint?"

"Why don't you ask her?"

Marek still hadn't mastered the art of communicating, especially not with Olive. Sometimes he still thought of her as an unachievable dream, even when she fell asleep in his arms. It felt so surreal sometimes as if she wasn't real. He could see, touch, and feel her, but despite their connection, she sometimes seemed so far away. He never knew what she was thinking.

As agreed upon, Abaddon and Nyx arrived for the Thursday night Open Jam. Abaddon wasn't even late because he had come with Nyx. Marek welcomed them with big bear hugs as soon as they walked in.

"Hey, man," said Abaddon. "Let up a little. It's not like I've arisen from the dead."

"Feels like it, though," said Marek.

They settled in at a small table near the stage. A warmth rose in Marek's chest as he watched Olive finish readying the scene, setting up microphones, and testing the sound with Ronnie. *That's my girl,* he thought. *She's mine now, not just a distant beauty.*

Noticing his gaze, Nyx asked, "How are you and Olive doing? I don't see you together often."

"We've both been pretty busy, but we still make time for each other," said Marek.

"You mean you've been pretty busy," said Abaddon.

Marek considered this observation. He had been busy. Lizzie Mae had slowly moved him from opening for other musicians to making him the headliner. The number of his fans had begun to grow, and there were a few regulars he began to recognize. Zads came out for most of them on the pretense that he was writing it up for The Peak, but Marek knew a friendship was growing there as well. He still hadn't introduced the reviewer to his other friends, but he knew it would likely happen at some point and that Zads would become a regular in the group. It was only a matter of time.

"Are you both playing tonight?" Marek asked, changing the subject. "Please tell me you're both playing." He glanced around for instrument cases then but didn't see them.

"Don't worry," said Nyx. "We brought our instruments. They're hiding backstage, though."

"Why's that?" asked Marek.

"Not sure if we're going to play them."

"Well, why not?" Marek leaned forward, resting his arms against the table. He reached out to catch one hand from each of his friends as if in shared prayer. "I need your support," he said.

"You don't need shit from us," said Abaddon, "And you know it. I'm not sure what kind of magic you've been using, but you are doing well, my friend. Just fine, it looks like."

Marek looked into Abaddon's face, searching for any suspicion of the spells he had been casting. It was just an expression, he reasoned. Abaddon didn't know anything. How could he when Marek hadn't told them? Then he wondered if and when he would ever tell them. Was this a secret he needed to keep?

Then the evening began with a welcome from Ronnie and a song from Olive. It had been a while since he had heard her sing. Her voice, so low and husky, always made him feel a certain way, shivers running up and down his spine. The little hairs on his forearms rose, forming goosebumps on the surface of his skin. He wondered, not for the first time if she wielded her own form of magic, but now that supposition came with greater understanding. Did she use magic intentionally, as he did? Could he share his secret with her without any strange looks or judgment?

After the song, Olive approached their table, casually reaching for Marek's whiskey and taking a swig. She grimaced after the swallow.

"Maybe that wasn't the best idea," she said. "I just needed something to wet my mouth."

Marek wrapped his arms around her waist. "You sounded amazing, as always."

She smiled shyly, leaning into his embrace. The others offered their compliments in turn. Then, Marek noticed her necklace, a pale pink stone wrapped in a silver wire attached somewhat haphazardly to a thin silver chain. He grasped the rock and pulled it up to get a better look.

"Is this new?" he asked.

"The necklace, yes. The stone, no," Olive said. "Do you remember the day we first found Herb & Altar? I got it then. Rose quartz. I just had a friend of mine make it into a necklace."

"I remember," he said. Jasper had also told him what rose quartz was commonly used for love spells. After all this time, was she still trying to attract him? Olive had claimed him the first time he heard her sing, maybe not on day one, but very close to it. What need did she have for more love spells?

Eventually, both Abaddon and Nyx agreed to play on stage. They were each a little rusty but played older pieces that were already familiar to them. Marek accompanied a few singers and other musicians, like in the old days, but admittedly he had gotten so used to playing solo that it was difficult to dull his shine enough for others to play over him. He actively tried not to use his magick, but it flowed from his fingers unintentionally. Soon he was swarmed with those who had heard him play, offering their compliments and asking where his next show would be. He felt a bit crowded but was starting to get used to all the attention. Like everything, it would come with time; eventually, he'd be willing to acknowledge his prowess. He wondered if it was his playing or the magick associated with it that caught people's attention.

By the end of the evening, the group of friends decided they would improvise a few songs together, Marek on piano, Nyx on flute, Abaddon on trumpet, and Olive singing. This time, Marek didn't bother trying to hold back. He played with an intensity that was new to him. He felt the heat rising in his hands and arms, climbing into his chest. It was a welcome heat, rather than a painful burn like the warmth one feels upon stepping inside from a snowstorm, drinking an Irish coffee with good whiskey. The shadow hands grew heavier, pressing his fingers down onto the keys with a ponderous weight. Despite this, he moved quickly, dragging the second set of hands. He set his intentions and played with an intensity that made him forget he was playing with other musicians – in his mind, it was just him, spotlighted on the stage, and the others faded, even Olive's sultry notes tugging at the edges of his heart.

As they finished the last song of their set, Olive came running to him, nearly throwing herself into his lap. He smiled, uncertain of this sudden affection but grateful for it. She almost smothered him with kisses and noticed a small strip of blue painter's tape peeking from the bottom of the piano's frame. Then he remembered the black-and-white paper bearing her visage, the remnants of the spell he had cast upon her.

Was all of the careless adoration she showed for him even real? Or had he unintentionally conjured it? He would need to remove that picture from the piano when no one was looking. While he appreciated the attention, he wanted it to be genuine, not something manufactured.

Ronnie approached the stage then, tossing half-wilted roses at their feet.

"What's this all about?" asked Abaddon, kicking them away in annoyance.

"Some old lady was trying to sell them at the door," said Ronnie. "I told her we had a no soliciting policy, but she looked so pathetic, I bought the whole lot."

Marek glanced down at the dying flowers and remembered the kingdom protected by fairies. He would give anything for some protection. He distrusted how good everything felt right now. Something was bound to go wrong soon.

2 1

The Page of Coins

Madame Rosivda turned the card, revealing a lush garden sur-rounded by an early evening sky. Standing in the garden was a young woman wearing a golden gown with layer upon layer of fringed fabric. She carefully examined a coin, considering the image on its face. It was the Page of Coins.

"There once was a poor woman with the most beautiful voice," said Madame Rosivda. "One of the King's men had heard her singing to her-self in the market as she worked at a vegetable stall. Her voice sent such a thrill through him that he offered to buy her entire stock of tomatoes if she would agree to follow him back to the castle. The woman was wary because she had never received such a gift, and the man's offer sounded too good to be true. She told him no, but gladly sold him a few tomatoes.

"The next day, the man returned. He told her she could sing like the angels and that the king would love to hear her. She explained that she did not have suitable clothing before the king, and he offered to buy her a new dress. She explained that she could not leave her family behind, and the man offered to bring them in a royal carriage. She said she could not accept such an offer.

"The next day, the king arrived, demanding she perform in his great hall, and she could no longer refuse. They provided her and her family with new clothing and escorted them to the castle. She could not believe her good fortune and feared it was a trick, so she sewed a few coins into the underside of her dress just in case before they left. If this was a trap, she might be able to escape and be prepared to make her way.

"Despite her worries, the trip went splendidly with no unexpected betrayal. She sang before the entire court in the king's great hall and received a warm welcome. She and her family feasted heartily on an elaborate spread of wild game and fresh bread, washing everything down with a sweet mead.

"As the sun disappeared over the horizon and dark came on, she broke away from the feast and wandered into the gardens. She pulled a single coin from the stash she had sewn into her dress and carefully examined it. It bore the king's likeness, and the resemblance was uncannily accurate. As she looked closely, the visage winked at her. Here, she could find success, earn the money to support her family, and make a new life for herself."

* * *

Olive invited Marek to join her at the amateur's circle at Herb & Altar. Although he had been using magick to enhance his performances, the other, more common kind felt ineffective. The candle spell Madame Rosivda had given him hadn't worked how he expected. It didn't seem nearly as effective as the music-based magic he now wielded. He agreed because she wanted to do it, and relationships were about compromises. Marek also knew Solomon would likely be there, and he had a few questions.

The evening began with calling the protection of the four directions and a brief meditation. Jasper led the call, his deep voice resonating with an ancient gong he rang to start the circle. Marek sat cross-legged on the floor with the others but struggled to focus. All he could think about was his next gig, the song he was trying to write, the melody running through the back of his mind. As he struggled to meditate, an intrusive thought, no, not even a thought, a voice entered his con-sciousness.

"What is it you most desire?" the voice asked. It was deep but not the same calm intonation of Jasper's voice.

Marek tried to push it down, deeper into his subconscious. It was just his thoughts materializing, he assumed. It couldn't be someone else talking to him.

"Everyone has desires," said the voice, more insistent this time. "There is no crime in embracing them."

Marek glanced around to see everyone else relaxed, their eyes closed, focusing on their breathing. The voice sounded so loud he wondered that only he could hear it. Where was it coming from? He closed his eyes, took a deep breath, and tried to relax.

"Life is not worth living if you are not striving for something," said the voice.

Marek tried to brush it aside. Who was doing this, sending these messages?

"You could be so much more, Marek."

He tried to think back at the voice without speaking aloud and found it challenging. He wanted to shout at it, to scream. He was happy with his life. He had enough. He had Olive. He had his music and was finally making good money at it. He had everything he needed. There was nothing else he wanted.

"Don't lie to yourself," the voice said. "You are hungry. You want more."

Marek looked around again, searching for someone who wasn't meditating. Olive opened her eyes momentarily and reached out to him, grasping his hand and smiling softly. She mouthed the words, "I love you."

He uncrossed his legs and began to stand up. He whispered down to Olive, "I'll be right back." She nodded and returned to a restful state.

When Marek snuck out the door, he realized he had been holding his breath. He took a few quick gasps and tried to regulate the air flowing in and out of his lungs. What was happening to him? Was he hearing voices now?

"Looks like he got your attention," said a voice above him.

Marek glanced up into the overhang to see Kevin perched there, staring down at him.

"Is Solomon here?" Marek asked, then wondered if the alchemist's mind-reading prowess extended to sending telepathic messages.

"He will be," said Kevin. "Flying is a much faster mode of travel." He stretched his wings, spreading one and the other to its full length, then glided down to land on a lower ledge jutting from a front window.

"How did he put his thoughts in my head?" asked Marek.

"The same way he does anything," said Kevin, then paused dramatically. "With magick!" He cackled at himself, sounding more like a bird than a human.

Marek sighed loudly. He hated all this mystery, all these tricks. "Why can't Solomon talk to me outright like a normal human?"

Just then, a shadow fell across the sidewalk at Marek's feet. He felt a heavy presence behind him. "What would be the fun in that?" asked Solomon.

Marek turned toward the alchemist, looking for all the world like a superhero villain with his long trench coat and black, flat-brimmed hat. "What do you want from me?" Marek asked.

"Why do you think I want something? Can't I just drop in for a friendly chat?"

Marek eyed him suspiciously. "What were you doing in my head?"

"It was just an easier way to communicate, to get your attention. Your lady friend doesn't seem to like me much." Solomon motioned to the witchy supply shop, where the meditation circle had finally broken up. Marek could see Olive cautiously looking around, looking for him to return. She crossed her arms over her chest and stared off into the distance. Immediately, he wanted to go to her to reassure her that everything was fine.

"What do you want from me?" he asked Solomon.

"You act like we're not friends," said Solomon. "Don't you owe at least some of your success to me? Wasn't I the one who helped you tap into your abilities?"

Marek had to admit that this was indeed the case, but he didn't like the idea of being beholden to somebody, especially this creep. "I appreciate your help, but I'm still the one setting myself on fire."

"Woah, woah, buddy," interrupted Kevin. "You do *what* to yourself?"

"Well, not actually," said Marek. "But it feels that way sometimes. It hurts to cast my spells. It requires effort and concentration. It saps something from me. It isn't easy."

"That's because you need to practice." Solomon grinned down at him, not in a friendly way, but in a way that made Marek feel like he was being mocked or made fun of. "I can help you hone your abilities if you'd let me."

"What do you get out of this?"

"Why are you suddenly so defensive?" Solomon asked. "Has she poisoned you against me?"

They both glanced at the window then, watching Olive wander the shop, looking at some of Jasper's new ingredients. Marek wondered what Solomon was thinking. Then the voice invaded his brain again.

"She's gorgeous, isn't she? It would be a shame if something happened to her," it said.

"Will you stop that?" Marek said. "You're right here, right next to me. Just talk to me."

"I wanted to make sure you got the message," said Solomon. "Loud and clear," he added telepathically.

Marek shook his head. "Again, what do you want from me?" he asked. "You must want something."

"Can't I just want to help a friend out? Out of the goodness of my heart?"

Marek glared at the alchemist, challenging him, but although he was defiant, he didn't feel strong. He felt weak, so frail, and tired of this game, the back-and-forth between them. Kevin hopped down onto Marek's shoulder. Marek tried to brush him away, but the crow took a small nibble of his ear before flapping up to the top of Solomon's head.

"Fine. Do you want to meet? Fine, but leave Olive out of it," said Marek.

"That's just it," said Solomon. "I need both of you."

"For what?"

"A ritual. I need both masculine and feminine energy to complete the ceremony, and due to circumstances beyond my control, I no longer have a coven to support me."

"I told you. Leave Olive out of it."

"What if I promised to teach her the same techniques I have taught you? You could be a duo rather than a solo act. What do you think?" Marek considered. It would be wonderful if they could perform together. They'd be able to spend more time together. And her voice - the things she could do with her voice. "I'll have to think about it," he said.

"There's a full moon coming soon, the best time for the ritual. Talk to her about it." Solomon leaned over Marek, fixing him with a stare. He felt immobilized like a statue. "I want you both to be willing participants."

"Or what?" Marek asked. "You'll force us to do it?"

"If you insist," said the voice in his head.

The door opened behind them, and Olive came onto the sidewalk, her face creased with worry. "I was wondering where you were," she said to Marek. "Who's this again?" she asked.

"Solomon," said Marek. "Solomon Dreyfus."

The alchemist bowed low and then kissed the hand Olive offered. "I believe we've met," he said. "But it is always a pleasure, Olive."

Marek watched, feeling helpless as she visibly recoiled from the tall man. Her words did not match the pained look on her face. "Likewise," she said, then turned to Marek. "Were you coming back inside?"

"Yes, you should go," said the voice in Marek's head. "But don't forget. I need an answer soon."

Olive glanced up at the crow on Solomon's head as if she had just noticed Kevin. Marek wondered if the bird would speak. Solomon reached up, allowing Kevin to step onto his hand, then lowered the bird to hip level. He stroked the black feathers as Kevin hopped impatiently from one foot to the other.

"Is he tame?" asked Olive.

"Quite," said Solomon. "Trained as well. Say hello, Kevin."

"Hello, Kevin," said the crow.

Olive laughed, delighted.

"He thinks he has a sense of humor," said Solomon.

"How delightful," said Olive.

You should hear the other things he says, though Marek. *You might not find him so delightful then.* "Well, we should be going," he said aloud.

"Yes. Next time," said Solomon and began walking down the street, Kevin still perched on his hand.

As they returned to the familiar scent of Herb & Altar, Marek wished he had a way to protect Olive, but Solomon insisted on including herl.

"He's an odd man, isn't he?" she asked.

"Who?" Marek's thoughts were elsewhere, wondering what the ritual might entail, trying to determine how he would introduce the idea to her.

"Solomon."

"Oh, yes. Pretty strange."

They were looking over the crystals again, or at least Olive was. "I've always loved obsidian," she mused. "But never had much use for it. It comes from volcanoes, you know."

"Yes," said Marek. "What is it usually used for?"

"Protection. It helps ward off negative energy."

"Why don't you get some, then?" he asked.

"But I don't need it."

Marek picked up the small, black stone, polished to a glossy sheen. "A little extra protection couldn't hurt. I'll buy it for you."

Over the next few days, Marek tried to devise a way to ask Olive about the ritual and encourage her to listen to Solomon's advice. Their meeting at the Herb & Altar seemed to have gone well, or at least as well as could be expected. Marek realized that if he wanted her to work with Solomon, to enhance her abilities, he'd need to tell her about the magick he had been performing as well. Or at least, he'd have to mention it. Otherwise, none of it would make any sense. He decided to invite her over with the promise of dinner so he could demonstrate what he had learned and show her how the magick worked.

He would make pasta, which is relatively straightforward. One thing Marek had never mastered was cooking, but he'd give it an attempt for her. By the time she arrived, he had put the water on to boil and invited her into the living room.

"What is it you wanted to show me?" she asked. She trailed behind Marek like an eager puppy dog. He only hoped what he had to show her warranted her level of excitement.

"I have a piece I'm working on. I just want you to listen."

She settled into a nearby chair, letting her dress settle into the curves and indents of her body. Marek fought the urge to grab and drag her to the bedroom with him. Even after all this time, he couldn't get enough of her. It was like an insatiable hunger. He sat on a stool before the keyboard and turned it on. It hummed to life, several lights illuminating its surface.

He played a few notes. He had been experimenting with incorporating more emotion into his songs, the same way he had reached in to tug at her heartstrings during his Royal Club concert. This one had no sense of loss but a triumphant melody meant to uplift and brighten. She began clapping along to the beat, swaying in her seat and when he finished, a broad smile crossed her face. She laughed with delight and then embraced him as he finished.

"How do you feel?" he asked.

"I can't quite put a word to it," she replied, but her face betrayed her jubilation. "Like a warm summer day, riding in a Corvette with the top down, my hair blowing in the wind."

"So, would you say happy?" he asked.

"More than that. Ecstatic."

"That's a good word. I'll have to remember it."

She beamed at him.

"Would you believe that I did that through magick?"

She stared blankly, not answering, then whispered, "What do you mean?"

"I channel an emotion into the music and then it reaches you, making you feel something."

"Isn't that how all music works?"

Then, he realized communicating this type of magick, even demonstrating it, wouldn't be an easy task. How could he make Olive understand? He tried playing a piece attached to a different emotion, something more solemn and sobering. He looked back at her, and her face had become a mask, pale and unmoving.

"Olive?" he asked. "Are you alright?"

A single tear streaked down her cheek. "That was so...I don't know...moving. But sad, too. It made me feel lonely, even though you're right here with me."

"I did that with magick."

"Yes, the magick of your music."

She was saying the right words, but he could tell she still wasn't quite understanding. He'd have to break it down for her but wasn't sure how. As he tried to simplify the process, he caught the glint of the rose quartz that hung around her neck. She used magick, too, just a different sort.

"Have you ever been part of a coven?" he asked.

"That's a bit out of the blue."

"No, hear me out. Have you?"

She pushed a lock of hair behind her ear. God, she was so gorgeous, he thought. "I consider myself more of a solitary practitioner," she said. "But if we could find one, I would gladly join. I'd like to learn from more experienced witches."

"What kind of spell-casting do you do?"

"Mostly affirmations. The words we say can have a strong effect on the way we think. They can change our realities."

"How does that work?"

"I decide what my intentions are for the day, and I shape those intentions into words I can repeat to myself throughout the day, especially if I struggle. It works. Usually."

He tried to echo her words by explaining the kind of spells he cast. "I decide what my intentions are for each song, how I want my audience to react, what I want them to feel, and then I channel those intentions when I play the song."

"Wait, so like real magick? It's not just mastery of the music?"

"Exactly." He was so excited he could kiss her but needed to ensure she understood.

"What is that like?" she asked.

"For me, it feels like my skin is burning every time I do it, but Solomon said it will improve as I learn to master it."

"Solomon?"

"Yes, he's the one who taught me to harness my magick, and he could teach you, too."

"My magick? Like affirmations that work?" she asked.

Marek kneeled at her feet, taking both her hands and drawing them toward his chest. "More than that," he said. "So much more than that. He could teach you how to use it when you sing."

"When I sing?"

"I think that might be your magick. It works for me, at least. Every time you sing, I get goosebumps, and I don't just mean that figuratively. All the little hairs on my arms stand on end. I get shivers listening to you."

She blushed then, the pink rising in her cheeks. "You're just saying that because I'm your girlfriend."

"I'm not. I think you might be using your magic unintentionally. It affects me like a spell, something I can't control."

"That's because you're in love with me," she said, kissing him.

"I mean, that part's true, but really, Olive, he can teach you. You can find success as I have."

"I have success. I like singing at the club."

"But you could have more."

She glanced around the room as if taking stock of the opportunity. "What's the catch?" she asked. "There's always a catch. I'm still not sure about this guy, Marek. Something about him just makes me uncomfortable. I'm not sure what it is."

"He's harmless," Marek lied. He wanted to heed her warning, but he also wanted to maintain a good relationship with the alchemist. Marek felt he would still be useful, could be a launching pad for both their careers.

"What did he ask for in return?"

"He wants us to help him out with a ritual. Didn't you just say you wanted to join a real coven - to meet with other witches?"

"I did, but where's his coven? I'd rather meet with a group from Herb & Altar."

"He is from Herb & Altar."

"Then why didn't he even come in the other night? Why did he lurk outside like a creep? And who has a crow as a pet?"
"I thought you liked Kevin."

"I can put up a good front. I was being friendly. Who has a crow as a pet and then names it Kevin? That's a human name, not a pet's name."

"I think that depends on who owns the pet. A person can name their pet anything they want."

"That's beside the point."

"Then what's the point?"

Olive glanced behind Marek into the kitchen, pushed him aside, and rushed to the stove. The pot of water was boiling over, overflowing onto the stovetop and sizzling as the water hit the flame.

Marek, coming in behind her, swore and turned off the burner. "Well, it's not ruined, just a mess. How do you feel about takeout?"

A few days later, Marek had a rare night off from his concert series and came to The Royal Club to listen to Olive sing. He sidled up to the bar, waving down Ronnie and ordering his usual. The whiskey glimmered, and a deep amber hue poured over the ice. It was smooth and needed. He rarely got the opportunity to sit and relax anymore.

"It's been a minute since I've seen you," said Ronnie.

"I've been busy." Marek took another swig, trying to decide if he wanted to stay at the bar and chat or find a place to sit in the ballroom.

"Seems like you've gotten too big for us," said Ronnie.

"What do you mean?"

"Come on; you know what I'm getting at." Ronnie smiled and twisted the ends of his waxed mustache into sharp little points.

"I wouldn't say that. I still play here sometimes."

"But this isn't where the money is."

"Ain't that the truth," Marek said. He took another swig of his drink. "Thanks for the libation."

Ronnie winked as Marek walked away. Marek settled down at a small two-person table and glanced at the intimate tea light burning there. After a moment, he let his eyes grow soft and tried to gaze beyond. Marek didn't know what he was expecting, but in his mind's eye, he saw the page of coins again, the young woman with the magnificent voice, and immediately knew that it had to represent Olive. With Solomon's help, she might become as successful as he had, and they could tour together all across the nation, making a life for themselves.

A spotlight appeared on stage, and Olive walked out. She wore a pale gold dress decorated with several layers of fringe. Approaching the microphone, Olive held it gently and began to sing. The song she sang was a blues ballad, heartbroken and melancholy, but the lyrics did not call out to any lover but to the need for money. Marek could make this happen - he could make them successful and wealthy, but he would need Solomon's help.

22

The King of Swords

Madame Rosivda turned the card, revealing a blue and purple night cloaking a dark courtyard garden. Sitting atop a purple branch adorned with pink flowers was a golden crow, illuminated with a golden and red halo. It wore a small crown, marking it as true royalty. On the ground, standing in a darkened doorway, was a small peacock that the crow had outshined. It was the King of Swords.

"There once was a crow," said Madame Rosivda, "that tricked an unsuspecting king. The crow could speak and understand human language and often wished he had a human form to use for his interactions with the world. Barring that, he wanted a power that seemingly couldn't be his own. He was one of an entire murder of crows that could communicate with humans this way, but he was the leader among them. Gradually, through several pecking fights, he ascended to the top ranks and became the king's primary consultant. Little did the king know, but the crows planned to take over the kingdom."

"First, the king crow planted seeds of ideas in the king's head: that he should run a peaceful kingdom and there was no need for a standing military presence, no need for guards or soldiers, and that they would welcome everyone indiscriminately.

"Other crows were dispatched to alter the minds of great leaders.

The head of the church, a haughty bishop who made his desires well known, soon promoted the spiritual abilities of animals, that they should be listened to and worshipped as messengers from God, especially the crows. Soon, many royals, as well as religious zealots, kept talking about crows as pets. The birds lived in a strange luxury and rode upon their master's shoulders.

"The people didn't realize that they were no longer the ones in control. The birds would whisper into their ears suggestions of what they should do, how they should act, and what they should say, and the people listened and followed these orders without question.

"When the king died unexpectedly, the crow, which had acted as his advisor, took the crown. There was no challenge, no question that this was the proper thing to do. After all, the crow was the mouthpiece of God, and they didn't dare anoint a human as the sovereign.

"Looking up at the Crow King, a small peacock shook his head in dismay. He might have taken his place if he had learned to talk and be clever like the crow. Instead, he was only a beautiful bird with no power or influence. The crows now ruled the kingdom."

Marek sipped down the dregs of his tea. "Maybe Kevin is actually in charge," he said to himself.

"Who is Kevin?" asked Madame Rosivda.

"The talking crow."

"So, you finally found him and talked with him?"

"A few times. Do you know him?"

"You seem to think I get out," said Madame Rosivda. "I tend to keep to myself. What do you know about this crow, though?"

"He belongs to an alchemist named Solomon. I mean, he's a familiar. I think he used to be human."

Madame Rosivda steepled her hands in front of her. "Interesting."

"Is that normal?" Marek stopped himself. So many things in his life had happened since he met Madame Rosivda that he wouldn't consider normal. "I mean, for a familiar?"

"Solomon must be a powerful magician," she said. "It takes a certain amount of power to call forth a familiar."

"Have you ever had one?"

"No. I prefer to operate on my own," Madame Rosivda said. She gathered her materials then, carefully storing the cards and the scrying bowl.

"Have you ever been part of a coven?" Marek asked.

"Once," she said. "When I was younger. It was good to connect with other practitioners when I didn't know what I was doing. Are you considering joining one?"

"Not quite, but Solomon wanted us to participate in a ritual in exchange for teaching us."

"Us?"

"Olive and me."

"I see. What kind of ritual?"

Marek hesitated. He wanted confirmation that this was a good idea but also wanted to go forward regardless. Did Madame Rosivda's opinion matter in this decision? He felt he could trust her, but would he change his mind if she warned him against it? He wasn't sure. "He said something about needing masculine and feminine energy."

Madame Rosivda nodded as if this also fell into the realm of ordinary things. "What is the purpose of the ritual?" she asked.

"I don't know."

"I think it might be important to ask that. You should know what you're getting into before agreeing to anything."

"What do you think he meant by harnessing masculine and feminine energy?" he asked.

"It might be sex magic."

Marek tried not to look surprised, but this knowledge shook him momentarily. He and Olive hadn't had sex since the incident at the drug dealer's house. They had done other things, intimate things that could be considered sex, but not intercourse. Olive seemed strangely shy about it, uncomfortable, and he hadn't pushed the issue. She'd let him know when she was ready.

A flood of questions coursed through his thoughts, but he couldn't seem to ask any of them. It would be fine, he tried to reassure himself, and besides, if it came down to it and they didn't want to move forward with the ritual, they could always back out. It was only reasonable, but maybe he should have another talk with Solomon and get some details from him.

The night of the ritual was fast approaching. Although Solomon had answered some of Marek's questions, his responses were cryptic. When asked about the purpose of the ceremony, he said it was for the "perfection of the human spirit." When questioned about masculine and divine energies, he merely replied that the ritual required a "balance of forces." He didn't say anything about sex magick, but why would he? Solomon was a clever man and knew how to set his trap.

Marek also didn't communicate his concerns to Olive, which should have been his first move. Instead, he kept all his worries to himself and played along when she expressed how excited she was to learn from Solomon.

"Tell me again what it feels like to channel magick through your music," she said over breakfast one day.

He didn't want to admit how much it hurt sometimes, but he could tell her the more pleasant bits. "It feels warm," he said. "Like when you come back in from the cold in winter. It starts slowly, gradually, from the tips of my fingers to my core. Sometimes it feels like someone else is sitting with me, guiding my hands. I think of it like a shadow connected to me."

"Do you remember that scene in Peter Pan?" she asked.

Marek shook his head, not understanding.

"His shadow could break free from him," she explained. "Wendy had to sew it back on so he wouldn't lose it."

"I feel connected to the shadow," said Marek. But when he thought about it momentarily, he wondered if that was the case. Could it break free from him and take on a will of its own? That would be terrifying, but he was the one who had created it, so that couldn't be the case. Could it?

"Are you ready for the ritual?" he asked, gauging her willingness to continue.

"Of course," she replied. She dug around in her yogurt with her spoon, prying a strawberry free. "Are you?"

"Yes," said Marek, but he wasn't sure. He took a sip of his black coffee. Everything would be fine, he told himself. There is nothing to worry about.

They met Solomon at his house, a large, sprawling estate on the edge of town. Most of the buildings in Horizon Heights stretched vertically toward the sky, so seeing a structure so low to the ground taking up more horizontal space was strange. Marek had only lived in a one or two bedroom apartment, even as a child. He wondered how the alchemist could afford the rambling residence stretched out before them.

Solomon was waiting outside already when they arrived. He wore a black cloak long enough to drag through the dirt, and Kevin rode upon his shoulder. Solomon had abandoned his wide-brimmed hat and instead revealed his bald head. He stepped forward to grasp Marek's hand in both of his as they approached. The cab which had brought them turned around in the semi-circle driveway and headed back to the highway.

"I hope your trip out here wasn't too much of a hassle," said Solomon. He looked to Marek and Olive as he said this, including them both.

"Not at all," said Olive.

As Solomon released his hands, Marek glanced over at Olive. She was smiling and seemed genuine. He knew that sometimes Olive was a people pleaser and said things just to make those around her comfortable, but he had spent enough time with her now that he could usually discern if it were for show or not. She returned Marek's gaze, and he could see in her eyes that she was ready and willing to move forward with their plan.

Spotting the crow, she jokingly added, "Hi, Kevin."

"Hi, Kevin," the crow squawked, mimicking her.

She laughed, but Marek wondered how long they would keep up the ruse that Kevin only parroted people rather than talked.

"Come, come," said Solomon, ushering them inside. "We have a bit of time before the sun sets. We'll be doing the ritual outside in my garden.

If we're lucky, the weather will hold, and we won't get rained on." He placed one hand on Olive's shoulder, guiding her to the front door.

Marek winced. He wasn't sure how he felt about Solomon familiarly touching her but pushed the thought down. It was nothing, he told himself. Everything was going to be okay. He was worrying for no reason.

Once inside, Solomon escorted them to his library, which held college-style bookcases reaching the ceiling. Some books looked ancient, and the titles had worn off the binding. Others were bound in black or brown leather. A small grouping of upholstered chairs sat at the far end, near a fireplace. Kevin flitted from Solomon's shoulder to a sizeable gilded cage hung from the rafters. Solomon motioned for them to sit and then rolled a small cart toward them. It was a tea service with a shining silver pot and several porcelain cups.

He served them, pouring the piping hot water over loose leaves. "Would you like any milk or honey?" he asked. Marek took his plain, but Olive requested honey. They settled into their chairs. The tea was delicious.

"What is this?" asked Marek.

"My proprietary blend," said Solomon. "Do you like it?"

Marek nodded, taking another tentative sip. The water was boiling.

"So, how will this work?" Olive asked. "The ritual, I mean. I'm more than willing to help, but I'd like to know what I'm getting myself into."

It was the same question Marek had been asking, with little feedback from Solomon. He wondered if she'd be able to get a straight answer.

"It's quite simple, really," said Solomon. "I just need you because a solitary practitioner can't perform it. It requires more energy than that."

"Yes," said Olive. "Marek told me you need both masculine and feminine energy. I would imagine that is where I come in."

Solomon nodded and then stood to start pacing across the room. He seemed to be looking for something. Eventually, he reached high on one of the shelves and pulled a book down. "This," he explained, "Describes the balance between the masculine and feminine." He brought the book to Olive, placing it in her lap.

Marek glanced over. The cover was faded and worn. As she turned to the first few pages, he saw diagrams depicting the naked form of a man and a woman. Was this related to sex magick, as Madame Rosivda had predicted?

"Don't worry," Solomon whispered to Marek. "You don't have to do anything you don't want to."

This reassurance sent a chill through Marek. He wasn't sure how to respond, and Solomon continued his speech to Olive without hesitation. "As human beings, we all start as female in the womb," he explained. "Then the testosterone kicks in, and some of us become male. It's simple biology. Some of us are even born intersex or a combination of the two. Despite what some may say, it's not entirely binary, one or the other."

Olive nodded, paging through the text, which Marek realized was more medical than anything else.

"Because of this," Solomon continued. "We each have masculine and feminine energies within us. For some, these energies lean further in one direction or the other, or can even be a fairly even balance."

Why was he focusing this on Olive? Marek wondered what Solomon was getting at.

"So you need Olive for her feminine energy?" he asked.

Olive grew very quiet then, her face turning a bright shade of red. "There's something I haven't told you," she said, turning to Marek. "Something I have hidden from you."

Marek waited for her to speak, completely confused by what was happening. How could there be something Solomon knew about Olive that he did not?

"I sensed it in you the moment we met," said Solomon. "I am good at reading energies, but you should tell Marek so he understands."

Olive set the book down and reached one hand over to Marek. She held his hand tightly and looked into his eyes. "Marek, I am sorry I didn't tell you sooner. I didn't think it mattered. I wanted to tell you but feared how you might react."

Marek squeezed her hand.

"I used to be Oliver," she said. "I was assigned male at birth."

Marek stared, taking in the beauty of this gorgeous woman, and couldn't reconcile what she had just said with how she looked. She was the most feminine woman he had ever met. How could it be possible that she was once he?

"I don't understand," he said to her.

She dropped his hand and looked to the floor.

"Because of her situation," said Solomon. "She has a unique blend of masculine and feminine energy."

"I would say more feminine," said Marek. He wasn't upset, just confused. Whatever Olive had been in the past, she was a woman now, and that was all that mattered. Why make it more complicated than that?

"I am a woman," said Olive.

"I'm not denying that," said Marek. "I'm affirming it. So what if you used to be something else? I don't care. I love you."

Solomon looked from one to the other. "I'm glad we got this out in the open. I didn't want you to think I was proposing some sort of sex magick." He laughed as if it were a joke.

"But you didn't need to out me, either," said Olive.

"You weren't going to tell me?" asked Marek.

She looked back at him, trembling now. "Not yet," she whispered. "I was going to tell you, but when the time was right."

They sat in awkward silence for a moment.

"Would you like more tea?" asked Solomon. They both declined the offer.

The sky had darkened, and it was almost time for the ritual. Even knowing that it wasn't sex magick, Marek still felt nervous. What did Solomon expect from Olive? Especially after her revelation, Marek wanted to protect her, hold her close, and reassure her that he loved her.

Solomon handed them both robes to wear. Marek's was a midnight black, matching the one Solomon wore, and Olive's robe was a pure white. Solomon stepped out of the room to give them privacy as they stripped down. They awkwardly laughed as they undressed, and Marek wondered how she could have ever been a man. If she hadn't told him, he would never have known, but he felt like he understood her better somehow, why she was sometimes a bit awkward and shy, maybe reluctant to reveal her new body to him, and he wondered just how unique this body was to her and why she had never told him.

As they finished and tied the cords around their waists, Kevin flew in tight circles above them, shouting, "Hurry! Hurry! Hurry!"

Olive giggled. "So he knows more than just his name!"

Marek wanted to explain that Kevin could say and did say so much more, but Solomon returned then, instructing them in the details of the ritual, where they would stand in the garden, and what he expected them to do.

"Remind me again what the purpose of this ritual is," said Olive.

Solomon seemed flustered then as if he wasn't sure what to say. Marek considered that he might be lying or not telling them the truth. He mumbled something about "reaching our highest human potential," but what did that mean? Nevertheless, they were in it now, and there didn't seem to be the option of backing out.

They stepped outside into the garden, and Solomon set up the circle with one tall pillar candle in each of the four directions. He called upon the spirits of his ancestors and the great God and Goddess in turn. The summoning circle still felt strange to Marek, who had only seen one drawn on a few occasions at Herb & Altar. Olive, however, seemed to be in her element. She gazed up at the moon like an old friend, her eyes shining. Solomon had pulled the hood of his robe over his bald head, and Kevin rode high on his shoulder.

After a series of low chants in a language Marek couldn't understand, Solomon focused on Olive. He directed her to kneel in the center of the circle and extend her hands as if she were the Virgin Mary offering her blessing. Marek stood aside, warily watching as Kevin flew into the space above their heads, circling once, twice, three times. Then he descended as if he were about to attack, and a dark smoke surrounded Olive, obscuring her entirely from view.

As the smoke slowly cleared, a lithe, dark-haired woman appeared opposite Olive, embracing her like a lover. She was entirely naked, and her pale skin seemed luminescent in the moonlight. As she untwined herself and stood shakily, Marek recognized something familiar in her eyes, her dark expression. She spun in a circle as if testing her body's abilities and then stared angrily at her breasts.

"Why am I a woman?" she demanded. "Didn't you say she had both masculine and feminine energies?" She turned on Solomon then, who was slowly backing out of the circle, his hands up in defense.

Marek hurried to Olive's side, wrapping her in a protective embrace. He wasn't sure what was happening, but she also looked stricken. Something had gone wrong, and she felt partially to blame even though she wasn't quite sure what was happening.

Solomon cowered as the other woman approached. "I don't know why it didn't work. I mean, at least you're human again?" He said it like a question, like he wasn't sure if the ritual had succeeded.

Still holding Olive, Marek addressed the naked woman. "Is that you, Kevin?"

She turned on her heel, fixing him with a glare.

"Is it you?" he asked again.

"This wasn't supposed to happen," said Kevin. Then he turned on Olive. "And it's all her fault."

"I never claimed I had masculine energy," Olive explained. "I have always been a woman, have always been feminine. I was born in the wrong body."

"Well, thanks to you, now I'm in the wrong body," said Kevin.

Olive shook her head, still confused. "I thought you were just a crow," she said.

Solomon stepped forward then, finding some of his courage again. He put one arm on Kevin's back, ushering him into the house. Kevin pushed him away. "At least you're human again," said Solomon, trying to reassure him.

"I might be human," said Kevin, "but I still don't have my body back." He strode back into the house, leaving the others staring at one another in awkward silence

23

The Hanged Man

Madame Rosivda turned the card, revealing an apple orchard cloaked in darkness. An agile young man swung upside down from his right foot at an intersection of tree branches. His left foot bent at an awkward angle, and his heel dug into the side of his knee. He stretched his arms over his head, touching the back of his hair and reaching toward the ground. His hair hung in thick messy waves from his head. He wore the livery of the king's court, a buttoned blue vest over a white tunic and yellow pants with a sharp crease down the front. It was The Hanged Man.

"There once was a servant of the king who possessed an unnatural degree of flexibility," said Madame Rosivda. "He could twist his body into such contortions that they looked impossible and incredibly painful. A few of the queen's ladies spied him in the orchard, practicing his gymnastics as they walked through. To spare the queen's delicate composure, they warned him to come down so that she would not be disturbed when she saw him hanging upside down and twisted in such a way.

"The servant refused, and when the queen approached and saw him hanging there like an unnatural, ghostly figure, she promptly fainted and fell to the ground in a swoon. Her attending ladies couldn't wake her, so they carried her back to the castle. The servant ran and hid then, but the ladies communicated what had happened to the king.

"When three days had passed, and the queen had still not awoken from her fright, the king sentenced the servant to death by hanging. The servant was captured and brought to the gallows, a tight noose fitted around his neck. The queen woke screaming as soon as the trapdoor opened up beneath him.

"From that moment on, she was haunted by nightmares of the servant, twisted into various impossible positions. Though he had died, his memory lived on through her. She saw him on the other side of her eyelids whenever she closed her eyes."

Marek didn't have any cheeky remarks for Madame Rosivda. After anticipating the ritual and its strange results, he hadn't been able to get much sleep.

He had joined Kevin for coffee a few days ago, and the interaction was uncomfortable. Kevin still seemed to blame Solomon, but also Olive for the mix-up.

"What does it feel like to be human again?" Marek asked, blowing on his too-hot coffee.

"Not what I expected," said Kevin. As if to prove the point, he attempted to pour some cream from a short pitcher into his coffee and managed to spill some down his shirt front.

Marek tried not to stare as the white fabric became transparent, and he could see the shape of Kevin's new breasts. He didn't appear to be wearing a bra.

"You said something about this not being the right body," said Marek. "I'm assuming you were trying to return to a male body?"

"No shit, Sherlock," said Kevin. His voice was still low and sounded male, but the rest of him was very obviously female. "Somehow, we managed to make me human again, but this isn't my body, and I don't know if there is a way to fix it."

"I don't understand how balancing masculinity and femininity was necessary. Wouldn't you have been better off channeling through Solomon? Or any male form?" asked Marek.

Kevin sighed loudly, his whole body moving with his breath. "It's complicated," he said finally.

Marek tried sipping at his coffee, and it scalded his tongue. He decided to try a different tactic. "Why do I feel you were in charge rather than Solomon?"

Kevin cackled. It was a sound that reminded Marek of the cawing of a crow, harsh and unfriendly. "Because I was," he said. What I miss most is the ability to fly around town, keeping tabs on everyone. It's frowned upon for a human to spy in people's windows and much harder to accomplish."

Marek nodded. "So the great plans you had for me were really for Olive? I was just a way to get to her?"

Kevin stared at him from across the table. Was it possible for a human to have black eyes? There may have been aspects of his crow form that had remained. "What do you think?" he asked.

Marek gave in, adding some cream to his coffee so he could drink it. He ignored the question. "So, what's next for you?" he asked. "Now that you're human again, I mean?"

Kevin looked off into the distance as if trying to decide for himself. "I'm not sure yet. I spent so much time trying to get here that I didn't think much beyond it. Do you have any ideas?"

Marek tried and failed not to glance at Kevin's chest again. "First off, I'd suggest investing in a few bras unless you want the extra attention."

Kevin shook his chest at Marek, the pendulous rhythm of his breasts catching Marek off guard. They took a few moments to stop swaying. "Maybe these could prove useful," said Kevin. "I hear women can be quite persuasive with their bodies."

A few nights later, Marek and Olive walked hand-in-hand down a dimly lit street. Some streetlights had burned out, so their shadows stretched in strange directions, growing like nightmarish monsters one moment and shrinking to hairline fractures the next. A strong breeze blew past them, and Olive gripped his arm tighter for warmth.

"Don't worry," he whispered to her. "We're almost there."

"Where are we going again?" she asked. Her voice almost disappeared into Marek's sleeve.

"It's a surprise."

They approached what looked like a giant, abandoned warehouse. There was no sign of life inside, but Marek knocked loudly three times on one of the side doors. A man dressed as a jester and wearing a black masquerade mask answered, ushering them through a long hallway that ended with a brilliantly lit big-top tent striped in red and white.

"What is this?" Olive asked again. Then, she saw Abaddon approaching them, wearing a pair of black angel wings made of what looked like real feathers. "Were we supposed to dress up?"

Abaddon embraced them both, winking at Marek. "You finally brought the lady out. I feel like I never see you two in the same place at the same time anymore."

"I've been busy," said Marek. "Playing the circuit. You know how it is."

Abaddon turned to him with a hurt look. "No, I can't say I do. I haven't played much lately, but I hope you both enjoy the show." He spread his arms, revealing his entire wingspan. The wings were impressive - you could hardly tell where he had attached them. They looked like they were growing from his shoulders rather than tied on like a cheap Halloween costume.

Olive and Marek found seats in the front row to see everything. Other audience members huddled together and murmured amongst themselves. There was a low hum, a buzz of anticipation around them. They ordered popcorn and waited impatiently for the show to begin. The lights dimmed, and a single spotlight came up, illuminating the center of the ring. It seemed strange to have a tent inside, but at the same time, it felt like the most natural thing in the world, like it couldn't exist anywhere else but in this place. A prominent figure entered the ring, wearing a red jacket with tails and brass buttons, a massive top hat, and thigh-high boots. She turned and smiled at them, a broad smile encompassing the entire room. When she winked, Marek immediately knew that it was Lizzie Mae. He nudged Olive, whispering to her that this was his fantastic agent. Olive nodded, and they watched as the show began.

It was a typical circus show, as much as any circus can be standard, but familiar faces populated the performance space. Abaddon graced the stage with his gorgeous black wings and performed an acrobatic act, twisting and turning through the air as if he could quickly fly through it. Abaddon invited Marek to the event, but the entire thing came as a surprise. All the acts seemed well-practiced, so Marek wondered how they had managed to keep it a secret, or maybe he had somehow unlocked a new level of friendship, including circus acts. Marek wasn't sure, but he was grateful to be invited and could share the experience with Olive.

After Abaddon's acrobatics, Ronnie entered the ring juggling three small beanbags. He looked more comfortable in this setting, his twisted handlebar mustache no longer looking out of place but a welcome addition. He graduated from juggling bean bags to knives and flaming torches and eventually requested the audience to toss him random objects to juggle. Some were small and more manageable, hats, shoes, a wristwatch. Then a businessman threw a heavy briefcase. Ronnie appeared to struggle with its weight for a moment, but it soon joined the other objects in the whirlwind of his hands.

Then he juggled what seemed to be an entire bag of popcorn. Each popped kernel flew from one hand to the next in a great stream of buttered loops. Marek couldn't count how many Ronnie had in the air at once; so many were flying by. At least they were light, he mused, but how did Ronnie learn to move so swiftly, deftly catching each kernel and then tossing it up again, as if he had never mastered anything but juggling, had dedicated his entire life to it?

The crowd erupted in applause and kept applauding when the next act began, a high trapeze act with Nyx as the star performer. A few others joined her in their swinging and flipping, but hers was the only face Marek recognized. She wore a tight body suit, which clung to her like the mini dresses she often wore at The Royal Club. If Olive hadn't captured his heart, Nyx might have been a top contender, but even now, he could see a sadness behind her eyes that never seemed to leave them.

Even high above the crowd, she looked like she would rather be buried underground with the child she had lost so long ago. He could tell the tragedy still haunted her, and would most likely never leave her. Despite this, she flew like a graceful swan, her cheeks glittering. In the end, she gave the audience a wan smile, as if someone had forced it out of her, as if it were painful to show her teeth, to bow and nod complacently. Marek wondered how things were going between her and Abaddon, how their living arrangement was working. He promised to ask later, but as soon as the next act began, he had already forgotten.

Marek glanced at Olive, who clapped and cheered with the rest of the audience. Taking her here had been a good idea. She needed something more light-hearted after the drama of the past few days, with the ritual and everything and the revelation of her trans identity. He still wondered why she hadn't told him sooner but acknowledged that it didn't matter. He loved her just like she was, regardless of what she may have been earlier. She caught him watching and blushed, the pink rising in her cheeks like paint spreading on a canvas. He reached for her hand and gently squeezed it. He hoped he could continue to make her happy.

The lights dimmed, and when they came back up again, Jasper stood at the center of the ring, his beard hanging down past his waist. Instead of a cane, he held a bullwhip and stood straighter than Marek imagined possible. The older man looked more youthful and roared out a welcome to two lions, a male and a female, who paced around him in menacing circles. The audience held their breath, waiting for disaster, but the lions were docile as kittens despite their violent claws and deep growls. The whip was just for show, and Jasper only used it for dramatic effect. He didn't touch a hair on those cats. Toward the end, the male yawned widely, showing his teeth but no aggression. They exited with a standing ovation, and Marek wondered what kind of magic made this animal mastery possible.

Ironically, the next act was a magician's act, but one which defied explanation. There were none of the usual bits – pulling a rabbit from a hat, sawing a woman in half, transforming scarves into bouquets. Instead, the tall man moved about the stage like a ghost, flashing in and out of the shadows, a spirit moving stealthily through the ring, popping in and out of the audience as if there was no such thing as space, time, and human movement. At one point, this spirit appeared immediately behind Marek, breathing down his neck like a clinging nightmare, and when he glanced back, he recognized the hollow eyes sunk into his face. It was Solomon, but it looked like all life had drained from him. His skin was pale and waxen, clammy as a corpse, and just as Marek was about to speak, his solid form disappeared only to reappear elsewhere in the tent.

Again, questions filled Marek's thoughts. Who had been the master, Solomon or Kevin? It was beginning to seem like the latter had been in charge. More importantly, who would show Olive how to harness her magical talents? It might be up to him to teach her, even after all they had been through. They both should keep their distance if this is what Solomon has become. But, more likely, this was just an act, a spooky silhouette to scare the audience. Indeed, it wasn't real, was it?

Before Marek could wonder any longer, red lights came up, illuminating the ring with sultry shadows, and a woman who appeared to be wearing little more than feathers and fringe descended from the ceiling. She floated down on a series of what looked like silk ribbons. She moved swiftly, her body twisting and turning in the silk like a serpent or like something liquid and far from human. Despite this, her black eyes gave her away. It had taken some time, but not long, for Kevin to embrace his new form, although Marek struggled to think of this woman as masculine. Everything about her exuded sex begged for touch, for all eyes to take every inch of her.

Olive also recognized Kevin. "I wonder," she said, "If he will still try to become a man again."

Marek tried not to stare at the female form wrapped in silk, undulating above them. "It's possible," he said. "But Kevin seems to be taking advantage of the opportunity presented to him. A female form can be very persuasive."

Olive elbowed him in the ribs, demanding his attention then.

Rather than wincing, Marek rewarded her with a kiss. Her lips felt soft and welcoming, like home, like everything he ever wanted, and he couldn't help but picture her naked, splayed open on his bed, giving herself to him. If she could just get over her insecurities, maybe it could happen. Perhaps they could finally reach that level again.

Not again, Marek reminded himself. He wished he could erase that first time from his memory, but it still lingered at the back of his mind, haunting him. Marek wanted nothing but to protect Olive, to make her feel safe in his arms. Never again would he threaten her that way or take what she hadn't freely given. Besides, sometimes a kiss can be even more intimate than other forms of connection. Olive had taught him this.

Marek glanced back to see two clowns enter the ring. One was short and fat, while the other was tall and skinny. They started with some simple slapstick and then brought out what could only be called a herd of poodles. The dogs were standard and miniature varieties and wore ruffled collars. The two clowns led them around; only the smallest ones could fit through hoops and elastic tunnels. It took until the end of their act for Marek to recognize the clowns, especially with all their pancake makeup. When he did, he couldn't stop his rolling laughter.

Olive nudged him again. "You like clowns?" she asked. "I don't think they're all that funny. Not that I'm scared of them, but you know."

Marek kept laughing and couldn't catch his breath until their act ended. "I – can't – believe –" He barely managed to get the words out between gasping for air. "That's my old boss. The fat one."

Olive stared, a smile finally breaking across her face. "That's Mr. Robins?" she asked. "Do you know the other one, too?"

"I'm pretty sure it's Timmy."

"Who's Timmy?" she asked.

"Well, he was my competition. He played in the lobby at the Ziggurat until Mr. Robins poached him."

They shared a laugh then, and Marek wondered if Timmy still played piano or if this was his new source of income. It wasn't strange for a musician to have several jobs, but seeing the two men dressed as clowns tickled him. In addition, some bizarre acts at this circus made him question whether he was dreaming. The whole evening felt so surreal.

Lizzie Mae stepped back into the ring to introduce the last performer, "Mr. Incredible," without further explanation. The average-looking man walked out into the spotlight and immediately stretched backward into an impossible bend that left his chin resting on the heels of his feet. The audience watched in awe as the contortionist twisted himself into pretzels until he eventually climbed up a pole to hang upside down on one foot. Marek didn't recognize the man's face but quickly realized the position. This contortionist was the hanged man who brought so much terror in Madame Rosivda's tale.

"Quite a show, don't you think?" asked a close voice, and then she was there, Madame Rosivda, her hair wrapped in a purple turban. "This is an entertaining dream, but it's time to wake up now."

Marek rolled over and nearly fell out of the bed.

24

The Lovers

Madame Rosivda turned the card, revealing a naked man and woman gazing lovingly into one another's eyes. They held their right hand over their heart, grasping the other's left hand as though they had made a solemn vow. Two ripe apples hung over them. In the distance, an angel slowly walked away on foot. The angel carefully examined the tip of an arrow as he left the couple to their designs. It was The Lovers.

"Many people believe," said Madame Rosivda, "That it was the serpent, representative of Satan, who led Adam and Eve into each other's arms, but that was never the case. Instead, it had always been natural for the earth's creatures to have sex. That was simply part of being an animal, one of God's creations.

"Some speculate that because God made humans in His image, that intercourse was not a natural act and somehow sinful, but that lie is far from the truth. How else would we be fruitful and multiply, as God had commanded?

"The serpent tempted Eve, and she ate the apple, became aware of her nakedness, and knew shame for the first time. From that shame arose sin. It wasn't until that moment that she questioned the shape of her body that she yearned to cover herself from Adam.

"So, it became Cupid's task to bring the two humans back together, to help them unite in the way that God always intended. They did so, however, not out of instinct or a desire to reproduce but to feel a deeper sense of connection. This communion was something that the animals did not share in their copulation. It was more than an instinctual urge for humans - what we now call love. That first union was part of something much more sacred, joining two hearts in a single beat."

Marek didn't know much Biblical lore, but this version of events sounded truer to him than he had previously heard about Original Sin. It made so much more sense. Sex had never been something to be ashamed of for him, not the act itself. Sometimes, Marek wished he could tone down his desire for it, but the best sex he had ever had always came as a byproduct of a connection he already felt for his partner.

After all this time, when he finally formed that union with Olive, he knew it would be an overwhelming experience. On the other hand, he hoped they didn't put too much pressure on it, expecting something magical that was still just a physical act grounded in mechanics. The emotion may be there, but there were also so many things that could go awry.

This time around, they talked about it. It wasn't the dark, sultry tones of dirty talk but an actual conversation and several discussions.

"I'm sorry it took me so long to come out to you," said Olive one morning over coffee.

"I'm glad you did, though, even if that wasn't your plan," said Marek.

She nodded, then admitted she might have waited longer if Solomon hadn't outed her.

"What were you so scared of?" he asked.

"I didn't know what your reaction would be."

Marek reached across the table to hold her hand. Her fingers felt small and cold in his. "Your past doesn't matter to me," he said. "I love who you are, here and now."

She drew back from him then, putting her hands in her lap. "But, in a way, my past is a part of me," she said. "If not for my past, I would not have become who I am."

Marek mulled this over for a moment. He loved how she looked first thing in the morning, still sleepy-eyed and childlike, her hair mussed and falling over her eyes. "I guess that's true," he said eventually. "Our past shapes our future, but I meant I don't hold it against you."

"Against me?" she asked. "Why would someone hold it against me? I had no control over the fact I was born that way. I never asked for it."

He had hit a raw nerve. "That's not what I meant."

"Would you still love me if I were a man?" she asked.

"That's a different question."

She wanted an answer. "What is it you love about me, then? I'm sure looks have something to do with it."

"Well, yeah. Of course, I'm human. I find certain things attractive. You have those things, but I'm not just talking about your body."

He was trying to find some sure footing, but it felt like this conversation was running away from him, that he was losing his grasp. Olive was crossing her arms over her chest. She was withdrawing into herself, closing off from him. What could he say to open her back up again? He wanted to reach out to her, to wrap her in a tight embrace, and never let go, but she didn't look very receptive.

"Just tell me what you want," he said.

"I don't want to have to tell you. You should be able to anticipate my needs."

"Olive, I can't read your mind."

"No? Solomon didn't teach you that?"

Not yet, he thought, then shook his head. That would just be an invasion of her privacy, and, in all reality, he probably didn't want to be able to read her thoughts. They needed to learn to communicate normally, like other couples. Why did their wires get so crossed, though, when they both had only the best intentions?

"Can we take a few steps back and start over?" he asked.

She looked reluctant. Her eyes and facial expressions always betrayed her.

"A fresh slate? No judgment?" he asked.

"Okay. Let's start over," Olive said. "Where did this start?"

"I'm pretty sure you were apologizing for not telling me you are trans. I'm not sure how it devolved into an argument."

She had somehow made her way to the sink as they sparred, but now, she returned to her chair at the table. "Yes," she said. "I guess you could say I'm still a little tetchy about it."

"Understandable."

"I just need to go about it at my own pace, I think," she said.

"Whatever you want to share or not share is fine by me," said Marek. "I just want to understand you. I just want to know how I can be a better partner for you, whatever that means and whatever that looks like."

"But you need me to tell you?" she asked.

"I have some ideas about how to love you, but you need to let me know if I'm not doing it right. Can you do that for me? Can you help guide me through it?"

"I think I can manage that."

"Thank you for being honest with me, Olive. I mean it, and I love you. We don't need to pretend our pasts didn't happen; I just don't want it to cloud our future."

"Okay."

"Good."

They kissed then, and it was sweet and good, and it felt like it might lead to something else until it didn't. Marek didn't think Olive meant to be a tease, but she was excellent at getting him excited and leaving him always wanting more than she had given. It was part of what kept their relationship exciting, but it also made him ache for her. Eventually, he would expect sex from her or feel unfilled. It was starting to feel like it was taking them too long to get there, but at the same time, he understood her reluctance.

They walked to the plateau's edge one afternoon to see the valley below. Horizon Heights provided only one exciting view, and this was it. It didn't require a hike because the entire city stretched across the elevated tabletop. They spread a blanket just feet from the edge and laid out their picnic lunch. Olive had packed BLT sandwiches and brought a bottle of wine for sipping. The weather was perfect, the sun shining down on them, a cool breeze playing across their skin.

"Have you always lived here?" she asked.

"I have," he replied. Marek surveyed the valley below, like Simba in The Lion King examining his realm. "What about you?"

"I came here when I was young. After my parents died."

"That's right. You barely knew your parents."

"I am so grateful for my Aunt Lucille. Without her, I would have wound up in foster care."

"Can I meet her?"

"Eventually. What about your family?"

"My parents... are demanding. My brother was always the successful one," he said.

"You have a brother?"

"Who is a doctor."

She leaned back, stretching out the entire length of the blanket. Marek stretched out beside her.

"Do you have any siblings?" he asked.

"None that I know of," she said.

"Did your aunt have any children of her own?"

"No, but I think I was enough to worry about." She propped herself up on one elbow. "Imagine a poor little orphaned boy who only wants to be a girl. My aunt had enough to deal with."

"So, you knew right away?"

"I did."

"How could you know that?"

She motioned toward the wine, asking if he wanted some. "I think we could use a drink for this conversation."

"I won't say no."

Once Olive had poured the wine and they had sipped at it for a minute, she told her story. "It wasn't just wanting to wear dresses or makeup or anything like that," she said. "Although, at the time, that may have just been considered gay. Not many people knew what it meant to be trans."

"I thought there have been trans people for centuries," said Marek.

"Well, there have. But medical intervention has been a relatively new thing. Aunt Julia found me an excellent therapist to talk to about my parents, but while I was in therapy, these other things came up, too, about my gender identity."

Marek took another drink of his wine, waiting for her to continue.

"They put me on puberty blockers. Getting other procedures approved took a little longer, but I never went through male puberty. It made things much easier."

"That makes sense."

She looked into his eyes, searching for approval there. "And it's why it was so easy for me to transition."

"I doubt it was easy."

"Well, easier anyway."

They sat in comfortable silence then, each sipping their wine, each staring off into the distance. White, fluffy clouds slowly skirted across the sky in a lazy race to the horizon. As they finished their drinks, Marek pulled Olive to him, and their lips met in a type of communion that felt more spiritual than physical. He felt more connected to her in that moment than they had ever been. She was no longer a tight bud but an unfurling flower, her petals slowly opening to him, and she smelled so sweet, so intoxicating.

"Do you have to work tonight?" she asked when they returned to Marek's apartment.

"No, it's a rare Friday night. I'm free," he said. "What mischief could we get into?"

"I was thinking just a night in."

"That's fine by me."

They ordered pizza delivery and found a movie to watch, a romantic comedy. It wasn't Marek's favorite, but Olive insisted. After eating, they cuddled up on the couch, Olive's head resting on Marek's chest as he played with her long, wavy hair. Halfway through the movie, she began to snore gently, but he didn't bother to wake her. Instead, he carried her to the bed and softly set her up on some pillows, drawing the blankets over her. She looked so peaceful, so perfect; he didn't want to disturb her sleep.

Instead, he lit a cigarette and stepped out on the balcony. He could get used to this, he thought, as he exhaled a cloud of smoke. Marek liked having Olive around; she fit into his life like a missing puzzle piece. Things felt complete with her. Even if it had taken a bit of magick to woo her, he felt there must be some element of destiny to their coming together. He didn't believe in soul mates, but he figured this must be what it must feel like if he did. He leaned against the railing, gazing out at the city lights, the nightlife of Horizon Heights just awakening.

Then he felt a hand on his shoulder. It was Olive, wearing only a loose silk robe. She let it open as he reached for her, revealing her bare skin. It wasn't that he had never seen her breasts before, but each time it felt like a revelation. His eyes also wandered to the curve of her stomach, the small valley between her legs.

Wordlessly, they made their way back to the bedroom. Her eager hands removed articles of his clothing as they got closer to the bed, first his shirt, exposing his bare chest, and then she worked on his belt, reaching one hand down to grasp his erection. Her touch felt electric, sending shocks throughout his entire body. It was everything he had been waiting for and more.

25

⚛

The Page of Chalices

Madame Rosivda turned the card, revealing a calm sea on the edge of a forest. At the water's edge, a small puppy greeted a mermaid who swam up to the beach. She wore a small crown, and her long hair trailed off into the deep. In the distance, the smoke from a wood-burning fire rose from a cabin where the puppy's owner lay, still fast asleep. It was the Page of Chalices.

"There once was a man," Madame Rosivda said, "who lived alone in a cottage on the edge of the wilderness, where the forest met the sea. He was an expert hunter and fisherman and kept several dogs to help retrieve his prey once he had killed it.

"He had become fierce and independent, relying on no one but himself. He grew a great beard that hung to his waist, and over the years, it faded into a colorless gray. Early one morning, as he fried up eggs for his breakfast, one of his dogs, an eager and rambunctious puppy, pushed its way through the back gate and trotted along the seaside beach.

"A mermaid swam up to the shoreline, and the puppy ran up to her to investigate. It barked gleefully, excited for the attention. The hunter heard him and glanced out the window but could not see the dog. He set his frying pan aside, threw water on the fire, and stepped outside to find the puppy.

"When he neared the shoreline, he finally spotted an eager tail wagging back and forth. 'What have you got there, buddy?' he asked as he approached. Then, he saw the mermaid, her hair floating all around her in the sea, her fluke occasionally slapping the water's surface. As he drew nearer, though, she slipped back into the sea."

"Then what happened?" asked Marek. He felt like he was in a state somewhere halfway between waking and sleeping. His life, when shared with Olive, felt like a dream. "Did they fall in love?"

Madame Rosivda winked at him, but he barely noticed. "Wouldn't that be another tragic ending?" she said, teasing.

Marek sipped the remnants of his tea and ignored her question.

"Tell me," she said. "Why do you still visit me?"

"What do you mean?" he asked, setting his cup on its saucer. "For guidance, for direction, all of those things."

"I feel like you have already gotten all you need from me."

"Maybe I like your company."

"I bet you like Olive's company better, though."

"Of course," said Marek.

They had moved in together. It was a slow process, like a trickling stream. Bit by bit, Olive began to settle into his space, bringing with her clothes, which she stored in a drawer he had set aside for her. She also brought her bathroom necessities: a toothbrush, deodorant, and a comb. Then, two men carried in some of her furniture, a favorite chair, end tables, and a few decorative lamps. The rest she sold at the end of her lease before officially changing her address.

They settled into a comfortable routine. Olive still worked a few nights a week at The Royal Club, and Marek played most weekends at various venues throughout the city. She would sit in the audience when she wasn't working, a built-in groupie for most performances. Sometimes, Olive would introduce him and make her presence known to any woman interested in her man. It was how she staked her territory.

Marek didn't mind the way she claimed him. It made him feel desired, even as he started to count the wrinkles forming at the edges of his eyes and the gray strands of hair growing at his temples. Eventually,

Marek knew he would also claim her with a promise and a ring, but not just yet. He wanted to make sure they were stable first, so he could provide for them if need be. Despite his success, they were still struggling a bit with money.

One late afternoon, while he practiced scales on the electric keyboard in his apartment, dreaming of when he could afford a larger place and an actual piano, even just an upright, he heard a scrambling on the stairs and a frantic knocking at the door.

He undid the latch and opened the door to see Olive grinning. In her arms, she held a small, wriggling, fluffy thing.

"Isn't she the cutest!" She nearly squealed with delight.

"What's that?" he asked, already knowing the answer.

She set the ball of fuzz on the floor, and it immediately started ransacking the apartment for anything chewable. "It's our puppy," she exclaimed.

They chased after it, petting its adorable head, tugging gently on its ears, all three wrestling. Eventually, the puppy slept, loudly snoring as it continued to play in its dreams.

"What should we name him?" Marek asked.

"Her," Olive said, correcting him. "I'd think you'd know your dog's anatomy."

"I can't say I noticed. What should we name her, then?"

Olive thought for a moment, then scooted closer to him. They sat cross-legged on the floor, and she crawled carefully into his lap. "What do you think?" she asked.

"What do you think of Rosy?"

"That sounds great."

The following day, Olive took Rosy for a quick stroll around the block before Marek woke up. When they returned, however, there were tears in Olive's eyes.

He grabbed the leash from her, unhooking the harness from the puppy. They sat across from each other at the kitchen table, and he poured her a cup of coffee. Olive wiped the tears from her cheeks and finally looked like she could speak again.

"What is it?" Marek asked. "Did something happen?"

"No, nothing," she said. "Nothing happened."

"What's wrong then?"

Rosy bounded into the kitchen, skidding into the trash can and toppling the entire thing. In moments, bits of paper and coffee grounds spread all over the tile floor Rosy. Marek and Olive laughed as they cleaned up the mess, and it wasn't until much later that Marek remembered Olive had been upset.

"How big is she going to get?" Marek asked, taking a break from his playing.

"Hmmm?" Olive barely looked up from the magazine she was reading.

The four-legged mayhem was sleeping again but had become a near-constant source of entertainment and conversation.

"Do you know what breed she is?"

"Not sure," said Olive. "Some sort of mix. I think the shelter said retriever, maybe Doberman? She might get kinda big."

"We might have to move before she gets much bigger then."

"I'm sure we'll figure it out."

He sat next to her on the couch. "Olive, I need to talk to you about something."

She set the magazine down so she could give him her full attention. "What is it?"

"Earlier, you were crying. What had you so upset?"

"I'm not sure I want to talk about it," she said, placing her hands in her lap.

He reached for one of them, squeezing gently. "Something had you upset. What was it?"

"I realized something this morning," she said. "About Rosy."

"What is it?"

"You realize this might be it for us, right?"

"What do you mean?" This conversation seemed to be turning ominous, but he had no idea what she could be getting at.

"I can't give you children, Marek," she said, staring at the carpet. "At least not biologically."

"Who said anything about children?" Then he saw her eyes, the way they threatened to well up again. "I mean, we're not at that stage yet."

"I just don't want you to get your hopes up," she said. "I saw a mother with a baby on her hip, and it just made me think about how... how that might never be us."

"There's always adoption," he said.

"You say that like you can just go out and buy a baby off the street corner."

"You can't?" He grinned at her then, hoping the joke would make her smile again. She gave him a slight pity laugh instead.

"We'll figure it out," he added. "Besides, look at Rosy. She's so freaking adorable."

They both glanced at the puppy, kicking and softly barking in her sleep.

"She really is, isn't she?" said Olive.

26

The Knight of Wands

Madame Rosivda turned the card, revealing a fairy sitting astride a golden bird. The fairy wore a sculpted helmet topped by a long, pink feather. He held his wand aloft as if riding into battle. The wind blew great gusts around them, sending fairy dust flying everywhere. It was the Knight of Wands.

"There once was a fairy who was a warrior," said Madame Rosivda. "Rather than flying with his wings, he trained a golden bird to carry him. He was the protector of his people. When he rode astride his bird, he became much more confident than his brethren, and anyone could see him from some distance away.

"At that time, a wizard had been captured in a magic circle. He was a threat to the fairies and had already killed one of them, albeit accidentally. Other fairies feared approaching the older man, but this one flew in defiantly to fix the situation.

"The wizard saw the bird approach and noticed the fairy riding it. The bird landed some distance away, and the fairy waited for the wizard to acknowledge him before entering the magic circle.

"'Why have I been trapped here for so many years?' the wizard asked. He did not understand his punishment.

"The fairy dismounted and stepped to the edge of a leaf at the

"

wizard's eyeline. The wizard had to strain to hear him as he spoke, but his words rang out clearly. 'You have killed one of our kind,' he said. 'And this is your penance.'

"'I have been so lonely, trapped here,' said the wizard. 'Please let me go free. I will do anything you ask.'

"The fairy considered this carefully. Wizards, such as this one, have been known to be crafty. What could he ask for that would be worthy of the fallen fairy? 'I ask for your protection,' he said. 'On our entire village, which stretches deep into the woods. Can you do that for me?'

"The wizard agreed, but as the fairy dropped the field which held him prisoner, he snatched the golden bird from the air, sending the fairy toppling to the grass. Before the fairy could regain his balance, the wizard had slipped the bird into his pocket. A golden bird like this would fetch a pretty penny at the market.

"'What about your protection?' the fairy asked, flying angrily into his face.

"'You seem to have things handled without me,' said the wizard, disappearing in a cloud of smoke. The fairies never saw him again."

* * *

"You still haven't answered my question about fairies," said Marek.

"What question was that?" asked Madame Rosivda.

"I wanted to know if they're real."

"What do you think, Marek?"

"After all I've seen, I wouldn't be surprised."

"Well, there you go then."

"That isn't an answer."

Madame Rosivda turned away from him, secreting away the tarot cards. Returning to the table, she asked if he wanted another cup of tea, but he declined. "After all this time," she said. "I have a question for you."

"Ask away," he said.

"What do you think of my stories?" she asked. "I've been told by so many that my methods aren't traditional, but usually, they still have a positive experience when I give my readings. What do you think?"

Marek leaned back, considering. "You've been spot-on for the most part. I think you have manifested so many things into my life."

"You think I have changed the shape of your fate?"

"Yes, I do."

Madame Rosivda shook her head then. "I don't shape anyone's fate but my own," she said. "And it is you who shape your life, Marek. I give you a glimpse at the possibilities."

Nyx called during the walk back to his apartment. Her voice was bright and eager for a change. "Have you read the latest issue of Rhythm & Muse?"

"Can't say I've had the time," said Marek.

"No one told you you're one of the featured performers?" she asked.

"What does it say?"

"Nothing but good stuff, but I'm surprised they didn't directly interview you. The article's written by a guy named Zads Abramowitz. I showed Abaddon, and he says the guy is one of his cousins."

"I've met him."

"Really? You're friends with the guy?"

"Not friends, really. We are more like acquaintances. I'll have to read what he wrote."

"Why don't you come over later? We can celebrate."

"Celebrate what?"

"You, of course. I'm so proud of you. Bring your lady. We'll make a night of it."

Marek walked the rest of the way, contemplating how far he had come from accompanying students to headlining sold-out shows. He hadn't celebrated. Not yet, anyway. He returned to an empty apartment. Olive must have taken Rosy out for a walk. He sat there silently and remembered that night when he first met Zads. He still had the man's number saved in his phone but never called it. Maybe now was the time.

The reviewer picked up after a few rings. "My man!" he exclaimed as if they had been hanging out regularly.

Marek wasn't sure what to say. "Is this Zads?" he asked. "I mean, Zadkiel?"

"Yes, Marek, how's it been?"

"You wrote a feature about me?"

"Sure did. Did you get the chance to read it?"

"Not yet. A friend told me about it."

"Great, great. Only good things, I promise. How have you been?"

Marek stretched out on the couch, kicking his shoes off. "Alright. I'm surprised you didn't set up an interview with me."

"It was a tight deadline," said Zads. "I didn't have much time to work with. Is there something that didn't read right?"

"I told you. I haven't read it. "

"Tell you what, why don't I buy you a drink sometime?"

Marek paused. He wasn't sure if that was something he wanted. Why had he bothered to call, then? "Are you related to Abaddon Navarro?"

"Sure am. Abaddon is my cousin by marriage."

"I was going to say. You two look nothing alike."

"Abaddon's on the Mexican side of my family. How do you know him?"

"He's a friend of mine." Marek wracked his brain. What else was there to say? "We're having a little get-together tonight at Abaddon's place. I mean this chick Nyx's place. They live together now."

"Really? I thought he was gay."

"He is." Marek sighed. What was he trying to do, invite Zads for a surprise family reunion? "It's complicated," he added.

"Sounds like it." There was an awkward moment of silence. "So, when should I stop by?"

Marek gave him the time and the address. This evening should be enjoyable. When Olive returned, he told her about what now seemed like a party. She was delighted and started making plans for what she would wear.

"Do you think we can bring Rosy?" she asked.

* * *

When they arrived at Nyx's place, the sky had darkened, the sun painting brilliant pink and orange hues across the sky. She greeted them at the door, wearing a bright yellow minidress that made her look like a Bond villain. She hugged them both, giving Olive cheek kisses as she entered.

"It's so great to see you," she said. "I feel like we only get to hang out when we make official plans these days."

"That's so true," said Olive as she sat.

"And who is this adorable little cutie?!"

Marek unlatched Rosy's leash, letting her run free. "This is Rosy. I hope you've got your place child-proofed. She's a menace."

As if to prove the point, the puppy raced down the hallway, attacking Abaddon as soon as he stepped out of the bathroom.

"It's such a beautiful night," said Nyx. "I was thinking we could have some drinks on the roof."

"Oh, could we?!" said Olive, nearly squealing.

"Sure thing, but we've gotta take the stairs. The elevator broke; I don't even know how long ago. Do you think Rosy can manage?"

"She's still a little scared of stairs, but I can carry her," said Marek. "She took care of her business on the way here, so she should be alright for a few hours at least. If not, at least she's little still and only makes little messes."

Abaddon scooped up the puppy then, turning her over and rubbing her tummy. "I got a call from my cousin," he said, almost absent-mindedly. "Sounds like we're gonna have a surprise guest."

Nyx glanced over at him and then laughed. "The more, the merrier, I guess. Who made that invite?"

"Me," Marek admitted. "He gave me his number once, a while ago, and I finally called it. I figured, why not. Thank him for that rave review, I guess."

"Just text him that we'll be on the roof. He might have to knock so we can let him up," said Nyx.

They grabbed a few plastic glasses and bottles of their favorite beverages before ascending the stairs. They were a ridiculous rag-tag group, chatting and laughing the whole way, but Marek hung back. He felt a bit self-conscious, even with the puppy in his arms, playfully gnawing at him. That was a kind of unconditional love and acceptance no human could replicate, not even Olive.

He questioned himself, why was he having doubts now? Why couldn't he just take an evening to relax with all his friends around him? It didn't make any sense. He had come so far, but his mind wouldn't let him just take it all in and be happy for once. He tried to push these doubts aside, to pay attention to the moment. Maybe he'd feel better once he was a few drinks in.

Abaddon opened the door to the roof, revealing a group of people all crouching and waiting and then shouting 'surprise' in a chorus of voices and noise-makers. There was yelling, laughing, and balloons, and Marek nearly dropped Rosy in the chaos. He gingerly placed her on the ground instead.

"What is all this?" he asked.

"I told you we needed to celebrate," said Nyx. "What do you think?"

"I'm a little overwhelmed," said Marek.

Olive stepped closer to embrace him, drawing him into a kiss. "You deserve this," she said. "You've worked so hard. We just want to celebrate you tonight."

Marek made the rounds with Olive, greeting each guest and eating or drinking anything handed to him. After a while, it started to become a blur. He knew most of the people there. They were friends, friends of friends, or regulars at any number of the venues he had played at. Eventually, he volunteered to take Rosy for a walk so he could get some fresh air. Although everyone had good intentions, he had been hoping for a nice, relaxing get-together with just a few friends, different from what felt like a giant crowd.

It was a trek back down to the ground floor, given that the elevator had broken, but he swept Rosy into his arms, and she wriggled impatiently. It was cute and annoying simultaneously, as he imagined many new parents must feel about their children. He snapped the leash on her collar, and they began their walk. Marek took a few deep breaths and barely noticed when Rosy started snapping at an insect flying around her head.

When he looked closer, he saw that it wasn't just a moth but a small human-shaped figure with wings. He blinked a few times, but the image didn't change. He tugged back on Rosy's leash, commanding her to sit. She hadn't attended obedience school yet, so it was only somewhat effective. The creature flew beyond the puppy's reach and hovered just inches from Marek's face.

"You better control your beast," the fairy said, nearly screaming. To Marek, it sounded like a high-pitched squeak. He strained to hear. "Do you know the consequences if it decided to eat me as a snack?"

Marek stared, unable to form words.

The fairy waved a small wand in his direction and spoke again. This time Marek could hear him without straining. "Do you see me, finally? Do you hear me?" he asked. The fairy floated closer, waving his arms frantically.

"Yes," Marek managed. "I can." This time it seemed much more accurate.

"Humans think they've got it made, but that's just because so many of us fae folk hide from you. You wouldn't know a mystical creature if it bit you in the ass."

"I'm sure I'd feel it, though," said Marek.

Rosy rolled over in the grass alongside the sidewalk, not noticing their exchange. Marek was grateful for that, at least.

"What do you want from me?" he asked the fairy.

"Me? Nothing. I just want to be relieved of your service," he said.

"My service? You make it sound like I've employed you."

"Well, not you, exactly. But it is only by your word that I can take my leave."

"What do you mean?"

"I have been tasked with your protection. But I told Madame

Rosivda you no longer need it, that you're fine on your own. You seem to have things figured out, don't you think?"

"She sent you to protect me?" asked Marek.

The fairy fluttered about anxiously. "I wasn't supposed to say that. There I go breaking the rules."

"What rules?"

"Do I have to explain everything to you?" The fairy started looking tired, flapping his wings frantically to stay afloat. Marek held out his hand.

"Here," he said. "Take a breather."

The fairy landed gingerly, gasping for air. "Thank you," it said. "You have no idea how much effort it takes us to fly." He paced back and forth across the length of Marek's index finger.

Marek waited for it to speak again.

"Madame Rosivda hired me to make sure you were protected. She knew a certain alchemist had his eye on you, and we were trying to ensure you didn't fall into the crevices."

"Well, you did a fine job there. We still went through with the ritual. Nothing bad happened, though. Not to Olive and me, anyway."

"I know. I was watching," said the fairy. "You think I wouldn't have interfered if things went south?"

Marek didn't have an answer.

"Anyway, it looks like you've got things handled, and I have other work to do," said the fairy.

"Is it always a fairy's job to protect humans?" Marek asked.

"Not just humans, but other magical beings, too. It's a pact we made long ago," said the fairy. "I wish it had not been the case, but now we are bound to it, or at least my particular clan is. But you've got this, Marek; you don't need me watching your every move. I already have a new assignment."

"You do?"

"I just need you to release me. Can you do that, please? I don't have to watch more than one human all day and night. One is plenty."

"Why did it take so long for me to become aware of you?" asked Marek.

"I want to say magick and that I've cloaked myself or something clever, but you just didn't look. You didn't see me because you weren't looking."

"I think I saw you once. It was quite a while ago, though." Marek remembered the small flying thing he had thought was a butterfly until it had gotten closer to him. He also remembered all the times he had asked Madame Rosivda if fairies were real, and she refused to give him a clear answer. She had been tricky that way.

The fairy continued pacing, then paused, staring up at him in expectation. "So... are you going to release me?" he asked.

"What do I have to do?" asked Marek.

"It's just a verbal confirmation that you no longer need my help. There aren't specific words, but they still need to be said."

"Alright," said Marek. He watched Rosy out of the corner of his eye, making sure she still wasn't paying attention. It would be a disaster if she suddenly decided to jump up and nip at the fairy. At the very least, it wouldn't bode well. "I am no longer in need of your protection. I release you."

The fairy nodded then, waving his small wand around his head with a flourish, sending sparkling dust cascading all around him. Marek thought he heard a small "thank you" as the fairy took flight, flapping his wings rapidly and disappearing into the ether.

Rosy came bounding back, eager to sniff more grass and trees. Marek ran his hand through her fur. He finally had confirmation fairies were real. At this point, he didn't find it all so surprising.

27

The Queen of Wands

Madame Rosivda had set up a table for readings on the rooftop. She brought less of her tools, but her deft hands shuffled through the tarot cards, allowing Marek to cut the deck.

"I'm surprised to see you here," he said. "I mean, I've told my friends about you, but I didn't expect you to be at this party."

"I come when I am needed," she said.

"Do you think I still need you?" he asked. "I met a little friend of yours who said otherwise."

"You met your fairy." She smiled. "You knew they were real, didn't you?"

Marek nodded. "I had a feeling."

"You can still come to me for a reading whenever you want," she said, "but I think there are others who might need my guidance more now."

"Like who?"

"I'm not telling."

She turned the card, revealing a winged princess wearing a crown and holding a wand—a swath of roses wound around her waist. A lion's big head leaned over her right shoulder, and she reached back to pet his muzzle. In the distance, three tall sunflowers grew toward the pink-hued sky. It was the Queen of Wands.

"There once was a queen who communed with nature," said Madame Rosivda. "She had a way of communicating with all the plants and animals, from the smallest ant or blade of grass to the tallest sunflower or predatory beast. She blessed and protected them, and they returned the same energy.

"The king grew jealous, fearing that she loved the whole of the world more than she loved him. After all, how could she divide her energy between all of them? He wanted more of her time, and every time she wandered out into the courtyards, to the gardens, to the edges of the castle grounds, he feared he would lose her. He thought she was careless and did not see the danger of a poisonous plant or a hungry beast. After all, nature could be ruthless and was not inherently kind to human beings, no matter what she might think.

"One fateful morning, he spied upon her from a distance. He watched as she removed her cloak, revealing a pair of gilded wings he had never seen before. Suddenly, he understood that the woman he had married was not a woman but a fairy who had taken human form, and he was afraid.

"He mixed a concoction for her to drink, which would put her into a deep coma, never to wake. He couldn't bear to kill her but feared her magical capabilities and worried about her intentions. They met for tea in the afternoon, and he offered her the glass. She sniffed it carefully but did not drink.

"'Why don't you trust me?' she asked him. 'I am your wife and your queen. What do you have to fear from me?'"

"He could not answer, just walked from the room for a moment, claiming he needed a moment to breathe. Before he returned, his wife had swapped their glasses. Not thinking, he took a drink and collapsed to the ground."

Marek hazarded a glance at Madame Rosivda. It was strange, not having his own cup of tea to drink. The tea had become a part of their ritual, and his hands felt incredibly empty.

"He should have trusted her," he said. "The queen, I mean. He should have trusted her, and everything would have been fine."

"Would it? The moment a person questions their lover, it might be the end of the relationship," said Madame Rosivda.

"What do you mean?" he asked.

"Keep your secrets close, but don't doubt the truth she tells you," she said.

Lizzie Mae pushed her way through the crowd then. "Marek! There you are!" She pulled him from his seat, ushering him away from Madame Rosivda's table. "It's an emergency!"

He tried not to grumble. He would have liked to sit and contemplate the reading for a moment. Usually, he walked at least a few blocks to mull it over. Now he was being pulled away. "What is it?" he asked. "Is someone hurt?"

But before his mind could start running down several disastrous avenues, she embraced him, nearly squealing in his ear. "It's a musical emergency!"

"Hold on." He managed to escape her grasp. "What's going on?"

"Have you ever done a dueling piano act?" she asked.

"No...why? What is it?"

"I need you to fill in," she said. "I know it's last minute, but you'll be fine. My guy had to drop out because he broke his wrist in a minor car accident. He can't exactly play piano with a broken wrist. You might even know the other pianist, Timmy Galanis. He used to play at The Zigurrat, but he's at The Den now."

"I know him."

"So you can duel him. It'll be a blast."

She turned to the crowd before he could even give her a definitive answer. "Hey, everybody!" she shouted. "Want to see Marek play?"

They rushed down in a great group to the Tickled Ivories piano bar, carpooling and cramming more bodies into cars than was reasonable. Marek squished between Lizzie Mae and Olive, who struggled to hold Rosy in her lap, along with Abaddon, his cousin Zads, and Nyx. It was a limousine with a professional driver, but it was still a tight squeeze with many adult bodies and a rambunctious puppy.

By the time they arrived, Marek was already sweating, overwhelmed by the sudden expectation to perform, but once they got him on stage and his fingers found the familiar shape of a piano's keys, he felt much more at ease. Timmy was already there, running scales. He looked a bit troubled when he saw he would be facing off against Marek. Before the show began, they shared a friendly handshake and wished each other the best of luck.

Marek was grateful he had done more improvising before finding himself in this situation. His dabbling in magick didn't hurt, either. As they played back and forth, he felt the warmth rising in his fingers, arms, core, and chest, inflaming his beating heart. This time, though, it didn't burn or rip his chest apart. It was warm, welcoming, and comforting but not painful.

The audience clapped along, mainly on the beat, because several were actual musicians. He drew from their energy and created riffs that blended and contrasted Timmy's music where they overlapped. One of the challenges here was not just that they were competing; they were feeding off one another, developing and expanding upon each harmony and melody, creating collaborative music, and building from one movement to the other to create a more cohesive piece. Marek felt like he was floating above the scene, watching himself play like a God contemplating the small machinations of a single human being.

When they finished, the audience erupted in applause, and it didn't matter who "won" or whether one was a better player. What mattered is that they connected people in ways only music could join them, creating a soul-level harmony in the hearts, brains, and bodies of so many beings. Pushing through the crowd, Marek found Olive. They crashed into one another excitedly, then melted in a soft embrace. Here, in this place, was exactly where and who Marek needed to be.

Acknowledgements

Once again, I would like to thank the indie authors I have met, especially those who are members of Studio Moonfall's Author Club Kenosha (SMACK) and the mad genius Donovan Scherer, who makes the magick happen, creating local book festivals where I sell my books. I never thought putting together a poetry collection last year would lead to a second poetry collection, a mystery novel, and now the first book of the Chords of Prophecy trilogy.

I would also like to thank my husband for reading the roughest of rough drafts and giving me feedback. Eternal thanks go to all my friends and family who have supported me in this journey. I hope you haven't gotten sick of me talking about writing yet because I plan to keep at it.

About the Author

Kaitlyn Bolyard teaches writing and literature at DePaul University and Carthage College. She lives in Wisconsin with her chef husband, who keeps her well-fed. In her spare time, she experiments with witchy things.

You can visit her at www.kaitlynbolyard.com.

Books by this Author

Mr. Wilson's Wives

Shunned by the women of her family for writing a tell-all memoir, Elizabeth Rodriguez escapes to northern Wisconsin for peace and inspiration. Before she can even get settled in, an obituary in the local newspaper catches her attention. As soon as she learns about Erwin Wilson and his twenty-three wives throughout his life, she makes it her mission to learn more. She begins by interviewing some of the locals and his remaining ex-wives, and she soon develops plans for her next bestseller. When her younger brother unexpectedly appears at her doorstep, she puts him to work helping her research and gather information. But with each mystery Elizabeth uncovers, she comes closer to the truth: maybe some stories aren't meant to be told, and maybe building family trust is more important.

Mystical Music Playlist

My readers may be interested in what type of music I listened to while writing this novel. Below are a few selections you might enjoy:

"Marie Laveau" - Vaud and the Villians
"Birds" - The Submarines
"Panoramic" - Lusine
"Muy Tranquilo" - Gramatik
"Miami Showdown" - Digitalism
"All Time Low" - Jon Bellion
"Lebanese Blonde" - Thievery Corporation
"Oh, Lover (NTO Remix" - Royskopp ft. Susanne Sundfor
"Do My Thing" - Estelle ft. Janelle Monae
"Four Walls and an Amplifier" - Brock Berrigan

I also listened to several Beats Antique, Pentaphobe, and NF songs. All of the above inspired the music my characters played and listened to and the novel's mood overall.

Author's Note

The tarot images used to inspire this text come from the Star Spinner Tarot by Trungles. Although the cards are traditional in name, some of the images incorporated are unique to this deck. For example, you will read descriptions of rabbits, crows, mermaids, and fairies, which do not necessarily appear in a classical Rider-Waite-Smith deck. The artist, Trung Le Nguyen, is a Phillipines-born Vietnamese comic book artist and illustrator. I encourage you to explore them yourself.